## THE ALMOST FINISHED
## YOUNG LADY

When Anne was summoned from the vicarage to take her place as the Earl of Bredon's ward on his country estate, the earl himself supervised the finishing touches in her upbringing.

He put her on a near-starvation diet to give her the slenderness that fashion decreed. He made sure her voice was trained to trill the songs that society salons applauded. And a veritable army of dressmakers set to work on a wardrobe that would dazzle all London.

Now the earl surveyed her from head to foot as they stood alone in a room lit by dancing firelight. And as she saw the unfamiliar gleam in the earl's cool gray eyes and the disquieting ghost of a smile on his handsome mouth, Anne felt a chill run through her—a chill that mounted to a trembling when his hand came to rest on her shoulder.

The earl had made her what she was—and now she suddenly feared what he wanted her to be. . . .

# The Rake's Protégée

# THE
# RAKE'S
# PROTÉGÉE

*by*

# Barbara Hazard

A SIGNET BOOK

SIGNET
Published by the Penguin Group
Penguin Books USA Inc., 375 Hudson Street,
New York, New York 10014, U.S.A.
Penguin Books Ltd, 27 Wrights Lane,
London W8 5TZ, England
Penguin Books Australia Ltd, Ringwood,
Victoria, Australia
Penguin Books Canada Ltd, 2801 John Street,
Markham, Ontario, Canada L3R 1B4
Penguin Books (N.Z.) Ltd, 182–190 Wairau Road,
Auckland 10, New Zealand

Penguin Books Ltd, Registered Offices:
Harmondsworth, Middlesex, England

First Printing, June, 1985
9  8  7  6  5  4  3

 REGISTERED TRADEMARK—MARCA REGISTRADA

Printed in the United States of America

BOOKS ARE AVAILABLE AT QUANTITY DISCOUNTS WHEN USED TO PROMOTE PRODUCTS
OR SERVICES. FOR INFORMATION PLEASE WRITE TO PREMIUM MARKETING DIVISION,
PENGUIN BOOKS USA INC., 375 HUDSON STREET, NEW YORK, NEW YORK 10014.

# PROLOGUE

*England, 1803*

The four gentlemen seated around the big mahogany table had finished dinner long ago, yet they lingered, drinking and talking in a desultory way. Although the curtains were drawn tight over the windows, they could still hear the sounds of the rain that had kept them from the hunting field for three long days. It hissed against the leaded panes and gurgled down the drainspouts as if it never meant to stop. The candles were burning low, and as one of them sputtered, the man at the head of the table raised a long white finger. His butler immediately hurried forward to snuff out the dying flame.

"More port!" the man seated on the left side of the table demanded, and the butler picked up the almost empty decanter and poured him another generous glass.

"I can't for the life of me see how you can continue to drink that stuff at this time of night, Hartley," the man across from him observed. "Some good French brandy is what you want at two in the morning!"

The man he had called Hartley admired the ruby color of his wine in the candle light, and then he swallowed half the glass. "I'll stay with the port, Reggie," he announced, his slurred words curiously light and high in pitch. "Only see what your brandy has done to Will!"

The brandy drinker cast a cursory glance at the figure who lay sprawled across the foot of the table, his dark head resting on his arms. A soft snore echoed through the room.

"Damned dull dog he is this evenin'," he remarked, moving his snifter in idle patterns on the dull, stained surface of the table. "Damned dull dogs we all are."

Hartley smiled. He was a tall, thin man with dark red hair

5

and a pair of narrow, cat-green eyes. In spite of his curving lips, the smile did not reach those eyes. It never did. "That's not what the *ton* calls us, dear boy," he reminded him.

Reggie looked up and grinned. "No, they do not, do they? But if the *ton* were to see us now, how they'd stare! No conversation, no plots, no escapades, and no wagers—why, there's not even a little ladybird or two within miles to amuse us."

"Yes, I have often wondered why you never let us bring some of the weaker, more delicious sex with us when we visit Cawfell, Hawk."

The man at the head of the table looked up from where he had been contemplating his nails. "Perhaps it is because, like the fox, I do not care to dirty my own earth?" he asked. His voice was deep in timbre, slow, and of a peculiar beauty. A woman had once told him it reminded her of a satin sheet that has been warmed by the fire.

The redhead chuckled. "Fastidious devil, ain't you?"

His host fixed him with a cool gray eye. "In some instances, extremely fastidious."

Hartley was reminded that he had once offered his current mistress to his host in payment for a debt, and Hawk had refused by saying, "I take no man's leavings, sir."

"But this ain't your earth, Hawk, Bredon is," Reggie protested. "You can't be thinking. Why, Cawfell's nothin' but a huntin' box!"

His blue eyes grew owlish and his florid, heavily jowled face grew taut as he opened his mouth widely and yawned. "Lord, I'm for bed soon." He stretched and then he sneered. "Satan's Rakes! Gad, what a misnomer that is tonight!"

"Shall we go back to town, then, before our reputations are quite lost?" the man at the head inquired.

"Can't do that, Hawk. Will's being hunted still for killin' his man last month."

His host nodded, a lock of blond hair that was almost white in the candlelight falling over his broad forehead. "I had forgotten. Perhaps we should go abroad with him and bear him company in his exile."

"As long as we do somethin'," Reggie persisted. "Why,

we haven't even had a good wager for a month. Devilish borin' we are, m'lord.''

"I think I have been bored for the past ten years," his host remarked, and both men laughed, for he was only twenty-four.

Anthony Hawkins, Earl of Bredon, snapped his fingers, and his butler hurried forward again to refill his snifter. As he tilted the cut-glass decanter, the gentleman on his right shifted sideways in his chair, and the toe of his polished boot caught the butler at the knees. The decanter shook as he staggered a little, and he sloshed some brandy on the table.

"Oi'm sorry, milord!" he gasped. "Oi'll mop it up instanter, sir! Hit was all moi fault!"

He backed away, bowing and scraping, and left the room to fetch a cloth, and Hartley, who had caused the accident, remarked, "I can't understand why you keep that old reprobate, Hawk. Jail bait, or I miss my guess, and his accent is more than a gentleman can stand. Dropping his aitches 'ere and putting them hanywhere!"

His host shrugged. "He's a good servant, and he's loyal. Besides, I know he will never rob me or disobey me.''

"Know somethin' about him, Hawk?'' Reggie inquired, leaning forward a little, as if he suspected a good tale was in the offing.

His host inclined his blond head. "You might say that, my friend. You might indeed.''

The butler returned then, and after he had wiped up the stain, his master waved him from the room. "Stay within call, Jenkins, but no eavesdropping.''

"Yus, milord, o'course, milord," he said as he left the room.

Hartley shuddered. "Just listen to him! Why, there is a gap as wide as the sea between that man and ourselves. The lower classes are so much lower, it is a wonder they are called 'men' at all. Even if you dressed him up in the best coat and boots and had Brummell himself tie his cravat, anyone would know his station in an instant. And, I daresay, before he even opened his mouth.''

"M'aunt Bess—the Marchioness of Sheldon, you know—

claims that education is all they need to make them our equals," Reggie said. "Bah! The woman's a muttonhead!"

"Perhaps she is right. If you get hold of them early enough, who is to say?" the earl asked.

"No, no, Hawk! It could never be done. There is that about them that will always reek of their birth. Assure you, dear boy," Reggie persisted.

The earl looked faintly amused. "Then we have found our wager at last, my friends. I will bet anything you like that I can take a servant and turn him—or her, as the case might be—into a personage fit to associate with royalty. A perfect lady or gentleman, in fact."

His guests broke into disbelieving laughter. "You'll never do it, Hawk! Beware we do not quite ruin you, dear boy," they cried, their animation revived at last.

"Shall we see?" he murmured. "Of course, there must be conditions set. The age is important, as I said. Our subject must be no more than twelve years old, and I will choose who participates in the experiment. Furthermore, it must be a wager that is not to be decided for seven years."

"Seven years?" Reggie asked, his blue eyes popping. "Why . . . why, we might all be dead by then, Hawk!"

"You most assuredly will be if you continue to swill brandy the way you do. No, I must insist on the seven-year term. It will add piquancy to the wager, to wait so long for its *dénouement*. And since I must produce an educated, well-spoken, well-set-up young person with excellent manners and versed in all the social niceties, seven years is none too long a time for the transformation."

"You're on!" Hartley exclaimed, pounding the table with his fist.

The noise startled Mr. William Ashton, who had been sleeping peacefully at the foot of the table, and he raised his dark head to stare with bleary eyes around the room. "What's the to-do?" he mumbled.

On having the wager explained by his host, he waved his hand and said, "Thass all right, then. But three 'gains' one—not fair. I'm in with Hawk." He dropped his head on his arms and promptly fell asleep again.

The earl looked at Reggie, now brooding down into his brandy snifter, his fat lower lip protruding at the earl's insult.

"M'lord Quarles, what is your pleasure?" Lord Bredon asked, his deep voice mocking.

"Aye, I'll wager you can't do it, Hawk. And Hartley can have my share if what you say is true and I am not above ground to collect it. But where will you find the slut or oaf you intend to make a member of the *beau monde*, m'lord?"

The earl was beginning to look bored again. "Why, anywhere you like. But stay! I have just remembered something that will simplify things. Jenkins!" he called, his change of tone so startling that Reggie jumped, and Hartley dropped the snuffbox he had been about to open. This time Mr. Ashton slumbered on.

The butler scuttled in and ran to the head of the table. He was a man in his fifties, short and thin, with balding gray hair and dark eyes set in large, heavy pouches. "Milord?" he inquired, bending forward in his anxiety to be of service.

The two guests who were awake settled back in their chairs and prepared to be amused.

"You have a daughter, Jenkins?" the earl inquired.

" 'Oo, me, sir? Nah, that Oi don't," Jenkins replied, shaking his head as if sorrowful he could not produce such an offspring at once.

"Then who does that wispy little thing I keep seeing in the hall belong to?" his master inquired.

"Oh, that's only Annie, milord. She's me wife's niece who we took in out o' the goodness of our 'earts when 'er ma went to the Americas last year."

"I do not believe I requested her life story, Jenkins," the earl drawled.

"Oh, nah, 'course not, milord," the butler agreed.

"You will fetch me this . . . mm, Annie, did you say? Just so."

The butler squinted in surprise and began to wring his hands. "Fetch 'er, milord?"

"There is something wrong with your hearing?" the earl inquired, his deep voice courteous.

His butler shook his head.

"Then go and do as I ordered. At once," Lord Bredon said. All during this exchange, he had not raised his voice or quickened the pace of his words, but now even Lord Quarles felt a shiver run down his spine.

"But, milord! The child's asleep in bed! Woi, it's afta two in the mawnin', sir!"

"I do not believe I asked for the time, either," the earl remarked.

The butler hesitated for a moment, but when he saw his master's blond eyebrow start to rise, he hurried from the room.

"A little beauty, is she, this Annie?" Hartley asked, his light tenor suggestive.

"Can't be. In this feminine desert, we would have noticed her," Reggie said.

"I do not know if she is well favored or ill, to tell you the truth. She is just . . . available for our purposes," the earl remarked. "And I do not believe you stipulated I had to turn her into an Incomparable as a condition of the wager. There are many 'ladies' who do not fit *that* category."

"Lord, yes. Hundreds of 'em," Reggie mourned.

"What amount did you have in mind to wager, Hawk?" Hartley asked.

His host looked bored. "I have no idea. Whatever you like."

"How about one hundred pounds each, then?" the redhead suggested.

The earl sneered. "Paltry, my friend, paltry for a wager of such magnitude. Shall we say a thousand pounds? It will add interest to the bet, and I am to be put to a great deal of trouble in the winning of it, after all."

The gentleman on his left narrowed his cat-green eyes until they were only slits in his long, narrow face. He was not as wealthy as his host or the two other gentlemen who made up the quartet the *ton* called Satan's Rakes. How like Hawk to put the wager almost out of his reach, he thought. The earl had come into his vast inheritance three years ago, on the death of his uncle. His father had died when he was still an infant, and his mother, Lady Gwendolyn Hawkins, had left him to her servants' care. Some said this lack of supervision was why the earl had grown up to be so wild and undisciplined and involved in constant scrapes and escapades. Although Sir Hartley Wilson was the eldest member of the group, he was quick to acknowledge that it was the Earl of Bredon who was its leader. Now he stared at the young man. He might be only twenty-four, but he looked years older with his cold, hooded eyes and the downward twist of his mouth. The life of dissipation he was leading had yet to leave any permanent marks, however, on his chiseled, handsome face.

Suddenly Sir Hartley remembered he would have seven years to accumulate a thousand pounds, and he smirked. He might even win some of it from his host, if the dice rolled for him, and honor cards continued to fall to his hand, and how satisfying that would be. Besides, he told himself, Hawk has about as much chance as a snowball in hell in pulling off this coup.

"One thousand pounds it is, m'lord," he said, and across the table Lord Quarles spoke his agreement to the terms as well.

The door of the dining room opened then, and the butler pushed a thin, sleepy-eyed child ahead of him into the room. She was barefoot, and wearing an ugly cotton nightgown over which she clutched a ragged blanket in her red, clawlike hands. Her face was narrow, with a sharp little chin under the snarls of her tangled reddish hair. The color of her eyes could not be determined, the lids were drooping so with weariness. She had been up since four-thirty the morning before, and since her aunt employed her as a scullery maid, as well as using her to fetch and carry hot water and chamber pots and coal when they had guests, she was exhausted.

The earl looked her over, and then he snapped his fingers, much as he would summon one of his dogs. "Come closer," he ordered, and then he murmured, "Thank heaven I did not say I would turn her into a raging beauty."

The other men laughed, and the child stared at them, confused and frightened. She did not move, and the butler pushed her none too gently toward milord. She stumbled over a fold of the blanket and fell against Lord Quarles's chair. He recoiled in horror.

"Get away from me, you dirty little rat!" he snarled. "Who knows what you've got? Fleas, no doubt, or something even worse!"

"You are harsh, Reggie," the earl remarked, beckoning with that long white finger. The child edged closer, never taking her eyes from his face.

She knew he was the Earl of Bredon, the man who owned the house. Her uncle had told her that. He was a very tall man with long legs and broad shoulders, and a supple, narrow waist. His face was cold and still, and now that he was staring at her, she shivered, although she didn't know why. He had never spoken to her before, or even seemed to be aware she was alive. She saw the way the candlelight turned his blond hair to silver, and imagined it would feel as rigid and chilly as the suit of armor in the hall, if she should touch it.

"What is your name, girl?" the earl asked.

The child swallowed. She did not like this place, or the men who stared at her so closely and who winked at each other and shifted in their chairs. There was something here that was evil, and she trembled. A loud snore from the other end of the table caused her to jump a little.

"I asked you a question. You will learn that I expect instant obedience," the earl said, his deep voice smooth, yet somehow threatening.

"An . . . Annie Ainsworth," she whispered.

Her uncle pinched her hard. "Milord," he hissed.

"Milord," she repeated.

"Hold out one of your hands," the earl commanded, and trembling in earnest now, she extended one scrawny, work-roughened hand. Lord Bredon studied it carefully, noting the broken nails and painful patches of chilblain.

"Come here and open your mouth," was his next order. Confused, the child did as she was bade, and then she was waved back.

"How old are you, girl?"

"Oi'm 'leven," she said, and then, as her uncle's wiry fingers pinched her harder, she gasped, "Milord!"

"Speak louder! When is your birthday, Annie Ainsworth?" the big blond man asked next, his hooded eyes intent on her face. She saw they were an icy gray, like the frozen skim on the water butt in the scullery on winter mornings.

"In March, me auntie sez. Milord."

"So, she is almost twelve. Close enough for our purposes, I believe. Well, gentlemen, have you any objection to my choice?" her master drawled, leaning back in his high-backed chair and ignoring her now as if she were not even there. She dug her bare toes into the soft carpet, feeling the thick pile surreptitiously. She had never been in this part of the house before.

"Object? I am more delighted than you can imagine, Hawk. But are you sure you would not do better with another specimen? We will quite understand, for I have rarely seen such an unpromising peasant," the redheaded man on his left said, sneering.

The man whose chair she had jostled put his handkerchief to his nose and shook his head. "You'll never win this wager, Hawk. Not in a hundred years, never mind seven. Look at her! Dirty, scrawny, ugly, and probably dim-witted as well!"

The earl turned slightly to see the child raise her eyes to the fat, florid man seated near her. For a moment, hatred gleamed there before she lowered her eyes again.

"We shall see, shall we not? Did you not notice how quickly she learned to say 'm'lord,' and after only two pinches, too?" the earl drawled. "All right, Jenkins, take her away. And have your wife see that she is ready to travel in a week's time. A bath or two might be in order before then, I believe."

His butler wrung his hands. "But, milord! Oi don't think . . . wot am Oi to say to the missus, then? Woi—"

"Did I ask for your comments? I am sure I did not," m'lord said. "You shall be well reimbursed for her loss, never fear. Now, leave us!"

Knowing how generous his master was when he was in his cups, Jenkins said no more. What did he care what the earl did with her? The child was nothing to him, after all, and he could tell from the way his wife treated her that Mabel didn't care for her either. It had something to do with her sister and the man she had married, who had gone off and left her even before Annie was born. And something to do with her sister's haring off to America and leaving the child on their hands. Probably Mabel would be glad to be shut of her, he thought as he pushed the child from the room and told her to get back up to the attic to bed.

In the dining room, Hartley inquired, "But where will you be taking her, Hawk?"

"Taking her? I have no intention of taking her anywhere," his host remarked, somewhat surprised. "I shall send her to one of my estates in the north and put her in the charge of the vicar and his wife there. Outside of yearly written reports from the good reverend, I do not intend to see her or think of her again until the wager comes due."

"But how trusting of you!" the redhead said in some surprise.

His host smiled a little. "Of course. If you employ good servants, you get good service. You really did not think that *I* was going to oversee her education myself? My dear Hartley! Surely you know me better than that. And besides," he added, his deep voice even smoother, "I cannot imagine that any of my instructions or expertise would be at all . . . mm, shall we say *appropriate* for a young lady of quality?"

Lord Quarles looked up from his snifter, a little bewildered. "But what will you do with her later, Hawk? I mean, if you do turn her into a lady? What then? Mind you, I don't think you can pull it off, now!"

Lord Bredon stood up to pour them all another drink. He shrugged. "I have no idea. Send her back here? Let her go? It is hardly important. Once she has won the wager for me, I do not care what becomes of her."

He lifted his glass. "I give you a toast, gentlemen. Let us drink to the year 1810—and the accomplished and elegant Miss Anne Ainsworth that is to be!"

# 1

*England, 1809*

In late August, Anthony Hawkins left the south of England, where he had spent the summer months, and traveled to Bredon in Leicestershire. He had not been to this, his principal seat, for over a year, and some vague stirring of conscience, plus the very real desire to make sure his agent was handling things in his usual excellent way, made him undertake a journey that he himself stigmatized as tiresome in the extreme.

The earl had no interest in his estate, beyond the monies that it provided for his coffers, but he knew his wealth depended on well-run acres, competent tenant farmers, and industrious servants. The impact of a visit from the earl himself was insurance, and the reinforcing of his agent's authority, that should not be neglected.

He left Lord Quarles and Sir Hartley behind him in Brighton, two of the men who made up the quartet the *ton* had named Satan's Rakes. William Ashton, the final member, had not been seen since early spring. His father had died, and he had been forced to forgo the Season, to handle estate matters that had fallen to his lot at last. His friends had been somewhat amazed that he lingered in the country for so long, but as Sir Hartley remarked, he had waited ten long years to come into his inheritance, and a little zeal must be forgiven him by his friends.

The pace the earl set was wicked, his coachman having been chosen for his ability to drive as if all the hounds of hell were snapping at the wheels. Inside the coach, the earl lay back on the squabs, his feet up on the opposite seat. His

beaver was tilted over his eyes, and his hands crossed carelessly in his lap. He looked completely relaxed. Barker, his
valet, clutched the strap next to him where he sat facing back,
and eyed his master with caution. He might be asleep, and
then again he might be staring right at him with those icy
gray eyes that were shadowed by the brim of his hat. The
valet swallowed and turned to look out the window at the
countryside they were racing through.

The pair had been silent for over two hours, for the earl
never spoke to his valet except to give an order. Barker had
often wished the salary was not so munificent, nor the earl so
satisfying to dress, for in that case he would have left his
employ without the slightest regret. But Anthony Hawkins,
the Earl of Bredon, was a delight to ease into a tight coat
from Weston. His aristocratic face under the silvery blond
hair was handsome, even wearing its customary bored sneer,
and there was nothing about him, from his broad shoulders
and narrow waist and shapely hands, to his long, well-muscled
legs, that would cause anyone to find a single fault with his
appearance.

And yet Barker could not help shivering sometimes when
he heard the earl approaching, or when those piercing eyes
inspected his face so carefully. He knew his master was a
harsh man, and some said an evil one, but he tried not to
think about the earl's behavior any more than he could help.
He might be Satan's Rake, but Barker had learned to ignore
the nickname. There were plenty of valets; there was only
one Earl of Bredon.

The sweating horses and dusty coach arrived at Bredon late
one afternoon. The grooms jumped from their perch at the
back, and one hurried to let down the step while the other
climbed the broad steps to give the knocker a mighty crash.
The earl had not been expected, for he never sent word of his
intentions ahead, but the butler who threw the door wide was
unperturbed. Bredon was kept as if the earl might appear at
any moment, and the only time the staff relaxed for even a
few days was right after he had concluded one of his light-
ning visits.

Now the butler snapped his fingers, and four footmen

appeared to line the steps and stand stiffly at attention. For long minutes there was silence, broken only by the chinking of the harness and the snorts of one of the tired horses.

Barker sat forward on the edge of his seat, clutching m'lord's dressing case to his thin chest. "M'lord," he said timidly, "we have arrived, sir."

The earl condescended to sit up and push back his tall beaver. He gazed without much interest at the scene outside the carriage door, and then he sighed. "Obviously," he said in his deep, mellow voice. Barker shivered.

The earl put out his hand, and the groom helped him to alight. He went up the steps at a leisurely pace, glancing at each footman in turn, but he did not speak until he reached the door, where his butler was bowing before him.

"Ah, Midler," he said as he handed this man his hat and gloves. "One of the footmen is missing a button on his livery."

His butler bowed deeper. The earl did not have to order him to see to it, or voice his disapproval in any stronger way.

Lord Bredon strolled into the great hall and looked around. More footmen stood to attention, and one of the parlor maids, caught before she could escape behind the baize door at the back of the hall, lowered her eyes and curtsied, trying to hide her feather duster behind her.

The earl stiffened, and never taking his eyes from the trembling maid, he said, "I am sure I made it a rule that I should never see a female servant in this part of the house."

"Yes, m'lord, you did, m'lord," his flustered butler said, hurrying into speech. "But not expecting you, Mrs. Westcott was giving the gold drawing room a good turn-out today, and the maids have been—"

He was stopped in mid-sentence by a languid wave of the earl's hand. Without another word, Lord Bredon went into his library, and the butler shooed the hapless parlor maid away, his face red and frowning. First the missing button, now the misplaced servant. It did not augur well for anyone's comfort during the visit. He gave the footmen soft orders to unload the coach, and then he hurried to bring a selection of wine and one of the best crystal glasses to the library. He knew he did not have to warn the other servants, not even the cook or the housekeeper, that the earl was back. Even now he was sure the word was spreading throughout the hall, and would be wafted, as if by a magic breeze, all over the several hundred acres that comprised the earl's seat. By dark, there wouldn't be a single soul among the earl's many dependents who would not know he was in residence again.

Lord Bredon stood beside his desk inspecting the afternoon post that had arrived an hour before. If he had not come, it would have been sent to London with the next post in the morning, from there to be forwarded to wherever he was at the time.

He pointed to the sherry as Midler presented the tray, and then he broke the seal of a letter from his friend William Ashton.

Will had written from his own estate, Ashton Abbey near Thetford. The earl's lips twitched as he read the enthusiastic, glowing sentences from the returned but unrepentant prodigal.

Mr. Ashton Senior had washed his hands of his only son after having to deal with a number of gambling debts and two duels fought before Will was even twenty. His acceptance into the ranks of Satan's Rakes had been the last straw for his none-too-patient father. Since the estate was entailed, he had not been able to disinherit the boy, but he had forbidden him to ever show his face at Ashton Abbey again. Will missed his three sisters a little, but since his mother had died when he was only ten, he had accepted his exile cheerfully. Released from his father's stern moralizing, and let loose among all the delights and immoralities of London, he had lost no time going to the devil as quickly as he could. He had a comfortable inheritance from his mother's brother, so he was wealthy enough to indulge himself. And now that his father had died, Ashton Abbey was his at last.

From all the earl could infer from reading his enthusiastic letter, Will had embraced his inheritance with a vengeance. A ghost of a smile twisted Lord Bredon's lips as he read the final page, and then he sat down at his desk and sipped his sherry, his gaze far away as he conjured up his friend's good-natured face.

He was surprised to find that he had missed Will's company. Two years younger, he was his most faithful follower, and without his wit and spirit, Lord Quarles and Sir Hartley had ceased to amuse. It was one of the reasons he had left Brighton so precipitately. Reggie seemed to be drunk most of the time now, and Hartley, with his excesses of other natures, could be tiresome.

Lord Bredon pulled a sheet of hot-pressed paper from the desk, and dipped a quill into the silver inkwell. He would write to Will and invite him to Bredon. It would give him someone to talk to, someone who would keep him company while he was here. And since Thetford in Norfolk was only a day and a half's journey, Will would not be put to any trouble. As he sanded his note, he smiled again. Not that it mattered. When he snapped his fingers, Will Ashton came, no matter where he was.

He rang the bell and ordered his butler to send a groom to Ashton Abbey with the note.

The butler looked out the long windows of the library. The sun, although it had not approached the horizon by any means, showed it was already late in the afternoon. "Er . . . now, m'lord?" he inquired.

Lord Bredon put down his sherry, one eyebrow rising.

"At once, m'lord!" the butler said hastily, and he bowed and left the room.

By the time William Ashton arrived at Bredon, some three days later, the earl was in a fierce temper. He was bored, of course, and when he was bored, he could be cruel. He had raised the rent of one of his farmers for no more reason than a fallow field, the parlor maid who had been in the hall when he arrived found herself sitting on her portmanteau in a carrier's cart, turned off without a reference, and the chef learned he was to be replaced. A dish of braised mushrooms in a wine sauce had given the earl heartburn.

Will found his host in the estate room, going over some papers with his agent, and he could not hide a grin at the discomfort on that gentleman's face, nor the relief written there when he saw the earl's friend had arrived. Lord Bredon left him abruptly, saying over his shoulder, "See that you take care of these matters without delay, Simms!"

Mr. Simms nearly banged his head on the desk, he bowed so deeply, and as Will took the earl's arm and strolled away with him, he laughed out loud.

At the earl's questioning look, he said, "I see you're still terrorizing the troops, eh, Hawk? I'll never understand how you manage to wring a groat from this place, the methods you use."

"It is because I terrorize them that they perform so well, my friend. But come! A glass of wine, and then I shall allow you to tell me everything about the abbey. I promise you will have at least ten minutes before my patience is quite exhausted."

As he motioned his friend to a seat, he thought he had seldom seen Will look better. Why, he was almost handsome. The pallor that was his usual complexion in London had been replaced by a deep tan, and his hazel eyes were alert and sparkling in the clear white that surrounded them. His face, although it had acquired some sun squints around those self-same eyes, had lost the lines that late nights and brandy had etched on his face, and he held himself erect, with barely controlled energy.

"Do sit down, Will. I find it fatiguing just looking at you, so full of vigor as you appear. Can it be possible that you *enjoy* country living?"

Will Ashton settled into a wing chair and crossed his legs. Although he was a sturdy man above medium height, he appeared shorter next to the earl's tall figure. Now he smoothed back his dark brown hair with a big hand that was as tanned as his face.

"I never thought to like it so well, Hawk!" he exclaimed. "There is such a difference now that the old man has gone. Ruth and Cynthia have married, but Margery remains at home. It has been a delight to make her acquaintance again. I vow you would stare to see how pretty my youngest sister has become."

"How old is she now?" the earl asked idly.

"Almost seventeen. I shall have to see about presenting her the next Season or so," Will said.

The earl chuckled. "*You* will present her? You'll have her on your hands forever if you do."

Mr. Ashton looked confused and the earl explained gently, "I hardly think one of Satan's Rakes . . . mm, a suitable sponsor, Will."

"No, of course not," Will said, frowning a little now. "But there's my aunt or my grandmother to do it. Margery will not have to suffer because of my reputation. Besides, I've been thinking, Hawk . . ."

"It is unnecessary to tell me, dear boy," the earl said kindly as his guest stared down into his wineglass as if hoping to find the words he wanted there. "You have seen the error of your ways at last. You have decided that from now on, as Mr. Ashton of Ashton Abbey, it behooves you to tread only a straight-and-narrow path, attending church twice on Sundays, and dispensing largess to the needy. No doubt you are even thinking of marriage to a suitably dull and worthy girl, and the birth of your heir shortly thereafter. Am I correct?"

Will Ashton's broad cheekbones were stained red now, at his friend's mocking words, but he looked into his icy gray eyes without flinching. "Yes, you are right," he said firmly.

The earl leaned his head back in his chair and closed his eyes. "Pray you will not quite desert your friends, Will. Without you to leaven the group, Hartley and Reggie grow tedious."

"I will never desert you, Hawk, you know that," Will said, his complexion reddened even more, that the earl should think him so careless.

Lord Bredon nodded at the compliment, and then he made a steeple of his hands and put them to his lips. "You have reminded me of something, Will. Something I have not thought of for a long time. There is someone other than your sister to be launched into society this year. Oh yes, we must make sure of that, for the girl is worth a thousand pounds to each of us."

"Whatever are you talking about, Hawk?" Will asked, completely at sea. "A thousand pounds?"

"Don't you remember that rainy night at Cawfell?" the earl asked.

His companion shook his head. "We are often at Cawfell. What was there about this particular night?" he asked.

"I had forgot. When the wager was made, you were fast asleep, your head on the table as a result of too many brandies. But you did recover your senses for a brief moment and came in with the rest of us. On my side, as well," the earl told him.

"A wager? What wager?" Will asked, getting up to refill his glass.

Lord Bredon smiled. "Hartley and Reggie bet me I could not take a little servant girl and turn her into a person fit to associate with the *ton*. I was to have seven years to accomplish the task—"

"Seven years!" Will exclaimed. "No wonder I don't remember it."

"The seven years will be up next spring," the earl said. "And then we shall see if we were victorious."

"And we bet a thousand pounds *each*?" Will asked, frowning a little now. It was not that he did not have the money, but he had several improvements he wanted to make at the abbey, and he did not want to have to delay them for a silly wager he had made when he was drunk seven years before. "Who is this girl, Hawk? And has your training succeeded?" he asked.

The earl heard the tension in his voice, and rose as the first dressing bell sounded. "I shall tell you all about it at dinner, my friend. That is, as much as I know. Since I have not seen the girl except that first night, I have no idea if I have succeeded or not."

He smiled a little and sauntered from the room, leaving a bewildered William Ashton behind him. To think that Hawk had made a bet of that magnitude, and never even checked himself to see what progress there was! He marveled as he swallowed his wine and prepared to go up and change into evening clothes. Shall I ever understand the man?

He could barely contain himself that evening until the covers were removed, the port served, and the servants dismissed. The earl had chatted lightly of this and that, seeming to derive a great deal of enjoyment from his guest's barely concealed impatience.

At last, as the door closed behind the butler and his minions, he smiled. "Very well, before you burst, Will! I have been thinking it over, and I believe I have recollected the matter now. The child was almost twelve, and a sorrier little rat you have never seen. She was the niece of my butler at Cawfell. I sent her to a holding I have in Durham County, to be raised by my vicar and his wife there. I relayed specific instructions for her care and training, so you need not look so horrified. And, of course, I have required a written report each year on her progress." He sighed and lifted his port. "I do not see anything further I could have done, do you? It seems to me I have been put to a great deal of bother as it is."

Will had to laugh at his tone of gentle complaint. "What does the vicar say?" he asked eagerly. "Is she . . . er, presentable?"

"According to his glowing reports, she has turned into a veritable princess from a fairy book." Lord Bredon sneered. "Of course, the man's enthusiasms must be taken with a grain of salt. He and his wife are childless, and from his letters I can only assume they have taken her to their hearts as if she were indeed their daughter."

"Does she know about the wager?" Will asked.

The earl shrugged. "I have no idea. She will certainly find out about it shortly," he said, his deep voice growing grim.

"But . . . but I cannot like this, Hawk! It seems to me that someone should make sure. After all, it is a sizable amount of money, and if there are a few little refinements to be made in her behavior, there is still time to do so."

"Excellent thinking, Will, excellent! May I suggest that when I go back to town, you ride into Durham and do the necessary?"

His friend opened his mouth, and thoughtfully shut it. "Yes," he said slowly at last, "I suppose I could do that.

After all, you have been put to all the expense and trouble of the wager up to now.''

The earl nodded. ''I am glad you are so quick in understanding, Will. I was dreading the possibility that I might have to point out your obligations to you.''

Mr. Ashton grinned at him. ''What is her name, Hawk?''

The earl thought for a moment, and then he shrugged. ''I don't remember. I shall have to look it up for you, but surely there can be only one such piece of perfection near Tow Law in Durham County. It is hardly a location that is overrun with the nobility or genteel society.''

''What am I to do if she needs additional training as a young lady of quality, Hawk?'' Will asked, his dark brows meeting in a frown.

''Tell the vicar to expect to be replaced within a fortnight, and then send the girl here. I'll have someone whip her into shape. And remember, we do have six months to do so.''

Mr. Ashton could not like the cold way his friend spoke about a young girl, nor the way he was prepared to let his vicar go. ''I am surprised she ever agreed to the scheme in the first place,'' he said in some wonder.

''Agreed? It was hardly her place, being only a servant and a child of eleven as well. If her uncle had no objection, what had she to say about the matter? Besides, she has had an exemplary upbringing for which thousands of wretched serfs would sell their souls. Enough to eat, and an education, pretty clothes, no work to do, and the love of her mentors.'' Lord Bredon sighed again. ''It appears to me I have been more than magnanimous—I have been downright saintly, a philanthrophist, in fact.''

Will laughed and covered his glass as the earl gestured toward the decanter. ''And what happens to her after the bet is won, or lost?'' he asked.

''If she is the vision of saintly goodness the vicar promises, perhaps I'll give her to you, my friend,'' the earl mused.

''Thank you, Hawk, but no! I want no mistress presented to me like some chattel!''

The earl waggled his finger. ''Not quite overcome by

morality yet, are you, Will? How disappointing! I meant her to be Mrs. Ashton, of course, not your light o' love.''

His friend stared at him, his hazel eyes darkening. ''Here, I say, Hawk!'' he exclaimed. ''I hope I know what I owe my name, sir! William Ashton to be marrying some little servant girl? Never!''

''I was only teasing, Will,'' the earl said, amusement warming his gray eyes. ''I am delighted to see that you rise to the bait as eagerly as you ever did.''

Will frowned down into his empty glass. ''Seriously, Hawk, what will become of her?''

Lord Bredon yawned behind a long white hand. ''I had no idea six years ago, and I have none now. Hire her out as a governess? Send her back to the vicar to find some hearty squire for her to wed?'' He shrugged, looking supremely indifferent. ''No doubt something will occur to me in time. You must remind me to think about it.''

# 2

Only a week later, Will Ashton found himself taking coach early one morning, to leave the comforts of Bredon for the earl's estate in Yorkshire. He had quite a distance to travel, and he knew he would have plenty of time to ponder this wager as his carriage rumbled northward. In the week since he had heard of it, he had come to think it not only mad, but cruel as well.

In fact, the whole venture made him uneasy, even a little ashamed. For the first time since he had met Lord Bredon as a green-as-grass eighteen-year-old, he found himself completely devoid of the hero worship the earl had always been able to inspire in him. He did not like the wager Hawk had made, not any part of it. He was surprised to discover that somewhere in the last few years he must have developed scruples. To be tampering with another's life for sport was repugnant to him, and he found it only added to the disquiet he felt when he remembered the girl was a servant. In fact, it made it even worse. Educated, advantaged people should know better than to exploit the helplessness of the poor and lowly.

And there was no use trying to defend himself by saying he had been drunk when the wager was made, and so did not know what he was doing. No, he knew only too well that all Hawk had to do was beckon, and, drunk or sober, he would follow his lead in everything. He had always done so in the past, and he had never imagined a time would come when he would not.

But now it appeared that that time had come indeed. He told himself he would see the girl, and he would talk to her.

26

He might have to explain the wager to her, although he had no intention of discussing it with the vicar and his wife, neither of whom, from what Hawk had told him, had any idea what was afoot. But if he felt the situation was impossible—if it seemed that any real harm would come from it—he would leave her there. When he got to London he would explain to Hawk why the wager could not be attempted, never mind won.

And then he stretched his sturdy legs out on the opposite seat of the carriage and tried to doze so as to forget these uncomfortable thoughts. Suddenly he had realized that growing up, at no matter what age it was attempted, was a painful process.

Lord Bredon had insisted he make himself at home on his estate. It was called "The Grove," and since he himself had visited it only once in the ten years of his inheritance, Will's stay would be in the nature of a personal favor. He had asked him to act as his agent, and he had authorized him to make any changes he felt necessary for future profit in the short time he was to be there.

Mr. Ashton had agreed cheerfully, although he felt Hawk much too careless a landlord to be ignoring even his northern-most estate this way. In answer to his query, the earl had said he thought it was sheep that turned him such a tidy sum each year, although he was not certain.

The earl had gone up to town the same morning Will Ashton left Bredon, and his last words still echoed in his friend's ears.

"I shall not tell Hartley or Reggie where you are, Will. I do not want to remind them of the wager until we see how the girl has fared. Be sure and write as soon as you have inspected her, and remember, she does not have to be beautiful, or even passing comely. The important thing is that she appears a lady, well-spoken and genteel. In this case her beauty is secondary. My, my! Surely this is a first for either one of us!"

He had laughed then, and entered his coach, leaving a perturbed Will Ashton to step into his own carriage and follow. They had separated at the end of the drive, Lord

Bredon turning left for the London road, Mr. Ashton to the right for Yorkshire.

By the time he was driven up the road that wound through the grove of trees the estate was named for, he was heartily sick of traveling. The roads had been dusty and rutted, but there was no relief from the occasional thunderstorms, for then the way turned into a muddy quagmire, and the pace had to be slowed.

A letter had been sent ahead of him, and he found an elderly butler smiling and bowing when he stepped down from the carriage and stretched. A young boy, his eyes wide with awe at the unusual visitor, ran out to take his bags as the butler welcomed him to the house. Will looked around. The Grove was built of stone, and had the feel of a place unlived in for many years, in spite of the cheerful fires that had been lit to take off the damp chill. It seemed clean enough, however, and the room the butler showed him to had a big four-poster with a good feather bed that was covered with colorful quilts.

He ordered some tea, and then a horse to be brought round. It was only three in the afternoon, and he had decided that if he waited till the morrow, it would only prolong the agony. No, he would ride to the vicarage at once, and get it over with.

The butler, who told him his name was MacCauley, was delighted to tell him the location of the manse, and the most direct route, as he served him his tea and some freshly baked scones. He was a garrulous old man, short and rotund and not much given to ceremony. Even as Will chatted easily with him about the neighborhood and the local weather, he wondered what Hawk would make of this elderly man who was so free and easy in his manner. Freeze him in his tracks, no doubt, with one of his icy glares, he thought as he wiped his mouth on an old darned napkin. The earl had never stood for familiarity from any servant.

The horse that was waiting for him at the front steps was a pretty mare, a chestnut with one white foreleg. She tossed her head and sidestepped nervously as he mounted.

"Aye, she's fresh, she is, sir, but she'll soon settle down," the groom told him in a broad local accent Mr. Ashton had trouble following.

As he set the mare to a walk, he wondered if this Anne Ainsworth he had come to inspect spoke the broad Yorkshire dialect. He almost hoped she did, for then his distasteful mission would be over before it began.

Horse and rider trotted down the drive and turned onto a bridle path through the woods. MacCauley had told him it was a shortcut to the village that was over the next hill, hidden from view. After he left the trees, he found himself in a broad field, cut with low, wandering stone walls that seemed to have no discernible pattern. Some little distance away from him was a large flock of sheep, peacefully grazing. They ignored him as he rode toward them. Will took a deep breath of the grass-scented air, cooler here in the north, and looked to the horizon and the rugged outline of the mountains the butler had told him were called the High Pennines. It was a beautiful day and a relief to get out of the coach at last, he thought as he urged the mare to a canter.

She jumped the low stone walls easily, and as he came to the brow of the hill, he pulled her to a halt. The village of Tees lay below him, and he was somewhat surprised at its size, and the height of the tower that graced the old gray stone church with its adjacent graveyard. A little distance away, he could see the manse, a long, low building with deep-set small-paned windows that was made of the same stone. It was set in a large garden and backed by an orchard. He turned the mare in that direction.

And then, out of the corner of his eye, he saw a cloaked and bonneted figure coming quickly down the hill in his direction. She carried a basket on her arm and there was a large dog trotting at her heels. He halted the mare and tipped his hat as she called, "Wait!" He could see she was frowning, even from this distance, and he wondered at it.

"Good day to you, ma'am," he called in return.

She came up to him in a rush then, and reached out to grasp the mare's bridle. "What do you think you're doing, riding White Stocking?" she asked in an indignant contralto. The dog growled a little at her tone.

Will had been busy trying to back his mount, afraid she might be trampled, but he stopped when the mare stood still and began to nuzzle the girl's arm. And then he forgot his concern for her safety and her rudeness as well as he stared down into what was surely the most beautiful face he had ever had the good fortune to see.

When he could separate the parts from the whole, he saw she had large dark blue eyes, thickly lashed and luminous. Her nose was straight and finely made, and her rosy mouth generous with an intriguing full lower lip. Her face was heart-shaped and ended in a firm little chin which she was raising at his scrutiny. On a pair of cheeks as soft and round as unblemished peaches, a blush was stealing, but he could not look away. He noticed that her hair was a riot of red-gold curls. Those that peeped from beneath her bonnet were turned to fire by the sunlight. He could not see her figure under the light cloak she wore, but she was above medium height, and she held herself proudly.

"I asked you a question, my good man," the vision demanded, her voice imperious now. Mr. Ashton noted her excellent diction, and the pure English she spoke, and he almost groaned aloud.

"If you are Miss Anne Ainsworth, I was coming to see you," he said, removing his hat and bowing from the saddle.

She looked surprised, and then she dropped the bridle and stepped back. The mare followed her, as meek as any lamb, and she patted her mane. "I am she," she admitted. "But who might you be, sir, to be riding my horse? Dismount at once!"

"Your horse?" he asked. "Surely she came from the Earl of Bredon's stable, ma'am."

Miss Ainsworth made a quick, impatient gesture. "I am the earl's ward, sir, and White Stocking is my mount. Whenever I ride, she is brought down to the manse for me."

"I see. I did not realize that you were Hawk's . . . er, the earl's ward. I am a friend of his come to stay at the Grove. William Ashton at your service, Miss Ainsworth."

As he spoke he dismounted and came to stand beside her. He noticed he did not have to look down very far to see her face, for they were almost eye to eye. The view, close up, was breathtaking.

"Sit, boy!" she ordered, and he became aware that the dog had risen and his growl was deepening.

"You must excuse me, Mr. Ashton. I did not know of your visit, for I have not been up to the Grove lately," she said. Will noticed that she was not at all flustered or shy, although surely Hawk had said she was only seventeen. Her self-possession was impressive.

"If you will join me for a ride someday, I shall forgive you," he heard himself saying. "I am sure there is another horse in the stable that I can ride."

Her laugh was a delighted musical chuckle. "Oh, there is another horse, Mr. Ashton, but I do not think you would care for him. He is an old, cantankerous gelding, and his gait leaves much to be desired."

"What is to be done, then?" Will asked.

"Are you fond of walking, sir?" she asked. "You might join Da and me for one of our rambles."

"Da is your dog?" he asked politely, and she chuckled again.

"King is my dog. Da is Mr. Davis Nettles, the vicar," she explained. "And that reminds me. I must get these berries to Aunt Ellen. She is making a special brew for one of our parishioners who is ill."

"Allow me to come with you, Miss Ainsworth," Will begged, hoping she did not hear the pleading note in his voice. "I must make the vicar's acquaintance, and extend Hawk's salutations as well."

"Hawk?" she asked as she started down the path, the dog pushing jealously between them. Will was left to follow, leading the mare.

"Anthony Hawkins, the Earl of Bredon," he explained. "All his friends call him Hawk."

"I see. I have not seen the earl lately," she said. Her voice was airy, and then he saw that little chin go up, almost defiantly, as she continued, "I trust you left him well, sir?"

"Very well. He is hoping to see you again before long," Will blurted out, wondering if there was anything in the world he could do to keep this beautiful, breathtaking girl away from his friend. Self-assured and confident she might be, but she was no match for the Earl of Bredon. And he was sure only one of Hawk's piercing gray glances would decide the issue. How could he not want her? Will was surprised at the stab of pain he felt at the thought. Now she was young and fresh and innocent. What would she be like when Hawk was through with her?

He was brought back to present company as she turned to face him, her dark blue eyes shining. "Is he coming to the Grove, Mr. Ashton?" she asked eagerly, for the first time betraying her youth.

"I am not sure," Will temporized. "I have not received any definite word as yet."

"We will all be delighted to welcome him at last!" Miss Ainsowrth exclaimed, almost skipping down the path now, her red-gold curls bouncing on her back. Will hurried to keep up with her.

They came to the vicarage through an old rose arbor that led into the garden. Miss Ainsworth took him to the kitchen door, where she deposited the basket of berries and wild herbs, and tied White Stocking to a fence. Then she insisted he come around to the front of the house.

"I cannot be bringing you in through the kitchen, sir," she explained, walking beside him now, the dog on her other side. "For one thing you are an honored guest, and for another it would upset Bessie. Bessie is the cook, and no one, not even Granny Nettles, dares to upset *her*."

As they strolled through the gardens, full of the fragrance of roses and lavender and larkspur, he heard the sweet notes of a flute drifting toward them from an open window.

"That is the vicar, playing his beloved Bach," she told him. "But he will be delighted to meet you, sir. You must not fear your visit is untimely."

She preceded him through the open doorway of the manse into a wide hall. The interior was a revelation. Whereas outside there had been ivy-covered gray stone, within all was bright and cheerful with sparkling white paint and colorful watercolors. On a polished center table of cherry was a large jug of flowers arranged with a loving hand. Without pausing, Miss Ainsworth opened the door to a parlor and indicated he was to enter.

"If you will wait, sir? I will tell the vicar you are here," she said, a smile curving those tempting lips. Will felt a lump in his throat and nodded, moving past her into the room.

Left alone, he looked around. The same loving touch he had seen in the hall was evident here in the shining furniture and old but well-tended fabrics. The Turkey carpet under his feet was worn in places, but it had mellowed to a series of soft golds and tans that was echoed by the chintz of the curtains and the soft pillows of the chairs. Above a large deep-set fireplace was an oil painting of the nearby mountains as a storm approached. He moved closer to inspect it. It was done by an amateur, but there was power in its rendering, and good color and composition. He stretched to see the signature, and was rewarded only with the two initials "D.N."

"Hmmmph!" came a ferocious snort somewhere near his left knee, and he almost jumped out of his boots.

Turning quickly, he saw the tiniest, oldest old lady he had ever seen. She was seated in a high-backed wing chair, her feet dangling above a footstool, and her faded blue eyes, set in a network of wrinkles, peered up at him in a ferocious frown.

"You've come for Annie, haven't you?" she asked in a quavering, cracked voice. "Don't take her, oh please, don't take her, sir!"

Startled, Will could not speak, but he stretched out his hand to her. At once she grasped it with surprising strength and turned it palm up. "Oh yes, I see," she crooned, bending over it until her nose almost touched his skin. "You were a wicked one once, weren't you, my fine boy, but now I see you are about to be changed. Praise the Lord! One of Satan's own has repented! Praise the Lord!"

Will felt a chill on the back of his neck, and wondered if the old lady was mad. Before he could wrench his hand from her grasp, the door of the parlor opened, and he turned toward it eagerly. A small man with graying hair hurried forward, exclaiming, "Now, Mother! Up to your old tricks again, I see. Let the gentleman go!"

The little old lady released Mr. Ashton with some reluctance, and turned away to stare into the empty fireplace, her lower lip pushed out in a pout.

Will went to join his host. "Vicar Nettles?" he inquired. "My name is William Ashton. I am a friend and emissary of the Earl of Bredon."

"Wickedness! Sin and wickedness, and death and destruction," the old lady keened behind them.

The vicar reddened. "Come into my study, sir," he said, leading the way from the parlor. Will was only too delighted to obey.

When they were both seated in the book-lined room, the vicar behind his desk, he rang a bell and then folded his hands before him and said, "I beg your pardon, Mr. Ashton. My mother is an old lady, and she is not well. Sometimes she says things—believes things—that are not so."

Will was reassuring the man that he had not taken any offense, when there was a soft knock on the door behind him. He did not have to turn to know who was there, for the vicar's eyes grew soft, and a warm, loving smile played over his lips.

"Anne, my dear, Granny is in the parlor and she has taken one of her dislikes to Mr. Ashton. Could you make sure she is not there when tea is served?"

"Of course, Da," her soft, low voice agreed. "I am so sorry, Mr. Ashton. Granny generally has excellent taste," she added, her voice demure as she shut the door.

Will felt the tips of his ears reddening, and he looked to the vicar, as if for instruction. That good man sighed.

"I must apologize for Anne as well, sir. The one thing I have not been able to teach her is how to control a sometimes unruly tongue. But you must tell me how I can help you. Perhaps the earl has sent you in person to see how his ward progresses?"

Will silently cursed Hawk as he tried for an honest, sincere tone. "The earl is naturally concerned about her progress, and since I was traveling this way, he asked me to look in on her—on all of you, sir!—and also on the Grove.''

"Are you sure he didn't put the Grove first, Mr. Ashton?" the vicar asked, his voice wry. And then he seemed to shake himself. "Ah, well, the secret was bound to come out sometime during your visit. You see now where Anne gets her pertness, sir. *Mea culpa.*"

At his rueful little smile, Will studied him more closely. He saw a man of about fifty years of age, with the fine, fresh complexion of the countryman. His clear blue eyes were intelligent behind his spectacles, and the pleasant lines forming in his face showed he was a man more prone to smile than frown. Will had already noticed his small stature when he walked behind him into the study, but his height did not seem to be particularly important. There was that about his manner that would make him noticed long before many taller men.

Will Ashton spent an uncomfortable half-hour alone with his host. Uncomfortable because he knew his errand, not from anything the vicar said to him. This good man talked almost exclusively about Anne Ainsworth—her beauty and goodness, her quick mind, her talent on the pianoforte and her sweet, true singing voice, and most of all, the joy she had brought into their lives.

At last he paused and shook his head. "You will be thinking her peerless, sir, too good to be true! And so I will tell you her faults. Besides her pertness, she has a hot temper that is sometimes too easily provoked. She cannot paint or sketch, her needlework is a disaster, and although she has a pretty accent in French, her Latin and Italian are shaky." He shook his head. "*Very* shaky. And then there is her inability to do more than the simplest sums. When I chide her with it, she only laughs. There, that is honesty indeed!"

He smiled at his guest and added, "But when Anne is near, none of these faults are the least little bit important, for she is like a ray of God's sunshine. My wife will be able to tell you more about that, Mr. Ashton," he said, rising as he heard some soft murmuring and the clinking of crockery in the hall. "Come, you must join us for tea, and meet her."

Will agreed eagerly, knowing Miss Ainsworth was sure to be present. He only hoped she had been successful in ousting the elderly lady who had startled him so with her unexpected yet accurate palm reading.

Teatime at the manse was a pleasant experience, marked with wit and laughter and an old-fashioned courtesy he had not seen for years. Mrs. Nettles had smiled when they were introduced. She was even tinier than her husband, but twice as round, and her face showed her good nature and kind heart. He thought Miss Ainsworth had been fortunate indeed in her adopted home.

He was the center of attention, of course, for he came from a larger, more cosmopolitan world than the village of Tees. Everyone had a dozen questions about new books and plays and music, the politics of the day, and what fashions were currently in vogue.

Miss Ainsworth had asked this last question, leaning forward a little in her eagerness. Now she had removed her light cloak, Will could see that she had a shapely figure, with a deep bosom and hips that swelled in luscious curves from a supple waist. In the eyes of the fashionable world, her charms would be too abundant, but he thought her perfect. She was tall, and she carried herself well, like a golden cornucopia of delightful richness. Besides, he remembered his sisters in their adolescence, and how they had slimmed down when they reached womanhood.

Miss Ainsworth was dressed in a simple pale blue gown, and she had brushed her curls into a more decorous style. Will could have told her it was no use. She could have worn her hair in the tightest, most severe bun imaginable, and its rich color would always betray her. Now a wandering sunbeam was captured in a few little curls above her brow, and he had difficulty concentrating on her question.

By the time his horse was brought round, he had accepted an invitation to dine the following evening, and a morning walk the day after, and he went away in a haze of delight and dismay.

Whatever was he to do? he wondered as he rode toward the Grove. Surely there must be something, some way he could keep Anne Ainsworth away from Hawk and the wager? He was determined to find it.

# 3

The next two weeks were almost dreamlike, they passed so quickly for Will Ashton. He spent a great many of his waking hours at the manse or with Miss Ainsworth and the vicar on long, rambling walks about the countryside. He had tea with them, and dinner, and he escorted the ladies to church and to the nearest market town to shop. Occasionally, stung by his inability either to confess his errand or to find a way to keep this golden girl from Hawk's attention, he tried to redeem himself by riding the earl's acres, talking to his shepherds, and going over the estate records with his agent.

Always his mind came back to Anne Ainsworth. He spent many long hours before a dying fire in the late evenings, planning and discarding a hundred different schemes for her escape from the earl and the wager. None of them were at all practical. Besides, Hawk was his friend. He found he could not serve him a backhanded trick, not even for Miss Ainsworth.

Still, he could not bring himself to write the promised report.

Sometimes he sat down to do so, telling himself he must be cold-blooded and firm, but page after page found itself in the fire instead of on its way to London. No matter how he began these letters, they always ended up a weak, whining plea that she be spared.

He knew her better now, and he admired her even more. He had seen her quick temper when they came on two boys torturing a mongrel dog. How she had descended on them, whipping about them with her walking stick, like some glorious avenging angel! And how they had run! Will found himself carrying the dog back to the manse so she could nurse it back to health, and he wondered what Satan's Rakes would have to say if they could see him.

And he knew her pertness and quick tongue, too. She loved nothing better than to tease him or catch him up with a gay remark. Hawk had called him gullible; how he would have stared to see how gullible he could be with this saucy young girl.

Many evenings he had sat entranced as she and the vicar played duets, he with his flute and she at the pianoforte. And late one afternoon after he had driven them all in his carriage to a nearby lake for a picnic tea, he had heard her singing a plaintive little melody that tore his heart, it was so sweet and true—so like she was herself.

He also knew many of her thoughts and fantasies. She confided in him as if she had known him for years, and they were the best and oldest of friends. Falling in love with her as he was, this was especially painful, but he reminded himself that she was very young.

He was astounded to discover that she had built up an image of Hawk in her mind that was totally false. To her, he was her guardian angel, the wonderful person who had swept her away from a life of poverty and hunger and hard, brutal labor and delivered her to people who loved her so much they never even scolded her. That he never came to see her, or even wrote, she excused with the airy, naive statement that "Surely earls, being such important personages, are *very* busy." And she never stopped asking if Will had heard from him, or inquiring about the date of his arrival, and Will was hard put to parry her questions. Once he had tried to tell her what kind of a man the earl really was, but she had refused to listen, claiming he was teasing her, and indeed he found it impossible to malign his friend, even to spare her.

The golden, bittersweet September days drifted by, and then the letter he had somehow expected, and was wholeheartedly dreading, was delivered to the Grove. After only the briefest of salutations, Hawk began, "I find it strange, almost sinister, that I have not heard from you, my friend. Is she so terrible, then? Is there no hope at all? I think it would be best if you bring her to Bredon, Will, and at once. I cannot come into Yorkshire at this time, and the problem must be resolved. I shall expect you, accompanying Miss Ainsworth, by the end of next week. I have sent a letter to the vicar explaining the visit, and mentioning that I think it is time the young lady was exposed to a wider society.''

Will groaned when he read that last sentence. He could almost see the twisted little smile Hawk must have worn when he penned it.

But whatever was he to do? Now that the vicar knew she had been invited, he could not hide it from them. By careful probing, he had discovered the Nettleses had no idea why they had been given Anne to raise, and more important, not an inkling of the kind of man Hawk really was. They had never met him, and the sobriquet ''Satan's Rake'' had not penetrated into the wilds of Yorkshire. He was grateful for that. For one brief, soul-searching moment, he wondered if he should go and confess everything to the vicar. And then, in his mind's eyes, he saw the cold, scornful stare the man would give him, and the hatred and disdain everyone at the manse would feel for him. It would put paid to any hope he had that someday he might marry Anne. Granny Nettles was right. He had been an evil man, involved in dissipation and duels and dalliance, but he could not admit it to these good people.

When he went for tea, he found the manse in a great uproar. As he stepped inside, Anne's maid, a dour country-woman named Mary Agnes, was coming down the stairs carrying a pile of gowns and muttering to herself as she did so. Upstairs, behind her, he could hear Granny Nettles crying, and in the parlor the murmurs of the vicar and Mrs. Nettles. The excited, tremulous chatter of Miss Ainsworth rose over their voices. He knocked slowly, and opened the door.

Anne jumped up from the footstool where she had been sitting at the vicar's feet. It was her favorite spot.

''Mr. Ashton!'' she cried. ''Have you heard the news? I am to go to Bredon. To *Bredon*, Mr. Ashton!''

She clasped her hands together and sighed with so much delight that Reverend and Mrs. Nettles had to laugh. Even

Will managed a weak smile as his hostess came forward to hug his arm and lead him to a chair.

"I am so glad you are to escort her, Mr. Ashton," this good woman said. "Such a young madcap as Anne is, I would not feel right sending her with only her maid and Miss Goodly."

"Miss Goodly?" he asked, feeling a tiny ray of hope.

Mrs. Nettles nodded. "Yes, a dear old friend of mine. She is a retired governess, and when she learned of our dilemma, she offered to go with Anne as her chaperon. Now, with the two of you to watch over her, the reverend and I can be easy."

Anne waved her hands impatiently at this dull talk of chaperons. "Shall I bring White Stocking, sir? And will an earl object to a *king*? I do not think I can leave my dog behind, not if this is to be a long visit, that is."

She looked at him with some concern, and he told her he was sure the earl would have no objection to a dog, but that there were so many horses to ride at Bredon, White Stocking would be superfluous.

Anne sank down on her footstool again and leaned her head against the vicar's knee. His hand crept down to rest on her red-gold curls, and Will saw the glitter of tears in the blue eyes behind his spectacles. "Do tell us all about Bredon, please!" she demanded. "Is it very big? Very grand? I do hope my clothes will not shame the earl, for we are not very fashionable here."

Will hurried into speech past the lump in his throat.

The evening before they were to leave Tees, he was invited to the farewell dinner at the manse. Here he was introduced to Miss Goodly, a tiny, dithery female in her fifties, who in his opinion did not look as if she could chaperon a kitten, never mind the dynamic damsel who almost crackled with her excitement as she sat across from him. However, he told himself, she was better than nothing.

After a short grace that asked the Lord to protect them on their travels, the vicar made a special effort to be festive. So did his wife, but Will saw her wipe her eyes more than once during the gala dinner. When at last the meal was concluded and the ladies rose, the vicar put his hand over Will's and pressed it. Then, when he had seen them out the door and closed it behind them, he returned to the table and poured them both a glass of port.

"I do not have to tell you why I have detained you, my boy. I am sure you can guess."

His smile was wry, and Will nodded and said, "Of course. You wish to speak to me about Anne . . . er, I mean Miss Ainsworth."

"Yes, it is about Anne. You have seen how precious she is to us, and I would ask a kindness of you. I do not know how long you will remain at Bredon, but I want you to let me know if Anne is not happy there. For any reason," he added, his voice stern.

Will looked into his clear blue eyes. It was obvious that the vicar had his suspicions about Bredon and its earl. Before he could speak, the vicar continued, "You see, outside of the money that is sent for her care, and the yearly reports I write to m'lord, there has been no communication between us. I have often wondered why he undertook Anne's upbringing and education, for he is not known as a warm, caring man. Several things have occurred to me, of course. Anne is so perfectly formed and lovely, so intelligent and talented, I can only assume she comes from a noble line. And the one thing we did not have to teach her was her regal bearing and manner. Perhaps she is a love child of one of his relatives? She is much too old to be one of his, unless he was precocious beyond belief."

He saw how uncomfortable Will was and chuckled. As his guest stared in surprise, he said, "I am constantly amazed at the way the laity assumes that men of the cloth must of necessity be innocent. My boy, in the nature of our calling, we have all of us seen more ugliness, more evil, than most men. Nothing surprises us, not after a few years in His service. But you must forgive me my disgression."

He took a sip of port and continued, "But if Anne is some wellborn bastard, why did she arrive the way she did almost seven years ago?"

He paused for a moment and stared into the candle flames,

as if lost in his memories. "It was very late at night, a cold, snowy night with a wind blowing that went right through you—typical Yorkshire weather in winter. She came on a carrier's cart wrapped up in a ragged blanket and clutching the only things she possessed in a shawl. Ellen cried when she saw her, and I, sir, am not ashamed to admit, was not far behind her. Such a scrawny little mite, almost starved and frozen as she was. Her hands and feet were covered by chilblains, but that was not the worst. I must tell you she had black-and-blue welts all over her body from being pinched and beaten. Do not ever doubt there is a hell after death for those who mistreat children, Mr. Ashton. God in His infinite wisdom will see to that."

He moved restlessly, and Will swallowed a sip of port to ease a suddenly dry throat.

"She could barely speak so as to make herself understood," the vicar went on after a moment. "And she was so frightened that it took herculean efforts over a long period of time before she dared to trust us. I thought to give her a puppy, and that opened the floodgates. Sad, is it not, a little girl who felt safe only in giving her love to the dumb animal she called King?"

He sighed and ran a hand through his thinning gray hair. "To add to our confusion, there was the earl's letter. It was so cold and businesslike! We were to educate and dress the girl as if she were a lady. She was to do no work—in fact, he ordered me to hire a maid for her when she was old enough to require one. That was one area where we did not succeed, Mr. Ashton. No one can stop Anne from helping when she sets her mind to it."

He chuckled a little and then he looked straight at Will. "Well, sir, we did not understand it then, and we do not understand it now. But it did not matter as long as our dearest Anne—our daughter—was with us. And once she realized she was safe here, that we would always love her, she became the young lady you see today. She is warm now, and trusting. Sometimes I think she is too trusting."

He shook his head. "It worries me. Anne throws herself at every experience as if she is trying to make up for her first eleven years. She runs after life and grabs it with both hands as if to squeeze all the juice out of it she can. It is almost as if she believes that nothing bad will ever happen to her again, that that part of her life is over forever. I fear that if she is not watched over, her enthusiasms may lead her into dangers and disappointments. You know her, you have seen how she is. Do you agree with me?''

Will nodded and then cleared his throat. The story he had just been told had affected him deeply. "I do, sir, and I can assure you that if it is in my power, I will not let anything happen to her. I will watch over her as if she were my own.''

"As if she were your own sister, Mr. Ashton?'' the vicar asked gently.

Will bit his lip. "Yes, sir, my own sister. For now,'' he could not help adding, and the vicar smiled at him.

"We shall see in time, my boy. Thank you for letting me tell you my concerns. I feel much better that you know and will be with her. And now, shall we join the ladies?''

As they walked together to the dining-room door, Reverend Nettles patted his arm. "Anne has promised to write often, but we would be pleased if you would honor us with a letter now and then, telling us how she goes on.''

"I shall, sir,'' Will promised, and then Anne was there in a whirl of skirts to smile at him and kiss the vicar, drawing them both into the circle near the fire.

Just before he took his leave, Will felt his eyes going to the wing chair where Granny Nettles sat, her hands plucking nervously at the shawl that covered her legs. Her faded eyes seemed keener tonight, and as she stared at him, he felt the challenge there. And then she nodded a little, as if satisfied with whatever she saw in his face, and Will was able to make his escape.

If the journey north to Yorkshire had seemed long and tedious, the journey south passed much too quickly for Will Ashton. Sometimes he rode beside the carriage, and sometimes, on rainy days, he joined Anne, her maid, and Miss Goodly, and a dog who seemed to have grown by several pounds and inches inside the rocking vehicle.

Anne had not been out of Yorkshire for almost seven years, and after the first day, when she was so depressed at leaving those she loved best in the world behind, she regained her spirits, thinking of the adventure ahead. Everything was new and fresh to her, and her exclamations and questions made it the same for the others. Will could see that Miss Goodly thought her much too coming, and once when she frowned, he leaned over and patted the older lady's hand in reassurance. Anne was no simpering miss, and he did not want her to become one. Slightly appeased, Miss Goodly held her tongue and ceased her remonstrances.

Will had brought a traveling chessboard with him, and he taught Anne to play, and sometimes she would read to them all if the light was good and the road smooth enough.

The inns where they stayed each night were a novelty to her, and she never left without a new friend or two behind her in the morning, for she was always smiling and kind.

Will wished the journey might go on forever, but of course, and much too soon, he found the carriage sweeping up the long drive to Bredon, an excited Anne all but pressing her nose to the window so she would not miss a single thing.

As he helped her down at the base of the broad front steps that rose up and up to the towering pillars of the front, he realized for the first time how impressive and intimidating Bredon could be, seeing it through her eyes. She looked around with her usual interest, pointing out a peacock on the lawn to Miss Goodly, and a folly peeping through the trees, but for Anne Ainsworth, Will thought her almost subdued.

The butler opened the door to his knock, and bowed. Not a smile creased his face, even when Anne gave him a most enchanting one of her own.

"Welcome, Mr. Ashton," this austere personage said, beckoning to what seemed, to a vicarage miss, to be an army of footmen. "His lordship is expecting you and the young lady. He is in the library."

Will asked him to show Miss Goodly to her room and to give his assistance to Miss Ainsworth's maid, and the butler raised an already lofty chin. "Of course, sir. It shall be taken care of at once."

He bowed and indicated they were to follow him, and Will felt a soft hand creep into his. He looked down and smiled. Anne was wearing a new blue traveling gown, with a matching half-coat and bonnet. When he had complimented her on her outfit that morning in the inn when she came down to breakfast, she had said she had been saving it for the day she came to Bredon at last. He thought she looked beautiful, and now he told her so again in a whisper, to give her courage. She smoothed the skirt with her free hand. "If only the earl agrees with you, sir," she whispered back.

With his heart sinking, Will knew she did not have to worry about that.

The butler announced them as they entered the library. Far away down a vast expanse of carpet, Anne saw the blond-haired man she vaguely remembered. He was writing at his desk, and he did not stop as they approached.

Then he laid his quill down and looked up, and she saw a pair of icy gray eyes sweeping over her from head to foot. One eyebrow rose a little as he came to his feet to stand leaning on the desk.

"Miss Ainsworth?" he asked, his voice noncommittal, but before she could answer, he turned to her companion. "Of course I understand now, dear Will. Oh, *how* I understand!"

As his glance returned to her face, keener now in its inspection, Anne sank into a deep curtsy. "M'lord," she said formally, and then, as she rose, she smiled. "No, that's not right at all," she said, and came toward him to sweep around the desk and reach up to kiss his cheek. Over the little blue bonnet, a pair of astonished gray eyes looked to his friend in what in anyone else would be called total confusion.

"That is a better greeting for one who has been so very kind to me for so long," Anne said, drawing away and blushing a little. "I cannot tell you how glad I am to see you at last, sir, so I might thank you in person for your care and concern."

Seeing that Hawk was speechless, Will Ashton strolled up to the desk. "Give me your things and sit down, Anne. I will order you some tea or lemonade. You must be thirsty after the dust of the road. I know I am."

As she removed her bonnet and half-coat and handed them to her courier, the earl found his voice at last. "Thank you, my friend. It is always so elevating to be instructed in my duties as host."

He turned to Miss Ainsworth again, his eyes going over her figure in the form-fitting traveling gown so quickly, Will was sure Anne had not noticed. "I am delighted to welcome you to Bredon, Miss Ainsworth," he said smoothly. "Why, you surpass my wildest expectations!"

Will noted the smile that accompanied these words, delivered in Hawk's deepest, most caressing tones, and his stomach tightened.

"But you must call me Anne, m'lord, for you are my guardian," she chided him with another sunny smile. "What a large room this is! And it has so many books! Da would be in heaven here."

"The Vicar Nettles, Hawk," Will explained, wishing he could relax and did not feel he had to perch on the edge of his chair like a dog guarding a meaty bone. Just then he remembered King, and he wondered what had become of him. He did not have to wonder for long.

Loud barking and the angry cries of several men came through the thick library doors, and the earl's face grew frigid. Anne jumped up, and picking up her skirts, ran down the room. The earl's expression did not even brighten at the sight of her neat ankles.

She threw open the door and the huge shepherd bounded in, licking her hands and wagging his tail as if they had been separated for years instead of only minutes. Behind him, the butler and four footmen crowded in to try to capture him again. King growled at them.

"Perhaps you will be good enough to explain this . . . er . . . this noisy intrusion, Midler?" the earl asked, icicles dripping from every syllable.

Anne rose from her knees and buried a firm hand in the dog's thick ruff. "I do beg your pardon, m'lord, and I must beg your servants' pardon as well, for it is all my fault. This is my dog, King. Mr. Ashton assured me you would not mind if I brought him, for I could not leave him at the manse. We have not been separated since he was a puppy.''

Will could feel Hawk's eyes flicking his face like an icy breeze and he was careful not to look in his direction.

Anne hurried on. ''In the excitement of our arrival, I forgot he was in the coach. He is not dangerous, you know. Stop that, King!'' she ordered as the dog curled his lip at the butler and growled again. ''It is just that he thinks he has to protect me, you see.''

''I suppose she has a dragon of a maid, as well,'' Hawk murmured to Will in a soft aside.

''And a chaperon, of course,'' Will told him, trying to preserve a sober face. ''She is a retired governess. Her name is Miss . . . Miss Goodly.''

When this information seemed to silence his host most effectively, Will was able to hear Anne say, ''I do hope he did not bite anyone?''

The warm concern in her beautiful face caused the youngest footman to thrust his bleeding hand into his coat, lest the sight of it cause Miss any distress.

''You may leave us,'' the earl snarled at his servants, and for a moment Anne looked at him with a little doubt. As they turned to go, the earl added, ''Some wine for Mr. Ashton, Midler, and some . . . er, some lemonade for Miss Ainsworth.''

The butler bowed, looking as if all this was not at all what he was used to, nor could ever approve, and then the earl added, ''And perhaps a bowl of water for the dog? Just so. One would not like to be deficient in any way to a guest, or I will have Mr. Ashton reminding me of my obligations again.''

His voice was sarcastic, but Anne did not seem to notice. As she led the dog up to be introduced, she laughed gaily. ''I am so glad you like to joke, Lord Bredon. I am always doing so myself, am I not, Mr. Ashton? And a sense of humor is so important, don't you agree?''

# 4

Anne settled down happily in a big chair with King at her feet, and proceeded to make the better acquaintance of this big, handsome man who was her guardian.

Will listened anxiously, but when Hawk behaved himself, making only a few cryptic comments that seemed to go right over Miss Ainsworth's head, he relaxed. He knew the time was coming when he would have to give Hawk a full account, and he began rehearsing phrases in his mind that would best illustrate what a marvelous girl Anne was, and why all thought of any wager involving her must be abandoned at once.

Anne told the earl the news of the vicarage, and all about her life in Tees, as if she were sure he must be interested in everything that had happened to her since last they met. Lord Bredon sipped his wine and studied her over the rim of his glass, coolly assessing her charms. She was certainly one of the most beautiful girls he had ever seen. That red-gold hair was distinctive, and he was surprised that the color attracted him. He had always chosen dark women, for he enjoyed the contrast between them and his own fairness when he held them naked in his arms. Anne Ainsworth would be gold to his silver.

He noted she was shapely, although his connoisseur's eye deplored her slightly overabundant charms. A sharp reduction in her food intake would take care of that, he told himself, and if that was the only fault she had, he could count himself fortunate indeed.

He applauded her excellent diction and pure accent. There was not a trace of Yorkshire in her speech, nor any of the lower-class patois he associated with her uncle. He must remind himself to reward the Vicar Nettles appropriately.

As she talked, he watched the color coming and going in her soft round cheeks, the sparkle of those dark blue eyes, her delicate arched brows and flawless complexion, and he wondered if the rest of her body would be as inviting. Somehow, he was sure it would be. And her full, rosy lower lip was entrancing, especially in a face so full of innocence it was obvious that no man had ever so much as kissed Miss Ainsworth. He decided that as soon as the wager was won, he would be delighted to be the first to do so, and to initiate her into all the wonders of lovemaking as well. He would make her his mistress.

When he remembered the way she had looked the last time he had seen her, he was filled with amazement at her transformation, and with his quick surrender to her charms as well.

He noticed that her dog never took his eyes from his face, and that although he lay in a seemingly relaxed sprawl near his mistress, his ears remained erect and pointed toward Lord Bredon's chair. And when he rose to terminate the interview, the dog was quick to rise too, a warning growl beginning deep in his throat.

"King!" Anne scolded him. "How dare you? This is our *friend*!"

She cuffed the dog and he subsided, although the earl was not fooled, especially when he saw that those dark, liquid eyes still followed his every move.

"I must apologize for King, m'lord," Miss Ainsworth was saying as she rose and shook out her skirts. "It must be because he is in a strange place. Neither one of us has ever been away from home before. He will soon grow accustomed to Bredon—and to you."

The earl smiled at her, a warm, lazy smile that was almost a caress. "I can only hope so, my dear Anne, since I intend to be at your side every minute I can."

He saw Will's sudden frown at his suggestive words, and added, "You must excuse Mr. Ashton and me now, however, for there is some business that we must discuss. I am sure you have some unpacking to do, and perhaps you would like to rest? Ask Midler to show you to your room and introduce you to my housekeeper. She will see you have everything you need. Dinner is at eight. We look forward to seeing you then.''

Anne curtsied. ''Of course, m'lord. But please do not treat me as a guest, for that is quite unnecessary. I look forward to exploring Bredon. It is so lovely. And I often spend hours alone; you must not feel I require your constant attendance or any special amusement.''

The earl hesitated, and then he bowed. Will was glad that the outrageous remark he was sure was hovering on his lips, about how delighted he would be to see to one very special kind of amusement, remained unspoken.

Both men watched her make her way down the expanse of carpeting, her posture regal and her round hips swaying in unconscious seduction. They did not move until she had shut the door behind her and her dog.

Lord Bredon sat down again then and motioned Will Ashton back to his chair. ''My dear Will, I cannot remember when I have been so stunned,'' he began. ''Completely stunned and amazed. As I mentioned in my letter, I was sure the girl had turned out to be so unsuitable for our wager that you did not know how to break the news to me.'' He smiled at his friend, and then he added, ''But of course, now that I have met the golden goddess, I see why you did not wish me anywhere in her vicinity.''

''I still do not, Hawk,'' Will said firmly. ''I see how you look at her, and it will not do! She is not like that, she is all goodness, and . . . and she is still only a child!''

''She has a very observant dog, Will,'' the earl remarked, as if he had not heard his friend. ''Did you notice how he never took his eyes from me the entire time he was in the library? I thought he had chosen Midler to be his enemy, but it is plain he has divined correctly the man he had best watch. He is very intelligent, for a dog.''

He laughed and waved his hand. ''As for her being a child, well, I have never seen such an *un*childlike form. She is extremely . . . mm, voluptuous, wouldn't you say? And still only seventeen, too.''

"It is baby fat, Hawk. My sisters were just the same," Will told him.

"Nevertheless, we shall put Miss Ainsworth on a reducing diet. It will be so much more effective to present Hartley and Reggie with an Incomparable rather than just a pretty, overweight lady, don't you agree?''

Will stood up and went to lean on the desk, his face only a few feet from his friend's. "Listen to me, Hawk! There must be no wager, no exploitation of Anne Ainsworth, do you hear me? She is too fine a person, and she has been through so much!''

"Yes, she looked as if she had been suffering," Lord Bredon replied.

"I meant when she was younger. The vicar told me her story, and it would break your heart, Hawk, to hear him tell of it.''

"I doubt it. I never weep, not even at the most affecting tragedies," the earl remarked. "Besides, I saw her at Cawfell. You did not. Now, go and sit down, Will. Your dramatics have no effect on me at all. I sent the girl to be turned into a lady to win us each a thousand pounds, you remember, and now that she is restored to me, she shall do just that. No, no," he continued, holding up a deterring hand when he saw Will about to break into impassioned speech. "No more. We shall have plenty of time to discuss this in the days ahead. And you need not worry that I shall seduce Miss Ainsworth. Not yet, at any rate. Until she has entered society as a sinless young virgin, and won its accolades, she is safe.''

"You are not fit to talk of her or even speak her name! None of us are, and if you hurt her, Hawk, I'll kill you!'' Will panted, not at all reassured by this generous forbearance on the earl's part.

One blond eyebrow rose, and Anthony Hawkins' voice grew cold, as cold as the icy glare in his gray eyes. "I shall forgive that outburst, Will, and put it down to the heat of your passion for the young lady. Passion you would be wise to temper, for she is not for you!'' Stern gray eyes stared into

defiant hazel ones as he continued, ''It pains me that I have
to remind you that Anne Ainsworth is my creature, Will. Oh,
yes, mine, and mine alone. I bought her for a handful of
golden guineas seven years ago, and she will do what I
say—in everything. And now you must excuse me, for there
is a matter of business I must discuss with my agent. He is
waiting for me in the estate room.''

He strolled away down the room, leaving a frustrated and
distraught Will Ashton behind him. Will went to one of the
long windows, to stare with unseeing eyes across the velvet
lawns of Bredon. Somehow, he must keep Anne safe.
Somehow, he must think of a way to get her out of this coil.
But how he was to write to the vicar and reassure him that all
was well with his charge before he had done so, he did not
know. He shook his head, and then he saw Anne coming
through the garden, King frolicking at her side. He leaned
closer to the pane, his eyes devouring her lovely face and the
sunlight playing in her curls. Only when she had gone around
to the front, did he leave his post.

When Anne had left the library, she heard the little whine
King always made when he had to go outside, and she led
him to the front door. The butler was there, bowing as she
approached. Not by a flicker of an eyelash did he acknowledge her dumb companion.

''I shall show you to your room, Miss Ainsworth,'' he
announced in the manner of one conveying a tremendous
boon.

''Thank you . . . er, Midler, was it not? I should be
delighted, after I take King for a short walk,'' Anne said, her
smile sunny.

The butler stiffened. ''That is not at all necessary, miss.
One of the footmen can see to the animal's . . . er, needs.''

Anne laughed, ''I doubt that, Midler, after the reception he
gave them earlier.'' She spoke with the ease of a lady born,
and then she said, ''I shall make their acquaintance tomorrow
and introduce them to King. For now, I had better take care
of him.''

She looked around at the footmen as she spoke, her warm
smile still lingering, and every man jack of them could hardly

wait for the morning. The youngest footman, his hand bandaged now beneath his white glove, made plans to beg a bone from the kitchen for the dog, hoping if he gained his liking, Miss would smile for him alone and make him her favorite.

Midler bowed again as he opened the door, and Anne went out, King at her heels. The dog ignored the butler as regally as Midler ignored him. When the butler looked back to survey the hall, one of the footmen turned a chuckle into a cough behind his gloved fist.

Anne was glad King had to go out, for she had a lot to think about. The earl was not at all as she had imagined he would be; in fact, she had never met anyone remotely like him before. It was plain to see that she must revise her thinking, for there was that about his manner that sometimes confused her. When he spoke to his servants, for example, he was cold and autocratic. She had not liked his occasional sneer, and some of his comments to her had made her uncomfortable, although she did not know why. And although she admitted his voice raised goose bumps on her skin, and was as warm and melting as the cheese she and the Nettleses sometimes toasted over the fire at teatime, it could also be cold and angry and abrupt.

Then, as King ran ahead of her down the path to the folly, she shrugged. He was the Earl of Bredon, and perhaps all earls behaved this way. She did not know. Mr. Ashton had not seemed upset, and surely he would know how earls and dukes and other nobles behaved. She would have to ask him about it when she got the chance.

When she reached the folly, she could not resist going up the steps and peeking inside. It was a round building with a small golden dome that was supported by pillars and latticework. Around the sides that faced the house, the lattice was covered with rambling rosebushes that still held a few late blossoms, but the side that faced the ornamental water had been left open so the view could be admired. Anne drew in her breath at the sight. There were no outlines of rugged mountains adorning a far horizon that she was used to in Yorkshire, but across the wide sheet of quiet water there was a large wood of huge old oak and beech trees. They looked as if they had been standing since the beginning of time. It appeared to be a wonderful place for a ramble, and she decided to take King there as soon as she had the chance.

She sank down on one of the wicker chairs with which the folly was provided, each one covered with plump, colorful pillows. She noticed there was a bell to summon a servant, a bowl of grapes and peaches, and a frosty pitcher of fruit juice on a table nearby, and she leaned back and sighed as she closed her eyes. Bredon was beautiful and so luxurious it took her breath away and made her stare. She would have to be very careful not to appear a country mouse in all this grandeur, she told herself, wishing she never had to leave it. There was something in her makeup that craved luxury and comfort, she realized, something she had never suspected to be part of her character before. The vicarage had been warm and lovely in its way, and she had not minded the shabby cushions or faded rugs, because it was safe, full of love, and her home. But here at Bredon, everything was ordered and grand and opulent, and she felt akin to it.

As she lay back in the chair, she dozed a little, and the dream that always came to her appeared in her mind. She was standing on a thick carpet, and there were men there, laughing at her and mocking her. She could not hear what they were saying, and she had no idea why she was there in the middle of the night. She was tired and cold, and her hands and feet were aflame with sores. Every time she moved, she could feel the scab on her back that had broken when Aunt Mabel took the switch to her that morning for spilling some milk. And then, the man at the head of the table spoke to her and beckoned her closer. He seemed bathed in a golden halo of light, like an angel, and his eyes radiated a cold glow like stars in the black sky of a winter night. She moved toward him and held out her hand. And then there was nothing. The dream ended abruptly, as it always did.

She felt King nuzzling her hand, and woke with a start. As she stroked his thick coat, she looked down at her well-kept hands. They were soft and white now, the nails pink and well manicured. Above her wrist was the satin braid that trimmed the cuff of her new traveling gown. Her soft lips tightened.

She would never go back to Cawfell, no matter what she had to do. She would never submit to being cold and mistreated and hungry again, she vowed, as she had so often in the past. The vicar and Aunt Ellen had never suspected how vividly she remembered her former life, nor guessed to what lengths she was prepared to go to avoid any return to it. She knew they loved her, and she had come to love them with all her heart, but still she could not help but mistrust the miraculous change in her fortunes, even after almost seven years.

The Nettleses had promised her she was safe with them and always would be, but those first eleven years were still etched sharply in her mind, and she could not forget. To the world, she appeared the serene young lady, smiling and confident, but underneath, the frightened child still cowered, waiting for the next blow.

When Anne came down to dinner just before eight o'clock, she was accompanied by Miss Goodly, dressed in her best navy-blue silk. This lady never stopped whispering her instructions, but even though Anne was impatient with her homilies, she was glad the chaperon was there to lend her support.

Anne had spent a long time trying to decide what to wear. Her maid sniffed when she finally chose her best gown of white silk, decorated with delicate embroidery around the narrow cuffs of the poet sleeves and on a double flounce at the hem.

"And is Lord Bredon giving a ball this evening, Miss Anne?" Mary Agnes asked, her rough voice sarcastic. "That is your best dress, and if you wear it tonight to dinner, what will you put on when there is a party?"

Anne looked mutinous as she held the gown against herself and stared into the pier glass. Imagine, a glass that showed all of you at once! What luxury!

"No, it will not do," Mary Agnes said, bringing her back to earth. Since she had once served as lady's maid to a baroness, Anne could not disagree with her judgment. The maid hooked her into a primrose muslin gown with a modest neckline and short puffed sleeves, and allowed her to put on the single strand of pearls that Mrs. Nettles had lent her.

Anne begged to have her hair put up, and Mary Agnes sniffed again. "It's not seemly, miss, for a girl your age. Do you want your guardian to be turning me off, then, for not knowing what is correct for a miss of seventeen? You'll put your hair up on your next birthday, and not a moment before!"

At last Mary Agnes declared she was satisfied, and let her go. Anne hugged the dour middle-aged woman and thanked her, and her maid gave her a little pat.

"Run along, now, Miss Anne, and mind that unruly tongue of yours," she reminded her.

Miss Goodly was whispering much the same advice when Midler announced them at the door of the drawing room, but the minute Anne stepped inside, she forgot. The earl was standing before the fireplace, resplendent in evening dress, but it was Will Ashton who drew her eye as he rose to greet them. She had never seen him in formal attire, the white of his cravat startling against his dark coat and tanned, good-looking face.

"How handsome you look, Mr. Ashton!" she exclaimed, and Miss Goodly moaned softly.

Will flushed and came to lead them both to the earl. Anne bit her lip when she saw his sardonic smile.

"And do I also earn your encomiums, my dear Anne?" he asked.

Anne studied him as he straightened up from where he had been leaning against the mantel. He was even more impressive than Will Ashton, with his long lean body and silver-blond hair, but somehow she did not want to tell him so. His gray eyes were amused as they lingered on her face, and she hurried into speech. "Of course, m'lord. You look just the way I remember you that night at Cawfell."

The earl bowed a little. "May I say you do not look anything like the way you appeared that night, Anne? And for that I am exceeding grateful," he added, his warm voice mocking. "Why, the ugly caterpillar has turned into a butterfly."

Anne did not know how to reply to this, so she said with a grave dignity, "May I present my chaperon, Miss Alicia Goodly, m'lord?"

The earl thought the picture they presented was more than a little incongruous, for Miss Ainsworth was well above average height and the lady at her side barely five feet tall. He nodded as she made her curtsy, and his words as he bade her welcome to Bredon were cool and indifferent. Will Ashton watched Miss Goodly, sure she was about to sink into a flutter of confusion and abjectness, but to his surprise, she drew herself up, her expression almost militant now as she stood even closer to her charge. One corner of the earl's mouth twisted, and then Midler announced dinner, and he bowed to Anne.

"You must allow me to take you in, Anne," he said, drawing her hand into the crook of his arm and pressing it. "Will, be so good as to escort Miss Goodly."

Anne noticed that the top of her head just barely reached his shoulder, and wondered why this should be so exciting. It must be that she was used to little people, she told herself, for the Nettleses had often joked about the Amazon in their midst. Now, as she walked beside him, fitting her stride to his, she had to admit she liked the feeling of being next to someone so tall. It made her feel smaller herself, and dainty and feminine.

The earl seated her at his right hand, in the luxurious salon that was the dining room. It was decorated in crimson and gold, the frescoes painted on the high walls and ceiling the work of Laguerre. Anne did not know that several leaves had been removed from the table, for she felt far removed from any of her companions. She looked at the array of plate and crystal before her, and was glad Mrs. Nettles' precepts were fresh in her mind.

"Observe what other ladies do, Anne, or watch the earl. He will demonstrate which fork or spoon or glass you should use, until you grow more accustomed."

It had been Mrs. Nettles' special charge to oversee Anne's

education as the lady of quality the earl demanded. She herself was the daughter of a viscount, and so she was perfectly at home with the manners of polite society. From her Anne had learned how to curtsy to every rank, how to walk and sit and dance, and how to converse at the dinner table, no matter how exalted the company.

The earl noted her poise was prodigious as she placed her napkin in her lap, not a bit awed by the service plate of gold before her, nor the huge gold centerpiece of sportive cupids and nymphs that was flanked by two high candelabra containing a dozen long wax tapers each.

Mr. Ashton installed Miss Goodly across from her, and Anne saw that it would be impossible for that lady to catch her eye through the massive decorations, and she smiled a little to herself.

Lord Bredon was impressed as he raised one long white finger, and a procession of footmen advanced from the sideboard bearing the tureens containing the first course. Midler came forward to get m'lord's approval of the wine.

As dinner progressed, Anne's eyes grew wider. She might have been able to keep her composure intact earlier, for Mrs. Nettles had explained the table service, but the delicious unknown dishes that were presented to her made her stare. She decided she must try a little of everything so she could write a full description back to the vicarage. Then she became aware that the earl's cool gray eyes were surveying her plate.

"I see you have a hearty appetite, Anne," he remarked.

Anne saw that he had taken only one slice of the salmon and a small spoonful of peas, and that he had ignored the white sauce with dill which she had spooned so generously over her fish. She had also agreed to a slice of oyster pie, some duchesse potatoes, and the carrots glazed with honey.

For a moment she felt embarrassed, but then she smiled. "It all looks so good, m'lord. I wanted to sample everything. It is true I have a good appetite, and I do enjoy my food."

The earl's eyes raked her shoulders and breasts. "Obviously," he murmured, signaling Midler to refill his wineglass.

Anne felt a flush begin in the pit of her stomach and spread upward, and she put down her fork. She darted a little glance at Will Ashton at the foot of the table, but he was talking to Miss Goodly and had not noticed the exchange.

The earl waited until Midler had withdrawn to the huge gold-leafed sideboard, and then he said softly, "You must forgive me for pointing it out, Anne, but you are much too heavy. Our society ladies all strive for a willowy look, for that is the vogue now. I do not think in your present state that you could be considered willowy by any stretch of the imagination."

Anne felt her throat grow tight with her incipient tears, and she lowered her eyes in confusion.

"Poor poppet," the earl continued, his deep voice warmer now. "Do not look so distressed! But before we go up to town, you must learn how to curb your appetite. I shall delay sending for the dressmakers until you have lost the weight that is necessary. You see, my dear Anne, I want you at your best when you meet the *ton*. It will make you look like a princess at the least, to say nothing of being . . . mm, more appealing, shall we say?"

At that, Anne raised her eyes to his face, searching as deeply as she could. There was a little mocking light in his eyes that did not reassure her, but then she scolded herself. The Earl of Bredon had done so much for her, surely she could do this little thing for him.

"Certainly, m'lord. I shall be happy to do whatever you suggest, of course. I . . . I did not know that I was fat . . ."

"How could you?" he asked, cutting his salmon now. "Lost as you were in the depths of Yorkshire. But all that will be changed now that you are at Bredon."

He ate his fish and then wiped his mouth on his damask napkin. When he saw her with her hands still folded in her lap, he said, "Eat your dinner, Anne. Time enough tomorrow to begin your course of self-improvement. We have several months before a most important day, my dear, and by then I am sure your figure will please even the . . . mm, highest stickler."

Anne Ainsworth started her reducing diet the next day, and
with a vengeance. She had been miserable throughout the
remainder of dinner, although she made a concerted effort not
to show it. She thought Will Ashton looked at her closely a
few times, his eyes going from her face to the earl's, conjec-
ture in them, as if he wondered what Lord Bredon had been
saying to her while he was doing the pretty with Miss Goodly.

He had scant time to question Anne, however, for the earl
made it plain that he had little or no interest in any conversation with her chaperon. Miss Goodly did not appear to be at
all upset by the snubbing she was receiving, and made a good
dinner. She confined her remarks to the earl to a compliment
on the expertise of his chef with the sauces, and a few
comments about the weather.

Lord Bredon nodded, but almost all his attention was
directed to Anne. He told her about London and the Season
she was to enjoy, and some carefully edited anecdotes about
the doings of the *ton*. By the time Miss Goodly rose and
beckoned to her, Anne was feeling a little more at ease.

She was glad even so that Mr. Ashton did not ask her to
play the pianoforte or to sing after dinner, and was delighted
when her chaperon excused them both early, claiming fatigue
from the journey.

When she woke the next morning, she was still feeling a
little depressed, and for a moment she lay still in the big
four-poster in the pretty blue and-white bedroom she had
been given, and wondered at it. She had been looking forward so to her visit to Bredon, to meeting the earl at last . . .
and then she remembered his criticism of her figure the

evening before. Under the blankets, her hands ran down her body, pushing here, pinching there. She did not feel fat to herself, but what did she know of the current vogues? And if Lord Bredon wanted her to lose some flesh, she would do it!

When she joined Miss Goodly at breakfast, she looked enviously at her plate. Little sausages and shirred eggs, fresh-baked scones, strawberry preserves that glistened with fruit—mmmm! Instead, she poured herself a cup of coffee, took one spoonful of the eggs and a small piece of Dover sole from the buffet, and told her chaperon she had eaten so much the evening before, she was not a bit hungry.

Miss Goodly nodded and buttered another scone. "Lord Bredon left a message for you, my dear," she said before she bit into her scone. Anne tried not to look.

"He said he had business to attend to this morning, but would expect to ride with you and Mr. Ashton this afternoon."

Anne smiled and sipped her coffee. "What are you going to do this morning, Miss Goodly?" she asked courteously.

"Mrs. Westcott, the housekeeper, is giving me a tour of the house. Should you care to join me, Anne?"

"I think I would prefer to explore the home wood and some of the grounds with King," Anne replied. "A brisk walk would do us both good."

"As you say, my dear," Miss Goodly said mildly. "I know you and the dear vicar were often abroad. Why, the Tees villagers used to say you were out in all kinds of weather."

"Da says a little mist or even rain never hurt anyone," Anne remarked. "I must remember to write to him and Aunt Ellen today, to tell them of our safe arrival."

"Do that, Anne. They will be so pleased and relieved to hear from you. I shall be writing myself in a few days."

There was a little pause, and then Miss Goodly asked, "Anne, do you think you will be happy here?"

Anne looked up from her empty plate. There was no gold centerpiece between them this morning, and she was a little surprised to see the shrewd, concerned look in the lady's brown eyes behind her spectacles.

"I am sure I shall," she said. "Bredon is so very luxurious, is it not? Who would not adore to visit here?"

"And the earl, do you like him?" Miss Goodly persisted.

"Well, he is different, a little more formal than I expected," Anne admitted.

"And quite a bit younger than I expected," Miss Goodly added absently. "Of course he is a stunning man with that blond hair and handsome face. It is too bad his manner is so cold and mocking."

"I think that must be because of his rank, don't you, Miss Goodly?" Anne asked. At the anxious look in her eyes, her chaperon bit back the quick retort she had been about to make. She had known many of the nobility in her lifetime, and not a one of them had been as cold, sarcastic, or conceited as their host. She did not like Lord Bredon, or the situation. Anne was too beautiful, too desirable, and the earl was, after all, an unmarried man. She had seen a look last evening in his hooded eyes that had given her pause. She was determined to watch over Anne as carefully as she could, for there was something about the master of Bredon that told her he was dangerous.

"I daresay," was all she replied, however, in a meek voice. Anne's smile was blinding as she begged to be excused.

When she reached the hall with King at her heels again, Midler was nowhere in sight. She went around in turn to each of the footmen on duty, asking their names and introducing them to King. King allowed them to pet him and make much of him, but it was the youngest footman who earned the most gratitude, by presenting him with a large bone. King wagged his tail and Anne smiled.

As King got a good grip on his bone, the footman told her his name was John Coombs. Anne liked him immediately. He had a fresh, open face and straw-colored hair with a large cowlick he kept smoothing down with one hand. His blue eyes were full of admiration for her.

"Thank you for King's bone, John," Anne said, giving him her hand. "You have made a friend for life."

She looked around as the door at the back of the hall

opened and Midler strode forward, his majestic gait only a little hurried.

"May I assist you, miss?" he asked, one eye watching King growling over his bone as if he was sure the butler had designs on it.

Anne could tell by his frigid accents that a large shepherd gnawing a disgusting bone in his hall was not at all what he cared to see, and hiding a chuckle, she told him she was about to take the dog for a walk. Midler hastened to open the front door, and King pranced by him as before, his bone held tightly in his big jaws.

It was some time before Anne could get him to abandon his treat and follow her to the home wood. They walked around the lake, enjoying the early October day. The sun was warm, and it glinted off the water, and this morning there was a little breeze that rippled the wide expanse. Anne held onto her broad-brimmed hat as she set a smart pace. Exercise was sure to make her thinner if she ate only tiny meals.

The home wood was beautiful. Strolling under the massive trees, the sun coming through the leaves in long streams of light, Anne felt she was in a cathedral. She wished Da was here, telling her about the trees and the various birds and small animals she saw. It was a little lonely by herself, and she was not sorry when she came to a cottage deep in the woods. Some distance away, she could hear a woodchopper at work.

A woman was hanging up clothes on a line near the cottage, and when she saw Anne, her mouth dropped open before she remembered to curtsy.

Anne introduced herself and asked the woman's name, and then she asked if she might have a drink of water. The woman nodded, and brought her an earthenware cup full, and a bowl for the dog. She was shy, and she seemed frightened of this strange and beautiful young lady, but Anne's artless questions about her life and her husband's soon had her talking eagerly. She had few visitors, and she was glad of the chance to sit down. Anne noticed she was with child and near her term, and she insisted on hanging up the rest of the basket for her, in spite of Mrs. Carter's protests.

When she left, she left a friend, as she almost always did, no matter where she was. She promised Rhea Carter that she would come back soon, and maybe next time there would be a baby to admire. Mrs. Carter's eyes were wide as she watched the tall redheaded lady walk to the edge of the clearing and turn to wave.

"They'll never b'lieve this in the village," she muttered to herself, darting a glance at the path where Anne had disappeared, as if she might have dreamed her visitor.

For luncheon, Anne had some fruit and a small piece of cheese. In vain did Will Ashton recommend the game pie and the apple tarts covered with clotted cream. The earl had not joined them, and somehow the atmosphere was lighter in his absence. Miss Goodly told them about her tour, saying she was sorry now she had not gone with Anne. Bredon was so big she declared she must rest for the remainder of the afternoon, being quite exhausted from the mile-long corridors and massive salons.

Mr. Ashton was more at ease with Anne's chaperon now. She had a dry sense of humor that he found refreshing, and she was not at all starched up and prissy, something he had always associated with governesses before. When he made a joke, she laughed even before Anne did, and it was a comfortable trio who sat on at the table, chatting together. Anne was still hungry, and she remembered her vow yesterday in the folly that she would never allow herself to be in that condition again. How quickly life changes, she thought as she went up to put on her only habit.

She was delighted with the mount the earl provided for her use. A mare as pretty as White Stocking, this horse was a darker shade of chestnut, chosen, if Anne had known it, to show off her red-gold hair by the contrast. Lord Bredon watched the way she rode for the first few minutes, but when he saw she could control her mount easily, and appeared comfortable in the saddle, he relaxed.

"Sit up a little straighter, my dear Anne," he said, and Anne straightened her back and squared her shoulders. Will Ashton frowned at this proprietary air, but the earl ignored him. "You ride very well. I am pleased," he said, and she smiled at him for the compliment. Will thought the whole situation disgusting, and made up his mind to speak to Hawk about it as soon as he got the chance. To hear him, the incorrigible rake, giving advice to such a good girl as Anne was, was too much for him to stomach.

Their way led them through the nearby village of Bredon, and Anne was treated to the sight of the inhabitants carefully bowing and making their curtsies as the earl and his party passed. She noticed that no one smiled at them. Perhaps they did not dare? she wondered. When she smiled herself, there were a few responses, gone before she could be sure she had really seen them. It appeared that Lord Bredon was respected but not much loved by his people.

It was late afternoon before they returned to the house. Anne expressed a desire to see the stables, and Will said he would take her. They left the earl at the front steps of Bredon and trotted on to the stableyard. It was a busy place, with the grooms and young boys caring for the many horses the earl kept. Anne walked through the yard and the various stables, admiring a pair of matched grays and a huge stallion kept in a special stall. She asked a great many questions of the head groom. He was a taciturn Scot, but he was not proof against her friendliness, and he smiled and tugged his forelock when she thanked him.

Strolling back to the main house, Will said, "Do you like it here, Anne? Do you think you will be happy at Bredon?"

She heard the doubt in his voice, and the little frown that creased his brow, and she wondered at it. The earl was his friend, and yet something seemed to be bothering Mr. Ashton.

"Miss Goodly asked me the same thing this morning," she said. "Bredon is very beautiful and very opulent. Imagine keeping all those horses. Why, the bill for oats must be prodigious!"

Her voice was awed, and Will had to smile. What a child she was, when all was said and done. "That is not what I asked, Miss Ainsworth," he said sternly. "Attend me, please! Do you think you will be happy here?"

Anne skipped a little beside him, holding the train of her habit out of the way. "Yes, I am sure I shall! I find I have a definite taste for luxury. No doubt Da would chastise me for it, but I cannot help it. I like hordes of servants and huge, impressive rooms. I like being waited on hand and foot, and having whatever I want brought to me.''

She did not notice that the frown was back on her companion's face. She picked up his hand and swung it as she continued, ''Now you must tell me something, Mr. Ashton. Why isn't the earl better liked? I noticed in the village that although he was accorded the deference his rank demands, he was hardly given an enthusiastic reception. Isn't he kind to his people?''

Will thought hard for a moment, squeezing the hand he held, and then he stopped. Anne turned a little to face him. ''I don't think Hawk has ever thought it necessary to be kind,'' he said slowly. ''He sees to their wants, and he is just. Most of the time,'' he added, remembering a few past instances.

Now it was Anne's turn to frown. ''He should be instructed in the error of his ways then, sir. And what better person to do it than his friend? I am surprised you have not pointed this out to him, for I am sure your people smile at you.''

Will tried to remember whether they did or not, and it seemed to him that perhaps they were a bit warmer, especially since he had remained at the abbey for such a long time after his father died.

''Anyway,'' his irrepressible companion continued, ''if you do not, I shall. It is too bad to let someone go on behaving badly all for the want of a little resolution. I daresay he does not even suspect his failing.''

''May I suggest you wait awhile, Miss Ainsworth?'' Will asked dryly. ''Hawk might take it amiss to be instructed by a girl of seventeen.''

''I am almost eighteen and a young lady,'' Anne said hotly. ''You heard what the earl said. I am to go to London, to the Season.'' She sighed in delight, and then catching his other hand up, she whirled him in a dancing turn, singing as she did so, ''To London, to London, to be a fine lady, with rings on her fingers and bells on her toes . . .''

Will caught her in his arms to steady her, and he could not help laughing at her delight. "And she shall have music wherever she goes!" he finished.

Both of them were laughing as they walked toward the house again.

In the library, the earl moved away from the window where he had been watching them. He was frowning and deep in thought. It appeared that Will was on the way to being more than just smitten with Anne Ainsworth, and he had no intention of permitting that. He must make sure he left Bredon, and sometime soon, lest Anne begin to return his love. The earl's frown deepened as he contemplated such an event, and that evening at dinner, his manner to Miss Ainsworth was warm and winning. Both Mr. Ashton and Miss Goodly regarded him with distrust and more than a little apprehension.

For the remainder of the week Anne was busy exploring Bredon and its village. She learned from John Coombs, the youngest footman, that his mother was ill. That same afternoon she asked the butler to order the dogcart and bring her one of the baskets of fruit that could be found on tables throughout the various rooms.

Midler looked a little surprised, but he did as he was bade. When Anne came down from her room, she was wearing a shawl and bonnet and pulling on her gloves.

"Thank you, Midler," she said. "I shall require John Coombs to accompany me," she added.

"Coombs, miss?" he asked, his voice stiff. He thought Miss Ainsworth much too coming, for it was his prerogative to appoint the footman who would go with her.

Anne gave an excellent imitation of Lord Bredon as she raised her eyebrows at his question and the tone of voice he had used. "Of course. Haven't I just said so?" she asked, and the butler was forced to raise a finger. The footman hurried forward.

"Ah, there you are, John. I have an errand in the village, and I need your help. Carry the fruit, if you please," Anne said, going before him to the door.

As she tooled the dogcart down the drive, the footman sitting up straight beside her holding the basket, he learned that she was going to visit his mother, and he was astounded. That Miss would condescend . . . be so kind . . . and bring him with her as well! He was lost in adoration in an instant, and he promised himself that if there was anything he could ever do for her, he would not hesitate for a moment.

When he tried to express his gratitude, Anne said, "Pooh! It is nothing. I was often going about on errands of this nature for the vicar at home, and I am sure the earl would wish me to do so if he knew about your mother. Besides, who is going to miss a little fruit?"

Her voice was more airy than she really felt. She had not asked the earl's permission, not for taking the fruit, nor ordering the dogcart, and she could not help wondering if he would mind. He had been abstracted the past few days, and sometimes she would look up to find his cool gray eyes studying her. She knew it was not because he was concerned about her weight. He saw the little she took at dinner, and her gowns were already looser. She wondered what was on his mind, and then she reminded herself that she was his ward. That must be his concern, and surely what she was doing today was her duty, helping him see to his people's welfare.

Mrs. Coombs was embarrassed when Anne entered her tiny cottage, but she soon forgot it in the joy of having her son beside her. John had only a few hours off every other week. She had not seen him since she had become ill, and she knew he had been worried about her. Now she assured him she was feeling much better, the influenza almost gone. Anne insisted on making tea for them all, and she was so easy and pleasant that the Coombses soon forgot the impropriety of Miss sitting down with a servant and his widowed mother.

After a little while, she announced she was going to walk to the vicarage and make the acquaintance of everyone there, and that she would not require John's services until it was time to start back to Bredon.

"What a good girl!" Mrs. Coombs exclaimed as the door shut behind her guest. "How thoughtful and kind she is!"

Her son stood by the window watching Miss Ainsworth make her way down the village street, stopping often to speak to everyone she met and to give them all a warm smile.

"She is an angel, Ma," he breathed. Mrs. Coombs hid a little smile.

That evening at dinner, Anne told the company what she had done. She saw Lord Bredon's fork stop halfway to his mouth for a moment, before it continued its upward path, but he made no comment.

"The vicar says he will be delighted to see us all at church tomorrow," Anne continued, wishing she had taken a larger portion of chicken. She felt as if she were starving, and these days she was just as hungry when she rose from the table as when she sat down. Sometimes, she even felt a little dizzy.

"At church?" Lord Bredon asked, his voice cool. "I am desolated to have to disappoint you, my dear Anne, but I do not intend to go to church."

Anne stared at him. "Not go?" she asked, her voice astonished. "But it is Sunday and the vicar expects you."

The earl's lips curled in a little sneer. "I doubt that very much, since he knows I never attend."

Anne opened her mouth, and then closed it. Lord Bredon saw the way her dark blue eyes flashed before she lowered them to her plate.

In the little silence that followed, Will Ashton hastened to say, "I shall be delighted to escort you and Miss Goodly, Anne."

Lord Bredon's sneer became even more pronounced. "Yes, you do that, Will," he said. "It will be such good training for your new role as saintly lord of the manor."

Anne looked from one to the other. The earl's voice had been sarcastic, and Mr. Ashton's face was flushed. She was glad when Miss Goodly changed the subject by asking the name of the artist who had painted the dining-room frescoes.

When the ladies withdrew, Will moved his chair closer to the head of the table. "Be so good as to dismiss the servants, Hawk," he said, his voice quiet yet determined. "There is something we have to talk about."

Lord Bredon sipped his port, and then he sighed. "Yes, I can tell you are anxious to continue the discussion we had the first day Miss Ainsworth arrived. Very well, it shall be as you wish."

He turned and waved his hand at the servants. "Out!" he snapped, and the room was vacated in short order. Milord appeared to be annoyed, and when he was out of temper it was better not to be found anywhere in his vicinity.

Will stared down into his glass of port as if to find the words he wanted deep in its ruby depths. Lord Bredon watched him, his lips curling in an amused little smile.

"Well, Will?" he asked after a moment. "You wanted to say . . . ?"

William Ashton looked up at the man he had idolized for so long, the man he had been so proud to call his friend. He felt a lump in his throat that their relationship had changed, even slightly. And then he pushed his glass to one side and clasped his hands together on the table.

"Listen to me, Hawk, if you please. I have watched you with Anne Ainsworth, and I can see that you want her, just as you have wanted so many other women. I grant you she is beautiful, but, Hawk, she is more than just beautiful and desirable. She is true and gay and lovely and fine, and she has had enough misery in her life. Give up this wager, I beg you! Give it up and let her go back to Yorkshire and the people who love her. I will even pay your share of the bet as well as my own if you will agree to my plan."

Lord Bredon's eyebrows rose in astonishment, and his smile broadened. "But, my dear friend, it appears to be a case with you," he said easily. "Can this be the man who said he would never marry a servant girl?" He paused for a moment, and then he added more softly, "The same William Ashton who declared in such ringing tones that he knew what he owed his name? My, my."

Will leaned closer in his agitation, his hands so tightly clasped the knuckles showed white. "I was a fool! If I could win Anne, I would ask for nothing more."

"So you do mean marriage. How extraordinary, when there is no need to marry the girl at all," the earl remarked, covering a tiny yawn with one hand.

"If you have spent all this time in her presence, and still do not see how fine and pure she is, you are a Rake of Satan indeed, Hawk!" Will said, his voice rising with his anger.

The earl stared at him with wintry gray eyes, and then he nodded. "I have never disputed the name of Satan's Rake, for I know it to be true," he said in a mild voice. "There is nothing fine or pure or good about me, nor about you either, Will. I have loved no woman, not ever. I use 'em, and when I tire of them, I discard them. Even Anne Ainsworth in her innocent girlhood has no power to move me, for eventually she will become like all the rest."

The earl sipped his port, and for a moment Will Ashton sat in a shocked silence. Then he asked, his voice quiet with wonder now, "Why do you hate women so, Hawk?"

The earl looked astounded at the question, and when he did not answer immediately, Will continued, "You have just admitted to using them as if they were not even human beings, just 'things.' Has no woman ever been able to command your love, not even your mother?"

Lord Bredon's laugh was disdainful. "I have never spoken of my mother to you, have I? Believe me, she would be the last woman I could care for. But why all this emphasis on 'love,' Will? Primarily, women were put on earth to propagate the species, and in doing so they amuse and satisfy men. They have fulfilled their destiny very well over the centuries. But neither of these occupations, worthy as they are, require 'love.' I outgrew any admiration I might have had for the opposite sex at a very tender age. You see, between my mean nanny and harsh governess, to say nothing of my indifferent mother, I had no one to inspire me. I have found that women, my dear Will, are not at all admirable. They are greedy and shallow and cruel; indeed I doubt if they even have souls. No, Will. But to say that I hate them is to use too strong a word. You have to care deeply before you can hate anyone or anything, and where women are concerned, I do not care a snap of my fingers. Rather, let us say that I am indifferent to them."

Lord Bredon noticed his friend's stunned expression, and he added softly, "And women are worse tools of Satan than we are, for look how one insignificant girl has been able to come between the best of friends and cause them to quarrel."

A flush spread over Will's cheekbones, but his hazel eyes

were steady on the earl's face. "I am your friend and I always will be, Hawk. But what you believe about women is not true, and what you plan to do with Anne is wrong. I cannot permit it, not and live with myself."

The earl's eyelids came down and hid his icy gray eyes. He could not remember that last time he had been criticized, and he found he did not like it a bit, especially from a man who had always admired him. Controlling himself with an effort, he said, "It is early days yet, Will. Perhaps by the time the Season begins, I shall have had a change of heart. Who knows?"

He saw the growing hope in Will's face, and he continued smoothly, "There is, after all, no reason Miss Ainsworth should ever learn of the wager and suffer disillusionment. In fact, I have come to think it best that she does not know of it, for I am not sure how good an actress she is. For that reason I want you to go up to town early next week. We do not want Reggie and Hartley posting down here to see what we have been up to, after all, and I hardly think the girl would care for their company."

Will set his jaw, looking stubborn, and the earl went on, "Miss Ainsworth is safe with me. Do not worry so! If her dragon of a maid and the dithery chaperon are not enough protection for you, you may comfort yourself by remembering that ferocious dog who guards her so constantly. He is still growling at me, and no doubt he sleeps beside her bed. In her innocence, Miss Ainsworth has protected her virtue most successfully, even from one of Satan's Rakes."

He smiled then and tossed off the rest of his port. "Come, Will. We must rejoin the ladies."

As they walked to the door, he threw an arm around his friend's shoulders and said, "If Miss Ainsworth does not know of the wager, there can be no problem. Besides, if we were to deprive her of her Season, I do not know what she would be apt to do, my dear friend. She is looking forward so to the treat!"

When Will chuckled, he relaxed a little, glad he had diverted his friend's mind so he would not ask again what Lord Bredon had in mind for Miss Ainsworth when that Season was over.

# 6

Miss Ainsworth and her chaperon, escorted by William Ashton, were driven in state the next morning to the village church. Anne's eyes danced when she saw the large coach, a footman seated beside the driver, and two grooms up behind, for surely this was excessive pomp for a journey of only a mile. In a short time they were seated in the Bredon pew at the very front of the church. Mr. Ashton was glad to see it had been dusted and that there were no mice making nests in the crimson velvet cushions that had been undisturbed for what he was sure was a very long time.

He had heard the soft murmurs of the villagers behind them as they took their seats, and as the vicar asked the congregation to bow their heads in prayer, he stole a glance at Anne. Her eyes were closed, and he let his own eyes caress that pure profile, the fresh complexion and red-gold curls, and the tempting curves of her figure, feeling safe from any prying eyes within the high walls of the pew. He was recalled to his surroundings only by Miss Goodly's little cough.

When the service was over, Anne preceded her companions down the aisle, stopping to speak to those villagers she had met, and to be introduced to others. She had a special word for the vicar and his wife. They looked bemused and more than a little pleased at this sudden interest from Bredon. The vicar prayed that it might continue, and smiled broadly as the earl's carriage drove away.

Down by the low stone wall that separated the church grounds from the adjacent graveyard, a small group of men had gathered to discuss the morning's most interesting event.

"They say she's 'is ward or summat," Mr. Pearsley, the blacksmith, announced.

"If she's 'is ward, then I'm the queen of the May!" the innkeeper scoffed.

"But the earl don't bring 'is fancies to Bredon, Mr. Booth. Nor do they be the type wot comes to 'oly services, if ever 'e should," the blacksmith persisted.

The other men nodded, and then an old farmer mused, his eyes dim with memories, "She's like a daffodil in the spring sunlight, ain't she?"

Mr. Pearsley nodded. "And she's too good to be a fancy piece, nice girl that she is. Why, did you know she stopped at Widow Coombs's this week, and brought Johnnie with 'er to see 'is ma?"

"Per'aps she is 'is ward, then," Mr. Booth conceded. "Not that *I've* ever 'eard 'e 'ad one, though."

The old farmer chortled and grinned. "And you, o' course, know all about milord, right, Mr. Booth? Calls you in for a chat once a week, no doubt, to keep you up-to-date on 'is doin's."

The other men laughed and clapped him on the back, but when the vicar turned to stare at this unseemly display of mirth on the Sabbath, they were quick to disperse.

Just then, Anne was being assisted from the carriage by the footman, unaware of the sensation she was causing in Bredon. "Thank you, Stanley," she said, her warm smile causing his chest to swell.

Then she caught sight of King. John Coombs had taken him for a walk, and she ran to meet him. The dog leapt up and tried to lick her face, and she held his muddy paws away from her pale green gown.

"Down, King!" she commanded. "Have you been in the lake, you naughty dog? How wet you are!"

John Coombs bowed. "I'm sorry, Miss Anne," he said breathlessly, for King had led him a merry chase. " 'E got away from me."

Anne laughed. "He gets away from everyone, John, but don't worry. He always comes home to me sooner or later."

She led the dog up the steps to where Will Ashton was

waiting for her, but when he asked her if she cared to ride that afternoon, she shook her head. "Not on Sunday, Mr. Ashton. No, I mean to write to Da and Aunt Ellen. They must be wondering why I have been such a poor correspondent."

She went past a bowing Midler into the hall, and handed her gloves and prayerbook to Coombs, who was close on her heels. And then the earl came out of one of the drawing rooms behind them, and the servants stiffened to attention. Everyone but John Coombs, that is. He was staring reverently at her belongings and did not notice.

King's growl brought him to his senses, and he turned to see the earl glaring at him. Catching his breath in fear, he bowed deeply.

"I wonder why the expression 'Better late than never' has never appealed to me?" the earl remarked as he came forward to take Anne's hand. His face was cold with his anger, and the footman backed away as he added, "I believe we will dispense with this man's services as of today, Midler. See to it."

Anne took his hand in both of hers and gripped it tightly. "No, no, m'lord! Whatever can you mean?" she asked. "John did not see you because he was helping me. You cannot be so cruel as to dismiss him for such a reason."

Her gaze held his, and he admired the flash of anger there, as well as the little pleading he could see deep in her magnificent blue eyes.

Disengaging her clinging hands, he turned away from her and said, "Remove the dog! He is dripping."

As a footman hurried to grab King's ruff, he added, "You must excuse us, Will. There is something I wish to speak to Miss Ainsworth about immediately. We shall join you for luncheon in a little while."

Will frowned, but he was powerless to prevent Hawk from putting a strong hand under her elbow and leading Anne away. As the library door closed behind them, the only sound in the hall was King's distressed whines. Will could see that the footman who was to be dismissed had paled and was swallowing hard.

"I should wait before letting the man go, Midler, if I were

you. The earl may be having a change of heart even now,"
he said.

In the library, Lord Bredon seated Anne on a sofa near the
fire. She folded her hands in her lap, but although she
appeared composed, Lord Bredon noticed her eyes never left
his face. He took the seat across from her, and only then did
he say softly, "Never do that again! I do not like to be
corrected, most especially not in front of the servants. And
when I give an order, I expect it to be obeyed instantly."

Anne felt a little shiver at his words. They were all the
more menacing for being spoken in such a quiet tone of
voice. She was sure she had heard them before, and she
wondered where. Taking a deep breath, she said, "No one
likes to be corrected, m'lord, and I apologize for speaking out
in front of the servants. But I was so distressed, I did not
think. You see, John Coombs is the sole support of his
widowed mother. I knew you had probably forgotten that, or
you would never have behaved as you did."

"Who is John Coombs?" he asked. "And what has his
mother, widowed or otherwise, to do with it?"

Anne's eyes widened. "Why, he is the footman you just
dismissed! Do you mean you do not even know his name or
his circumstances?"

The earl's shrug was impatient. "I see no reason why I
should clutter up my mind with such trivia. It is enough that
he knows my name and serves me well. That is all that is
required."

Anne looked horrified, but her firm little chin rose. "But it
is not kind to treat servants as if they were cattle, m'lord.
You cannot have thought—"

"I think of servants as little as possible and I am never
kind," he snapped, but then, when a stricken look came over
her face at his ruthless words, he said more easily, "I suppose you know all their names? It is not at all necessary, my
dear. You can say 'Here, you!' and you will get the same
instant service. At least you will at Bredon."

"But that's terrible!" she said. "Why, we are God's
creatures, no matter how high or low our station."

The earl waved a white hand. "Spare me the sermon, Anne. I had forgot you have spent the morning at church."

Anne rose then and came and knelt before him, raising her heart-shaped face so she could search the handsome, haughty face above her. She looked very beautiful with her red-gold curls tumbling around her face and her full lips parted a little, and the earl found himself wanting to reach out and pull her into his arms. He made himself sit back and cross his arms over his chest lest he give in to the temptation.

"Please, m'lord," she begged, "take John back. He is a good footman, and he is kind to King."

Now the earl's smile was mocking. "Of course he is. King is *your* dog, and that is enough to ensure the most careful care. The footman is a man, my dear Anne, and you have quite an effect on men, no matter what their station. I daresay there isn't a footman out there who wouldn't walk through hot coals for you."

She blushed a little, and for a moment her dark lashes fluttered on her cheeks.

"I cannot tell you how much it has amused me to see how their eyes follow you, so full of dumb adoration. I shall have to begin calling them 'Anne's Army,' " he added, his voice derisive.

She looked up then, and he saw the challenge in her eyes. "Then if they are my army, and I am the commander in chief, surely I can insist that John Coombs remain in the ranks, m'lord," she said, her pert words spoken in a demure voice.

Lord Bredon looked at her coldly. "You are a baggage, miss," he told her, but when she nodded in complete agreement, he found himself chuckling at her wiles.

After a moment he seemed to recall himself, and he said with cold contempt, "How typical! Like all women, if you cannot get your own way by right and intellect, you begin to wheedle and tease to gain your ends. In this case it will not do."

Anne rose to her feet at his stern expression and retreated to the sofa again, her eyes puzzled. "I do not understand, m'lord," she said in the silence that followed.

"Then I shall explain it to you," Lord Bredon said, his gray eyes never leaving her face. Anne could not look away. "Know that I am master here. When I give an order, it is to be obeyed without question. It is certainly not open to discussion or revision, not even because you wish it, my dear Anne. No. If you will just accept this one simple fact, we will all get along so much better."

Anne felt herself stiffening with rising anger, and before she thought, she said hotly, "But John Coombs will not get along better, nor will his mother! And to be dismissed for such a little thing—because he did not bow in unison with the other footmen. Why, even royalty would not demand such homage! It is nothing but pride, and willful vanity, and . . ."

She stopped abruptly as the earl came to his feet in one quick, fluid motion and strode over to grasp her hands and pull her upright. Those gray eyes were not cold now, she noticed through her panic. They were burning with a strange light, and his mouth was set in hard, taut lines.

"Be quiet!" he ordered, his normally melodious voice harsh with his anger. "How dare you say such things to me?"

As he spoke, his long hands gripped her shoulders, and it was all she could do not to cry out at the pain. She tried to pull away from him, and he shook her. "Never speak to me that way again," he ordered through gritted teeth.

She could not help a little gasp as his hands tightened even further, and suddenly he let her go and stepped back. She noticed he was breathing hard and that a silvery lock of hair had fallen over his brow. When he reached up to smooth it back, she saw that his hand trembled with his rage, and she was frightened.

They stared at each other, the only sound in the room the ticking of the mantel clock, and then he said in a cold, icy voice that was more menacing somehow than another man's bellows of rage, "There must be no repetition of this scene. Watch what you say to me, and how you say it, for I will not stand being chastised by a . . . by my ward."

Anne wondered what he had been about to call her before

he remembered she was his ward, and then he asked, "I trust I have made myself clear?"

He glared at her, and she nodded, unable to speak.

"You will answer me," he ordered, his tone still arctic.

She saw that he would not be content until she agreed verbally, and she made herself say, "Of course, m'lord. You are Bredon, and Bredon is yours to do with as you will. I beg your pardon."

Somewhat mollified, he came toward her again and grasped her chin to tilt her face up so he could look down into her eyes. He saw rebellion and stubbornness there, but he also saw resignation to his will, and he nodded carelessly, satisfied at last. "Good! How fortunate that you are a quick study. Now, shall we join the others?"

He took her hand in his arm, and as they walked to the door, he said, "As a reward for your obedience, the footman may remain. Do not ask me for such a boon again."

"Thank you, m'lord," Anne whispered. She felt cold all over, as cold as she had ever felt coming down a windy Yorkshire hillside in January with sleet falling and striking her face. The earl had never shown her this side of his character before, and the kind guardian angel she had thought him was wearing a tarnished halo. She had made him into such a hero all these years, that seeing him off his pedestal upset her. Then too, he had frightened her. For one mad moment when he was hurting her, she had been reminded of her childhood and her aunt.

Now, as they walked through the hall, he left her for a moment to have a quiet word with Midler. The butler's face was scornful as he looked at Miss Ainsworth, but he nodded and bowed.

In spite of the hunger that gnawed at her so constantly these days, Anne had very little appetite for luncheon, and she was relieved when the others conversed and left her to her thoughts.

Will Ashton left the next day. He told Anne that he had business in London, but he promised to return quickly. Anne found Bredon depressing and lonely without him, for she was avoiding the earl's company as much as she could. True to his word, he had had John Coombs restored to his duties, but although she was grateful to him, she could not be comfortable in his presence. She spent her mornings with her chaperon, reading and doing needlework, she took long walks with King, and late each afternoon she retreated to the folly by the lake, where she could be alone and think.

She noticed that Lord Bredon watched her coldly. He was courteous when they were together, but he did not seek her out. Anne wondered if he was regretting inviting her to Bredon, or even making her his ward at all, and a cold little shiver ran down her arms at the thought that he might be contemplating sending her away. But even if he did, she told herself, she could not have held her tongue on Sunday. What the earl had done was wrong and cruel, and with the vicar's training, and the words "Do unto others" ringing in her ears, she had had to speak out. She had thought she would do anything to avoid a return to Cawfell, but it seemed there were some things she could not do after all. Closing her eyes to injustice was one of them.

One afternoon in the folly, she was practicing one of the songs Da had taught her when the earl came back from a ride. As he handed his reins to a groom, he heard the sweet, plaintive notes, and for a moment the harsh planes of his face softened.

He made his way through the gardens toward the sound, admiring her soft, true tones. He knew she was unhappy, and he was surprised to find that he was sorry for it. He missed her bright smile and sunny ways, for in some way Bredon had returned to the cold formal atmosphere that had always prevailed before Anne Ainsworth's arrival. It was not that she was boisterous or loud, but he had not not realized how much he had come to listen for her musical laugh, her happy voice when she called her dog, and the little snatches of song she hummed as she ran down the stairs.

Suddenly he stopped, an intent look in his eyes, as he realized how much he wanted that laughing girl to return. He smiled to himself then, for he did not doubt for an instant that it was in his power to bring her back. Anthony Hawkins had a great deal of experience dealing with the opposite sex, and Anne Ainsworth, for all her self-possession, was only a very impressionable, very young lady. He considered the methods he would use. Now that Will had gone off to London to still any qualms the other members of Satan's Rakes might be having at his long absence, he had the perfect opportunity to begin. He had only to find her alone, out from under the watchful eyes of her chaperon and without that damned dog, and there would be no hindrance to his plan.

Since he had not heard the dog barking, and knew Miss Goodly was taking tea at the vicarage, he realized he could begin at once.

He waited until she finished singing and the last notes of the melody faded away, and then he climbed the shallow steps, applauding as he did so.

Anne put a trembling hand to her mouth. She was wearing a soft cashmere gown trimmed in moss-green ribbons, with a matching ribbon threaded through her hair. As she leaned back in surprise, the sun over the lake lit her curls with liquid fire. The earl felt a slight constriction in his throat at the sight.

"Congratulations, Anne," he said, coming to take the wicker seat beside her. "How is it I have never had the pleasure of hearing you sing before this?" he asked, a little smile curving his lips. "You do it so well!"

"You never asked me," she said baldly, and then she flushed at her gaucheness.

He bent closer and took her hand, holding it warmly. "I shall have to discover what other delights you have that I have never 'asked' you about," he remarked softly. He was about to raise her hand and kiss it when he saw the confusion in her eyes, and he let her go and rose to pour them both a glass of lemonade.

Anne watched him doubtfully. She had never been treated to the sight of the earl in full pursuit; he seemed a completely different man.

"Do you find the folly pleasant, Anne?" he was asking now.

"Yes, I do. It is so peaceful here," she said, wondering if

she had imagined the dangerous light she thought she had
seen in his gray eyes.

"You will not be able to enjoy it much longer, my dear. I
fear the autumn storms are drawing close. But perhaps in
cooler weather you might investigate the *orangerie*. It is only
when the trees are blooming that the scent can be somewhat
overpowering."

They chatted for several more minutes. Anne could feel her
mood lightening at the earl's good humor. Not even King's
growl when he bounced up the steps, fresh from hunting
rabbits in the home wood, seemed to annoy him. He laughed
at the dog while she scolded him, but she noticed he did not
offer to pat him.

Dinner that evening was pleasant, more pleasant than it had
been for over a week. The earl divided his attention equally
between Anne and Miss Goodly, and he seemed especially
talkative and full of amusing anecdotes. He did not linger over
his port, but came almost at once to the drawing room.

"I discovered Anne's vocal talent only this afternoon, Miss
Goodly," he remarked. "It makes me wonder how I could
have been so remiss as not to inquire more particularly about
her other skills. For example, I do not even know if you can
dance, Anne, and if not, we must do something to remedy the
situation at once, before the Season begins."

"Of course I can dance," Anne said. "Aunt Ellen instructed me, didn't she, Miss Goodly?"

The older lady nodded, an amused little smile playing over
her lips at her charge's indignation.

"Perhaps we can persuade Miss Goodly to play for us, so I
might judge for myself?" the earl asked. "I should warn you,
however, that I am known to be hard to please."

Anne jumped up, her eyes sparkling at the challenge, and
she herself led Miss Goodly to the piano and selected the
music, while the earl called for another branch of candles and
had the footmen take up the carpet.

When the music began, Anne found it exhilarating to be
held in his arms and to follow his lead as he took her through
a country dance. She had never danced with a man before,
for there had been no one but Da to partner her. Besides

being in holy orders, he had pointed out the disparity in their height, so Anne had had to learn her steps alone. Now she found out how delightful dancing could be.

The evening ended with the earl's compliments and his promise that he would undertake to instruct her in the waltz himself, that daring German dance that was taking London by storm. Of course it had never been performed in the village of Tees in Yorkshire. To have Lord Bredon's arm around her waist, his hand pressing her back, to be so close to him— why, no doubt the vicar and Aunt Ellen would think it scandalous.

As she went up to bed, Anne realized she could hardly wait for her lessons to begin.

# 7

Anne's happiness returned during the following days. Sometimes she would remember Lord Bredon's former arrogance, but when he smiled at her and teased her, she felt her heart warming and opening to him as if he had never been harsh and cruel at all.

And then, one rainy afternoon when she climbed the winding stone stairs in Bredon's highest tower with him, she disgraced herself by fainting. He had set a brisk pace, and for a while she had kept up with him eagerly, but near the top of the last flight, she felt herself growing dizzy. As she reached the last step and took the hand he held out to her, his voice grew dim in her ears, the stones of the tower seemed to move as if they were underwater, and she slipped to the floor.

The earl caught her up in his arms, his brows contracted in a frown. Laying her gently on the stone floor, he knelt beside her to rub her hands. She regained consciousness almost at once, and tried to sit up, one hand going to her head.

"What happened?" she asked, bewildered.

"You fainted, my dear," the earl told her, one arm going around her shoulders to support her. "Do not attempt to stand until you are sure you have regained your strength. Do you do this often, Anne?"

"Often? I have never fainted in my life!" she said, her voice indignant.

The earl's handsome face was close to hers. She felt breathless, but somehow she knew this had nothing to do with her physical condition.

"Then we must investigate further," Lord Bredon said next. Held against him, Anne could hear the echoes of his warm voice, deep in his chest, and smell the lotion he used. She told herself she must stop being so silly.

"Have you ever felt dizzy before this?" the earl asked next.

"Why, yes. But just since I began to eat so little, m'lord."

Suddenly she gasped as he sat her up and ran his hands slowly down her body. She could feel his fingers touching the sides of her breasts for a fleeting moment before they continued down to her waist and hips. She knew she should protest, but something she seemed to have no control over kept her still. Where his hands touched, her skin seemed to glow under her clothes. He ended by spanning her waist with his big hands, and he looked surprised.

Then he drew her back into his arms and cradled her against his chest. "Poor Anne," he crooned as he rocked her to and fro. If she had not been so distraught, she might have noticed that his voice was ragged and totally unlike his usual bored drawl.

"You have obeyed me with a vengeance, I see," he continued. "I did not mean that you should fast until you fainted, my dear. But come! Has no one spoken to you about it? Miss Goodly or your maid?"

"Mary Agnes did scold me, m'lord," she managed to whisper. "But I told her it was your wish."

"I hope you will always yield to my wishes, every one of them," he said, his voice caressing. Then he hugged her and put her away from him. Anne wondered why she wanted to throw herself back into his arms. Whatever was happening to her?

"Since you obey me so well—and I cannot tell you how that pleases me, my dear—I am sure you will heed me when I tell you you must lose no more weight," he said. "I can tell how much thinner you have become, and I am sure it is more than adequate for our purposes."

"Do . . . er, willowy ladies have a tendency to faint, m'lord?" she asked, her eyes mischievous.

"I have no idea," he said, ignoring the sparkle in her eyes. "I shall send for the London dressmakers this very day. In the meantime, ask that maid of yours to make over some of your gowns so they fit you. It is a wonder I did not notice, as loose as they are.'' He paused for a moment, and then he asked, ''Are you feeling better? Can you get up?''

Anne stood up when she heard his brusque tone. He was there beside her to steady her as he said, ''In a little while I will help you down the stairs, and this evening I myself shall tell you what to eat. We cannot have you fainting in a London ballroom or falling ill from lack of nourishment,'' he scolded her.

Anne felt a rush of joy at his concern. How could she have thought him cruel and unfeeling? Just look how he worried about her. Why, surely the way he had behaved over the matter of John Coombs had been only a momentary lapse into bad temper.

This delightful state of affairs continued throughout the week. The promised dressmakers arrived, and as well as taking in all her old gowns, they began a number of ball gowns, walking dresses, and habits that had her glowing with pleasure. Lord Bredon himself approved every design, and chose the fabric and the color, under Miss Goodly's watchful eye. He had just selected a gown with a daring neckline and narrow skirt to be made up in a dark brown silk that was shot through with gold threads.

''I cannot think that dress at all suitable, m'lord,'' Miss Goodly said, frowning as she studied the fashion plate. ''A young girl in her first Season—why, it is not at all seemly.''

The earl was turning the silk this way and that, admiring the change of color, and he answered absently, ''I quite agree with you, Miss Goodly. But she will look stunning in it later.''

The chaperon stared at him, and then at the drawing again, and her lips tightened. To her mind, the dress was not suitable for anyone who called herself a lady, but indomitable as she was, she was not brave enough to incur his wrath by pointing it out to him.

The following afternoon, Lord Bredon took Anne for a drive in his racing curricle. He had chosen this vehicle for two reasons. It was not only unsuitable for an older lady, there was no room for her, or for the dog either.

Anne looked disappointed as she glanced over her shoulder to where King was howling disconsolately, held tightly in the grasp of two of the footmen, but soon she faced front again and prepared to enjoy herself. The October day was pleasant, with a little bite in the air that told you winter was coming, and she was wearing a new blue gown and pelisse with a dashing bonnet that tied under her chin. She knew she looked her best, for she had seen the approval in the earl's eyes when she came down the steps, and felt the way he pressed her hand as he helped her to the perch himself.

Now he pointed out various points of interest in the countryside, and kept up a light conversation. Anne could feel his shoulder pressed against hers in the narrow carriage, and she tried to pretend that she was not conscious of it, nor of the powerful thigh that was touching her own. Surely it was wrong to feel this way about your guardian, and she scolded herself and resolved to do better. The earl smiled to himself, well aware of her dilemma.

At length he stopped in a pretty little village that was bordered by a wide stream and suggested they stroll about and investigate. He left the rig at the inn, ordering refreshments for their return, and then he took her arm and they walked until they reached a path that followed the riverbank.

"How delightful this is, m'lord!" she exclaimed.

"Do you think you could possibly bring yourself to call me Hawk?" he complained. " 'M'lord' is so formal."

"But you are my guardian, sir. It would not be correct. Besides, I don't like that name. It reminds me too vividly of a predatory bird."

"Then call me Tony or Anthony," he suggested, but when she shook her head shyly, he did not press her.

"I wonder if Da is out walking this lovely afternoon," she said after a moment.

Her voice sounded subdued, and Lord Bredon curbed his impatience. "You miss him very much, don't you?" he asked, his voice uninterested.

Anne did not notice. "Yes, and dear Aunt Ellen too. But

my stay at Bredon has been so exciting, I am afraid I do not miss them as I ought,'' she said, determined to be truthful.

The earl laughed. ''You remind me that I have not asked about your schooling, Anne. I am most pleased with everything I have learned about you and plan to reward the vicar for his care. But what did he teach you, I wonder?''

''I can speak French, but my Latin and Italian are not very good,'' she confessed. ''I also have some botany and history, and I have read a lot of English literature, of course. But I pray you will not ask me about my sums. I am very bad at sums!''

''Now, what is this?'' he asked sternly. ''I see I must look into this failing of yours, Miss Ainsworth. Tell me, if you please, what are one and one?''

She laughed. ''One and one are two, of course. Even I know that!''

Lord Bredon stopped and turned her to face him on the narrow path. For a moment he looked down into her merry face, and then he said softly, his deep voice as smooth as cream, ''Yes, one and one are two. But that is not always true, my dear.''

She looked confused, and he added, ''Oh yes, Anne, as you will discover someday under my expert tutelage, one and one can also make a delightful and exciting . . . mm, one.''

He saw she did not understand, and he chuckled. ''You do not know what I mean now, but it shall be my great pleasure to show you.''

''When?'' she asked, her blue eyes direct. Her heart was jumping in an alarming way, and she was well aware how lonely a spot this was, but she was helpless to suggest they return to the inn.

One blond eyebrow rose. ''Someday, when you are a little older,'' he said. ''My promise on it.''

Then he bent his head and kissed her cheek, one arm going around her waist to pull her close to him. Anne closed her eyes.

When he raised his head, he saw the thick lashes hiding those glowing blue eyes, and the way her breath stirred her gown. He also saw that her lips had parted ever so slightly, and it was all he could do to give her a careless hug before he said, "Come, my dear. It is time we return to the inn. I have no desire to drive in the dark. Not in my racing curricle behind my blacks."

Anne noticed he was quieter on their return, and that sometimes his brows contracted with some secret thoughts, and wisely she did not chatter. She did not know that the earl was deciding to leave Bredon, and Anne Ainsworth, before he forgot his original plan. She was much too tempting and desirable for him to remain and keep himself under control.

Anne herself had a lot of thinking to do. She was remembering the way his lips had lingered on her cheek, and how she had felt pressed against all the hard, long length of him. Being held in his arms during a waltz paled in comparison. And although he was her guardian, he was not so very much older than she was herself. She wondered why he had never married, and then she was glad the approaching dusk hid her flushed cheeks as she contemplated what being his wife would be like.

The earl left only a day later. He had announced his intention of going up to town at the dinner table after they had returned from their outing. Anne could not help giving a little cry of distress, but he noticed Miss Goodly took the news with the air of one having a burden lifted from her frail shoulders.

"Do you have to go, m'lord?" Anne asked, her blue eyes pleading. "I will miss you so!"

Lord Bredon's fingers tightened on the stem of his wineglass.

"Anne!" Miss Goodly admonished her. "What m'lord does is not your concern. Indeed, you should be grateful he has been able to spare you so much of his time up to now."

Anne subsided, but she did not look happy. It was too bad! And just when they were getting to know each other better, too.

"I do not know when I shall return," Lord Bredon was saying, and then he surprised himself by adding, "I will miss you, too."

The following day, Anne came out to wave good-bye to

him, and as the carriage disappeared from sight around a
bend in the drive, she knelt beside her dog and buried her
face in his ruff.

"At least I still have you, King," she whispered. "But
how lonesome Bredon will be without the earl."

King settled down on the top step, his paws hanging over
the edge, and he gave a huge yawn. The ears that had always
stood at attention whenever Lord Bredon was near Anne,
drooped.

In the days after the earl's departure, Anne made herself
keep busy. She practiced her singing and the pianoforte, she
read for an hour each day, and she began to embroider some
slippers for Da and a pillow for Aunt Ellen as Christmas
gifts. She also made it her special duty to call on any of the
earl's pensioners she knew were ill. When she heard Rhea
Carter, the woodcutter's wife, had had a baby boy, she
begged a length of fine white flannel from the housekeeper,
and a basket of delicacies as well, to take to the new mother.

She also wrote each week to Lord Bredon, but his replies
were brief and sporadic, and somehow unsatisfying.

Everyone, with the exception of Midler, was very fond of
Miss Anne, as she was known to the staff, and pleased that
she remained in residence. Bredon Hall was so much pleasanter,
now Miss had come to stay, and although no one knew why,
they did not question her presence, either at the hall or in the
village.

One cold November afternoon that threatened snow, Anne
was curled up in a big wing chair in the library, reading,
when Midler knocked and announced a caller.

Anne looked up, surprised. No one ever called at Bredon.
It was something she had wanted to ask the earl about many
times. She knew his parents were dead, but where was the
rest of his family?

"A caller, Midler?" she asked, rising to smooth her dress,
wondering if she were to meet one of them now.

"A Sir Hartley Wilson, miss," Midler informed her. "He
is an old friend of the earl's, and finding he was not in
residence, he asked for you by name."

Stranger and stranger, Anne thought, but she nodded and

said she would receive the guest. As she waited for the butler to bring Sir Hartley to her, she wondered if she should not have insisted Miss Goodly be present as well, but when she saw the middle-aged man who entered the room, she did not think such a precaution at all necessary.

Sir Hartley came toward her frowning, and that frown did not lessen as he gave her a slight bow. Anne thought him an ugly man with his long lined face and narrowed green eyes, the receding red hair streaked with gray, and the sneer that seemed a permanent feature of pale, thin lips.

She curtsied and then held out her hand. "Welcome to Bredon, Sir Hartley," she said, and his frown grew even more ferocious. Behind them, Midler was closing the library doors.

Unlike Mr. William Ashton or Lord Quarles, Sir Hartley had not forgotten the wager, nor the name of the little servant girl Hawk had found at his hunting box. He was a shrewd man, and his fortunes had not prospered since then. He knew he could not pay the wager, but more important, he was determined to win it any way he could. Now he came close to this stunning girl, noting her red-gold curls, and said, "You are Anne Ainsworth?" His light tenor was somehow disbelieving.

"I am she," Anne agreed. "Have we met before, sir? I do not remember the occasion."

"Then we have met, but whether you are Annie Ainsworth still remains to be seen." He sneered, throwing himself down in a chair and crossing his legs. His rudeness, while she was still standing, offended Anne, but she took a seat near the bell in case she needed to summon assistance. What an unpleasant man, and what a strange friend for Lord Bredon to have ! And whatever did he mean?

"Now, my good girl," he continued as his green eyes raked her face and figure, "since I am sure Hawk is paying you very well to play this part, I will not ask you your real name. I do wonder where he found you, though. You are perfect—refined, genteel, well-spoken—and I might have known he would have a trick up his sleeve. Hawk doesn't like to lose. Not at anything."

"I do not understand you," Anne said, wondering if he were mad.

He laughed, a cold bark of derision. "Come, come, my dear-whoever-you-are! There is no need for all this posing, not with me. I know when I have been bested, although I hope to find a way out of the tangle even now. Tell me, what sum is Hawk paying you to pretend to be Annie Ainsworth? Perhaps, between Reggie and myself, we can come to a more profitable arrangement for you."

Anne took a deep breath to steady herself. "You have been misinformed, sir. My name is truly Anne Ainsworth, and I am the Earl of Bredon's ward."

Sir Hartley leaned forward and slapped his knees, his jeering laughter echoing through the room. "His *ward*, are you? I will grant that you might be his latest *mistress*, but his ward you are not."

Seeing her face stiffen with shock, he added, a wheedling note in his voice, "Come now, m'dear. Where did Hawk find you, and what is he paying you?"

"I have told you who I am. I see no need to repeat it," Anne told him, and then she reached for the bell. "I do not care to continue this discussion. I find you rude and insulting, sir."

In a flash he was out of his chair, his fingers closing around her wrist until the pressure forced her to drop her hand back in her lap. With his other hand he put the bell out of her reach. She opened her mouth to call for help, and as quick as the cat he appeared with those strange green eyes, he clamped a hand over her mouth.

"Not yet, my pretty wench," he crooned. "You will be glad you did not call out after I have told you the whole story. Did Hawk tell you about the wager? I was sure he must have. And a thousand pounds is a lot of money. If you come in on my side and Lord Quarles's, I'll see you get a quarter of our share. Now, that's something to consider, is it not?"

He took his hand away from her mouth, and when he saw she was not going to cry out, he strolled over to the drinks table and poured himself a glass of canary. Behind him,

Anne's brain was working feverishly. What wager? What did he mean?''

Sir Hartley resumed his seat and sipped his wine before he said, ''Aye, I see that offer's given you pause, hasn't it? Never met a woman who didn't have her price.''

''What wager?'' Anne asked, ignoring his sneer and going straight to the heart of the matter. Her words sounded stilted, her lips were so stiff with shock and pain. Sir Hartley had hurt her, and he had seemed to enjoy doing so.

Her unwelcome guest studied her white face, and he saw the way she was clasping her hands in her lap to keep them from trembling.

''So you don't know?'' he asked, his voice wondering. ''Can it be possible that he really did accomplish it?''

''Accomplish what?'' Anne managed to force out.

''Seven years ago, the four of us friends the *ton* calls Satan's Rakes made a wager at Cawfell, Hawk's hunting box. He and Will Ashton bet that if they took a servant under the age of twelve, they could turn her into a lady. Reggie—Lord Quarles—and I bet it was impossible. The wager comes due this Season, which I assume is why you are here at Bredon.''

''Cawfell . . .'' Anne whispered. ''The dream.''

Sir Hartley shrugged. ''It will be no dream for me if Hawk wins the bet. I will be honest with you, since I am sure I can convince you to be my conspirator. I don't have the thousand pounds to pay it, and Reggie's so sodden most of the time, he's no help. I posted down here to find out what was going on after Will let slip Hawk was entertaining a guest. Oh, he covered up right away, pretended you were just one of Hawk's fancies, but I knew better. Hawk never brings his whores to Bredon. He's too fastidious.''

He snorted and took another sip of wine. Anne stared past him, frozen with shock. ''It was only for a wager'' pounded in her head over and over again.

''So, Annie Ainsworth, or whoever you are, shall we do business?'' Sir Hartley demanded. ''Or has Hawk seduced you indeed to the point you will not betray him? He's a handsome buck, I'll grant you that.''

Anne brought her wide-eyed gaze back to his sneering

face. "I am Anne Ainsworth," she repeated, almost as if she were beginning to doubt it herself. "It is true that I was a servant at Cawfell, but . . : but I cannot believe the earl would do this to me . . . treat me this way . . . or Mr. Ashton either."

Her voice died away as Sir Hartley chuckled. "Oh, Hawk and Will will go to great lengths to win a bet. I told you he hates to lose, and Will follows him in everything."

"But what will happen to me after the wager?" Anne could not help asking.

"Who knows?" he asked, his tone implying that he cared very little. "Perhaps he'll set you up as his mistress. You're comely enough, even though you are nothing but a servant slut. How amusin'! An educated slut. It might add spice to the relationship for him."

Anne did not hear him. In her mind's eye she could see the way the earl had looked at her, and she was remembering some of the things he had said. That he wanted her to look her best when she met the *ton*, that he would not stand for being scolded by her, and the little hesitation before he called her his ward. And she remembered how he had said he hoped she would always yield to his wishes, and that he was going to tell her how one and one could make one someday when she was a little older.

Her face grew even paler, and her lips looked as if they had been chiseled from cold marble. Sir Hartley eyed her with unease. Was she going to faint? Have hysterics? She certainly appeared to be in shock, so perhaps she was truly Annie Ainsworth after all, and Hawk had let her remain in ignorance of his real purpose in overseeing her upbringing. But if that was the case, he told himself, he might be able to convince her to run away. After all, if no servant-turned-lady could be found, he would win a thousand pounds. Feeling a little better, he went to pour her a glass of wine, and came to put it in her hands.

Softening his voice, he said, "Drink this, dear lady. You look as if you need it. I am beginning to think Hawk very remiss not to have told you the whole story. No doubt he imagined you would be able to play the part of lady better if you continued to believe you were one. But I see I was wrong about you, and I apologize for calling you those names. No matter what your background, you are a lady now, and as such should not have to submit to such indignities. If I were you, I would go away from here at once. It would serve him right, after the way he has treated you!''

He paused, staring at her face through narrowed eyes, wondering if he had said enough to convince her.

Then he reached into his pocket and pulled out a purse. ''Here, take this. It is only fifty pounds, but consider it a down payment on your share, if you will leave Bredon and hide. As soon as I hear you have disappeared, I will send you more. Here's my card. Write to me and give me your direction, but on no account let Hawk know where you have gone.''

He paused, and then he added, his light tenor menacing, ''Do not try to trick me, Annie. I will find you if you do, no matter where you go. And it would be such a shame if someone as lovely as you are were to be scarred.''

He reached out and ran a harsh fingernail down her cheek. Anne did not move. He put the card and the purse down on the table beside her. ''I shall leave you now, to consider and make your plans,'' he said.

He waited, but when she had no comment, he bowed and went away, shutting the door of the library softly behind him.

As he tooled his rig down the drive and away from Bredon, he was smiling as he had not smiled for a very long time.

# 8

A few minutes later, John Coombs came in to make up the fire. He almost dropped the hod of coal he carried when he saw Miss Anne, her face so pale and immobile she seemed like a marble statue. He knew Sir Hartley Wilson had called and asked to see Miss Ainsworth, and he had been anxious for her. Coombs was familiar with all the men the *ton* called Satan's Rakes, and he felt Sir Hartley much the worst of them. To even think of him in the same room with Miss Anne had upset him, and he had not liked the pleased little smile the rake had worn as he was leaving.

Now he emptied the coal into the box much more loudly than he ever would have dared in Midler's presence, but even the noise it made did not rouse her from her abstraction. Coombs poked the fire until it was glowing again, and then he came to stand before her, hoping the butler would not come in and find him.

"Miss Anne?" he asked as loudly as he dared. "Are you all right?"

For a moment he thought she was not going to reply, but then she turned her head and looked at him. He clenched his fists when he saw the wounded expression in her eyes and the droop to her mouth.

"Are you all right, miss?" he asked again, bending closer in his anxiety.

"Yes . . . no . . . I don't know," she said in a sad little voice that was totally unlike her usual cheerful tones.

John made so bold as to reach out and pat her hand. "Shall I fetch your maid, miss? Or Miss Goodly?" he asked.

She stared at him for a moment more, and then she sighed. "If you please, John."

She turned away toward the fire, and he could tell she was lost in her thoughts again and had forgotten him. Bowing, he went to the door. That man had done something to hurt and upset her, and he wished with all his might that he had him standing before him right now! He walked through the hall, pausing beside his friend Stanley to whisper, "Find Miss Goodly, Stan, and ask her to go to the library. Miss Anne needs her. I'm off to fetch her maid."

Stanley looked at him, his brows coming together at the distress he saw in his face, but before he could ask what the matter was, John was climbing the stairs.

It was only a few minutes before Miss Goodly and Mary Agnes entered the library. The footmen had not been able to tell them what was wrong, only that Sir Hartley's visit had upset Miss Anne.

Mary Agnes went to her mistress and knelt before her. As she picked up her hands to rub, her shrewd eyes assessed her carefully. Miss Goodly took a seat nearby, and much to the maid's surprise, took command of the situation at once.

"Now, Anne, pay attention, if you please. John told me you had a visitor—an old friend of the earl's, I believe?"

She paused, but when her charge only nodded, she said briskly, "Come now, my dear! You must see that if you do not explain, there is no way your maid and I can help you. Who was this man? What did he want? And why has the visit discomposed you?"

Her voice was matter-of-fact, and Anne obeyed without question. "It was all only for a wager," she said sadly, and a little tear ran down her cheek.

"What was?" Miss Goodly persisted. "Start at the beginning, Anne, or we will not be able to make heads or tails out of your story."

Anne told them what had happened. Mary Agnes sat back on her heels, but she did not look at all aghast as the tale unfolded. She had never been able to fathom some of the things gentlemen considered amusing, and although she was sorry for her mistress, knowing society and men as she did, she was not surprised.

Miss Goodly shook her head a few times and made a disgusted cluck with her tongue every now and then, but she did not interrupt. When Anne finished, there was silence for a moment, and then the chaperon said, "It appears that I was right in my first assessment of he earl's character. That gown he chose for 'later'—I should have known."

The maid handed Anne a handkerchief. "Satan's Rakes!" she exclaimed. "Aye, that they are indeed, to do such a thing."

"But what am I to do?" Anne asked in a pitiful little voice. She felt just the way she had when she was eleven, alone and frightened and cowering. All those happy years at the vicarage had been erased from her mind as if they had never been. She had been tricking herself in thinking she was safe and beloved, and that happy state would never change.

It was obvious that she had been transformed into a lady for one purpose and one purpose only. The earl did not care for her—why, even his concern after her faint had been in case she would not be able to win the wager for him. And after it was won, he had made it very clear what her role was to be. She still could hear his deep voice teasing her about the sum of one and one, and she shivered.

Now she tried to pay attention to a very militant little Miss Goodly as the woman said, "We must go away, and as soon as possible. I cannot, with a clear conscience, allow you to remain at Bredon, Anne. The vicar, dear Ellen—why, everyone's feelings must be offended if you did!"

"But I cannot go away," Anne said in despair. "Where would I go? If I return to Tees, it is the first place the earl will look for me, and it will get Da in trouble if he gives me shelter. And Sir Hartley warned me that the earl must not find me. He left me money so I could hide somewhere, and he threatened to hurt me if I tried to trick him."

Mary Agnes' eyes were snapping, and she tossed her head. "I'd like to see 'im try it, miss, with Miss Goodly and myself to protect you," she said, her voice indignant. Then she thought for a moment, before she turned toward the chaperon and asked, "But where can we go, if not to Tees, ma'am?"

Miss Goodly waved a careless hand. "Some place will occur to me, no doubt, but the important thing is to be far away before the earl returns. Come, Anne. We shall go up and start packing immediately. Mary Agnes, have some tea brought upstairs. There is nothing like a good hot cup of tea when you have had a shock."

Still speaking, she led a dazed Anne to the door. Mary Agnes took her upstairs while Miss Goodly paused to exchange a quiet word with a hovering John Coombs. Seeing the question in his worried eyes, she whispered, "She will be all right, John, but we may need your help before much longer."

"Anything, Miss Goodly," the footman breathed. "I'd do anything to help Miss Anne, and so will all the others."

The chaperon looked around to see the other footmen on duty looking stern and resolute, and she smiled a little. She had heard the earl's sarcastic references to "Anne's Army," and it appeared they were a devoted group indeed. She was to discover how devoted a few minutes later when one of them brought up the purse and Sir Hartley's card, which had been left in the library. Miss Goodly took these things with reluctance. If Anne had not been so depressed, she would have laughed at the way her chaperon held the purse gingerly by two fingers well away from any contact with her gown, and her sniff as she set it on a table.

"Much as it pains me, we will have need of this money," she said. "I do not have much with me, and Mary Agnes, of course, none."

Since Anne refused to take any of the gowns the earl had chosen for her Season, the packing was soon accomplished. Then the three of them sat around the tea tray making and discarding plans.

"Wherever we go, it must be some place the earl would never think of looking, or Sir Hartley either," Miss Goodly said.

"I would like to go back to Cawfell first," Anne announced after several silent moments while the others tried to think of a place of sanctuary. "I want to know who my father is, and where he is now. And perhaps my mother has returned to England. My aunt and uncle are the only ones who can tell me, and I do not think the earl will suspect I might return to Cawfell—at least not at once."

Mary Agnes' brow was creased in deep lines. "But, Miss Anne, Miss Goodly . . . how are we to leave?"

She pointed to the various trunks and portmanteaus, looking completely confused.

The chaperon smiled. "That is the easiest part of all. We simply tell Midler that one of the earl's carriages will be required early tomorrow morning. I shall tell him we have had bad news from Yorkshire and must return at once. There will be no difficulty about that!"

She nodded decisively, and Mary Agnes looked relieved, but Anne exclaimed, "But that would be stealing, dear ma'am! To take a carriage and team, a coachman . . . we cannot do it!"

"I think the earl must agree he owes you that much, my dear," Miss Goodly said. "Especially after he reads the letter I intend to leave for him. I cannot tell you how much I look forward to the writing of it."

Her little eyes were snapping now behind her spectacles, and Mary Agnes nodded her approval.

In a few moments she went away to begin this happy chore, and the maid left Anne to go and pack her own belongings. Anne wandered over to the window of her room and stared down into the gardens and lawns of Bredon. She had been so happy and content here, until she found out the earl's true purpose. And Will Ashton's, too, she reminded herself. She did not think she would ever trust any man again. They were all of them evil and devious and cruel.

Anne and Miss Goodly had a quiet dinner, served by the superior Midler himself. Exactly as Miss Goodly had claimed, he did not ask any questions about the carriage she ordered, and he even unbent to the point where he said he hoped the bad news would not be as serious as they expected. Anne thanked him, feeling like a hypocrite.

Her chaperon went to bed very early, in preparation for the

morrow's traveling, but Anne lingered in front of the drawing-room fire, staring into the flames. She seemed to be able to see the earl's face there, first stern and cold, then warm and caressing before it changed into a mocking sneer as he laughed at her, and she cringed. And then there was a knock, and King, who had been dozing at her feet, sat up and growled, his ears coming erect as he faced the door.

Midler entered and bowed, his eyes never leaving the alert, growling dog. "The earl has arrived, miss," he said, his voice haughty and cold once more. "He wishes to see you in the library at once. Without the animal," he added. Behind him, Anne could see a distraught John Coombs.

Anne's hand went to her heart. Why was he back again? Had he learned of Sir Hartley's visit?

Numbly she got her feet, her hand automatically going to King's ruff. As she turned him over to John's care, the butler added, "I have had the carriage you ordered canceled, miss, at the earl's orders."

The disdain in his voice was easy to read, but Anne only nodded as she passed him. Somehow, she was not afraid, and in some strange way even a little relieved at the coming interview. She had not liked the idea of disappearing before she saw Anthony Hawkins again. She wanted to hear from his own lips that what Sir Hartley had told her was true; she wanted to search his face for some clue that he was sorry, that he regretted the wager and would release her from it. Perhaps she was being naive, she told herself as she made her way across the wide hall, not even seeing the commiserating glances the footmen gave her as she passed, but maybe she had wronged him after all. Perhaps it was not what it seemed; perhaps Sir Hartley had lied to her, or the earl come to care for her.

With a lighter heart, she went into the library and shut the door behind her quietly. Lord Bredon was standing before the fire dressed in riding clothes, his boots dusty and his hands clasped behind his back. He did not speak, nor did she as she came toward him and curtsied, trying to still the little leap of her heart at the sight of him. Her eyes never left his face. She saw he was angry, very angry indeed, for his gray eyes were cold and furious, and his mouth was set hard.

"I understand you were planning to leave Bredon tomorrow, Anne," he began, his deep voice tightly controlled.

Anne folded her hands before her and nodded. "I was, m'lord."

"But I do not believe I gave you permission to do so," he said. "You seem to have forgotten that I am master here. You will go only when I tell you you may, and when I order. I did not have you raised as a lady to defy me. No, in this, as in everything, you will obey me, instantly and without question."

Suddenly Anne was as furious as he was. She drew a deep breath and said, "So Sir Hartley was telling the truth after all. You only sent me to the vicar so you could win a stupid wager, didn't you? You never cared about *me* at all, just your thousand pounds."

The earl stared at her. The sudden anger in her voice and the way her blue eyes sparkled with scorn held him silent.

"How could you do such a terrible thing, m'lord?" she asked, speaking quickly now in her distress. "To befriend a child, letting her think you cared about what happened to her, raising her above her station and allowing her to dream of a nonexistent future . . . It was cruel! Nay, more than cruel! You are a fiend!"

The earl interrupted. "I am hardly a fiend, my girl. Why—"

She interrupted him in turn. "Perhaps I should have called you Satan's Rake, sir? I see very little difference after all, and the sobriquet fits you so well."

He bowed a little ironically, but she saw a muscle quiver for a moment beside his mouth.

"I do not think I have ever hated anyone the way I hate and despise you now, m'lord," she whispered.

"That is quite enough!" he said in a harsh loud voice, and her hand went to her throat in surprise. "You forget your place!"

"Which place is that, m'lord?" she returned quickly. "The lady or the scullery maid? Or perhaps you meant the place you had in mind for me to occupy when the wager was won?''

When he did not answer, she added, ''And if you did not want me to forget my place, you should never have given me ideas above my station.''

''It would be well if you did not anger me further, Anne,'' the earl retorted, stung by her defiance. ''I bought you for a handful of golden guineas, and you belong to me.''

He moved forward as he spoke, and grasped her arms, bending his head to glare down into her eyes, now only inches from his. Anne stiffened. ''I belong to no one but God and myself!'' she cried.

He shook his head, and Anne itched to slap him. ''The courts would not agree with you, Anne. You are as good as my slave. I have a paper signed by your uncle that makes your position very clear.''

When she opened her mouth to dispute this, he added quickly, ''Slavery has always existed in the world. It is not only the unfortunates from Africa and Asia who find themselves sold into bondage.''

She stared back at him, her blue eyes still defiant, but now somehow saddened and regretful. For a moment, he felt unaccustomed remorse at what he had done seven years ago.

From a drunken Lord Quarles he had found out that Sir Hartley had posted down to Bredon. He had followed him at once, leaving a message for Will Ashton to come on the morrow. If the other two knew of Anne's existence, there was no more need for secrecy. When he arrived at Bredon and found Sir Hartley had come and gone, and spoken to Anne as well, he had been surprised at the amount of relief he had felt that she was still here, and unharmed. The last few miles he had ridden like a man possessed, afraid that Hartley would take her away before he could save her. It was only his concern for the wager, of course, he told himself, but then he would remember some of Hartley's less charming methods of dealing with women, and how he always seemed to enjoy hurting them, and he would spur his horse to a gallop again.

When he discovered from his butler that Miss Anne, her chaperon, and the maid were planning to leave Bredon in the morning, his fury had returned. How dare she try to thwart him? How dare she even think of escape? She was his and she would do what she was told, even if he had to take his whip to her himself.

Now he glared at her as she said, her firm little chin still tilted in revolt, "You have had me brought up as a lady, not a slave, sir, and a lady I remain. But I could almost wish you had left me at Cawfell. Even my aunt's cruel beatings, the hunger and overwork, were better than being made your possession. Have you no shame? No remorse at all? Can it be possible that you really believe you can own another human being? God help you!"

His hands clamped tightly on her shoulders, but she did not notice.

"You will be silent, girl!" he thundered.

"I will never be silent!' she retorted.

Goaded by her blazing, condemning eyes, he pulled her roughly into his arms and bent his head still further to cover her lips with his. His mouth was hard and demanding, and she tried to pull away. His hands tightened even more, holding her crushed against him. Realizing there was no way she could escape him, she went limp in his arms, willing herself to ignore the strange feelings that were coursing through her as his kiss deepened. When he realized she was fighting him no more, he loosened his hold and moved his hands up and down her back in a caress. At last he lifted his mouth from hers and stared down into her face. She was white from shock, her thick lashes resting on her cheeks and hiding her eyes. He saw the way her half-open mouth quivered as she fought to catch her breath, and unable to resist its full pink contours, he bent again and covered it with his own. This time his kiss was gentle and soft, and when he let her go, she opened her eyes and stared at him in silent wonder.

Lord Bredon smiled down at her, and one finger came up to trace the tears that were running down her cheeks. "Go to bed, Anne," he said, his voice husky. "I did not mean to do that, but it seemed the only way to keep you quiet."

Anne stepped back, still staring at him, and her hand went out to grasp a chair back as she stumbled a little.

"I will see you in the morning," he said, turning away from her a little so she could not see for herself how much she had affected him. "Perhaps then we can continue this discussion more quietly, and with the dignity a *lady* and gentleman should employ when they converse."

As he stopped speaking, Anne seemed to come out of her trance, and she turned and picked up her skirts and fled to the door. Almost, he thought as he watched her fly down the length of the library, as if she imagined I might force her into an embrace again. But are you flying from me, or from yourself, my dear? he asked silently as the door closed behind her.

He went over to stare down into the fire, amazed that his icy fury had melted so quickly in the warmth of their embrace. Since he had come of age, no woman had dared to scold him or take him to task the way Anne Ainsworth had. If they tried it, even in a spirit of teasing fun, he had walked away from them without a backward glance. But he knew, even if there had been no wager to consider, he could not walk away from Anne. Admitting this was not only unpleasant, it was painful. As a boy, punished and bullied by the prim nanny his mother had hired to see his upbringing, and scolded and ridiculed by his stern governess, he had vowed that never again would he put himself under any woman's power. Only once had his resolution slipped. When he was seventeen, he had fallen desperately in love for the first time. The lady was some years older, a houseguest of his mother's, but she had encouraged him to believe she returned his regard. There were a few stolen meetings and at last she had taken him into her bed and let him make love to her. Lost in passion for the first time, and with a boy's ardor, he had written her a poem. In it he had poured out all his deepest feelings and laid bare his soul. The next afternoon, hidden in the garden so he might catch a secret glimpse of her, he had heard her reading his poem aloud to the other guests, and laughing as heartily as they did at his boyish enthusiasm. Even his mother thought it was amusing, he noticed before he fled.

Since that time, no woman had ever touched his heart. no one, that is, until Miss Anne Ainsworth had come to Bredon.

The earl shook his head and went to pour himself a glass of
wine. As he sipped it, he told himself he was being ridiculous.
She might seem different, but she was only a woman after
all, and as such not to be trusted.

In the hall, Anne went over to where John Coombs was
holding a whimpering King. Midler was watching, so all she
was able to do was whisper, "Come to my room as soon as
you can do so without being discovered. Do not worry if it is
late. I will be awake."

He bowed, and she snapped her fingers to King, trying to
move up the stairs at her usual pace. When she reached her
room, she did not ring for Mary Agnes at once, but sank
down before the bedroom fire to bury her face in the dog's
thick fur.

She had not known that kissing a man would make her feel
like that, she realized. Even though she had willed herself to
remain stiff and unyielding, her body had defied her. Of its
own volition, it had pressed close to the earl's caressing
hands, and her treacherous lips had opened under his in a sigh
of pure delight. She wondered what he must have thought of
her, after all her brave defiance, and she squirmed a little.
King moved restlessly as she hugged him tighter, and she
made herself get up and ring the bell. Now she knew how
thin her defenses were, it was all the more important that she
escape Lord Bredon before they crumbled completely.

Anne was relieved to learn that Mary Agnes already knew
about the earl's unexpected return, and had been making new
plans.

"Since we can't take the earl's carriage, and since he is
sure to have you watched from now on, we must leave here
tonight," she said, her voice determined. "You're not safe at
Bredon, miss. Not anymore."

"I know," Anne whispered. "But how can we escape?
Where can we go?"

"We must go on foot, so we will have to leave most of
your clothes, and mine too. I thought of that woodcutter's
wife with the new baby that you befriended. Do you think she
would give us shelter, just for tonight?"

Anne rose to pace the room. "I don't know, Mary Agnes.

I did ask John Coombs to come here as soon as he can. Perhaps he can help.''

The maid was already emptying a portmanteau and repacking it with necessities. Discarding flimsy morning gowns and lace-trimmed petticoats, she put in a warm shawl and a walking dress. As she packed, she asked, ''But what are we to do about Miss Goodly, miss? She won't be able to walk very far, for she is older, and unused to rough living.''

''We cannot leave her to face the earl's anger,'' Anne said. ''We must find a way so she can come along too.''

When John slipped into the room two hours later, he discovered all three women dressed for traveling, and waiting for him. Told of the situation, he nodded.

''Yes, you go to Rhea's tonight, Miss Anne. She's my cousin, I know she will take you in. And then tomorrow we'll see about getting you away from Bredon.'' He eyed the older chaperon with some doubt. ''You can't walk away, that's sure. Would you object to a farm cart?''

''The very thing, John!'' Mary Agnes exclaimed. ''And if we were to disguise ourselves, we may make a clean escape even now. The earl will not be looking for countrywomen. But we will need some old clothes; at least Miss Anne and Miss Goodly will.''

''I'll see to all that, never fear. Now I'll show you how to get out of the house without anyone noticing you. Can you find your way in the woods at night, Miss Anne?''

Anne pressed his hand. ''I am sure I can, John. Besides, I have King to help guide us.''

The three picked up their bags, but this John would not allow. ''Don't worry about your things. Stan and I and the other footmen will bring them to the cottage as soon as we can,'' he said.

As quietly as they could, the little cavalcade crept down a back stairway behind the young footman. Anne could not help smiling a little when she saw his cowlick waving over his head like a flag. In his concern for them, he had completely forgotten to smooth it down. There was no way she could ever thank him, she realized, but she gave him her warmest smile as she slipped out a side door to the gardens behind her maid and Miss Goodly, a silent King at her heels.

Their way was not difficult until they had walked around the lake and were about to enter the home wood. Anne paused for a moment then, and stared back at Bredon. It bulked tall and massive and proud against the sky. The brilliant lights in the earl's library were reflected in the dark lake. It seemed to Anne as if they were shimmering fingers, reaching out for her in a desperate search.

She wondered what Lord Bredon was doing. And then she waved her hand in farewell. In all likelihood she would never see Bredon or the wicked earl again. The pang she felt as she whispered good-bye made her square her shoulders before she turned to lead the way on the first part of their escape.

# 9

Shortly after twelve the following afternoon, an old farm cart, pulled by a tired, decrepit plowhorse, made its way slowly through the village of Bredon. It was loaded with full gunny-sacks that were somewhat protected from the elements by a ragged tarpaulin. Two women sat on the narrow plank that served as the seat. The driver was middle-aged and she wore an old-fashioned bonnet and an old shawl. Her companion was so bent over as to appear crippled, and as the cart continued through the rutted street, she waved and called out to the children playing around the cottage gates. All of them stared at her and pointed, although a few of the younger ones ran crying for their mothers. The crone's gray hair floated in wispy strands around a vacant face, and every so often she would give a screeching cackle, but whether it was of delight or just the result of an empty mind was difficult to tell. The driver was seen to scold her passenger more than once, as if impatient with her senility.

There were a lot of people abroad that cold November day, but although the cart drew many glances, no one's eyes lingered on it for more than a minute. Even the earl's agent, who was questioning a group of men outside the village pub, gave the conveyance and its unusual occupants no more than a cursory glance.

The cart lumbered away behind the plodding steps of the old horse and was soon lost from sight.

In the smallest cottage in the village, Mrs. Coombs twitched the curtain back over her front window and breathed a prayer of thanksgiving. She would have good news to send to John and the others at the hall, she thought as she put the kettle on for tea. And that sweet Miss Anne was safe, something she and several others of the villagers had worked throughout the morning to ensure.

"Are you all right, Miss Anne?" the driver of the cart asked softly over her shoulder as she guided the horse along the road. "We are away from Bredon now, but I think it best you stay hidden."

"I'm fine," one of the gunnysacks replied. The one next to it moved impatiently. "King is a little restless, though," Anne added. "Can I let him out to run alongside?"

"Not yet," Mary Agnes ordered. "We are much too close to the village. Keep him still awhile longer, miss."

Then she looked at the elderly crone beside her, and there was new respect in her voice as she asked, "All well, Miss Goodly?" She had been horrified at the role the chaperon had chosen to play during their escape from Bredon, claiming it would just call attention to them. Besides, she was not at all sure the prim, refined former governess could do it in a convincing manner. Miss Goodly had insisted.

"If we skulk through the village without a word, it will be very suspicious. This way everyone will be looking at us, but no one will suspect such a complete turnabout," she had said. Now Mary Agnes had to admit that Miss Goodly had been proved right.

The older lady straightened up and pushed her loose hair away from her face. "I am perfectly all right, thank you," she said in her normal, correct accents. "However, I will be glad when I can don my spectacles again, for I find it difficult to see. Then too, this seat is most uncomfortable!"

"Poor Miss Goodly," the sack sympathized. "We must find you a cushion somehow. But oh, how I wished I might have seen you when we came through the village! You sounded perfectly demented!"

"I have always enjoyed amateur theatricals," Miss Goodly admitted primly, smoothing her patched gray linsey-woolsey gown as she did so.

A reminiscent smile lit the maid's usually dour face. "You were a sight, ma'am," she said. "Good as a raree show, you were."

Miss Goodly permitted herself an answering smile. "Well, we are safe away, all thanks to John and the rest of Anne's Army. I never thought we had a chance of success until I saw how they sprang into action. Imagine, bringing all our things in these sacks, one at a time, and providing us with food and old clothes, and the cart and horse as well!"

Mary Agnes glared at the tired old horse. "I wish they'd found a better animal, though," she muttered, calling for him to giddyup.

The old plowhorse tossed his head and snorted, but he did not increase his pace, and the maid sighed and settled back, trying to make herself more comfortable on the narrow plank. "It's a good thing we don't have far to go today," she remarked.

"Yes, we may be thankful that John Coombs's supply of relatives seems endless," Miss Goodly declared. "I'll be glad to find this farm he sent us to, and his Aunt Sarah as well."

They passed other carts and riders along the way, and once a group of horsemen wearing the earl's livery cantered by. Miss Goodly was quick to resume her acting whenever anyone was in sight, but by the time Mary Agnes turned the horse and cart into the narrow track that led to Hill Farm, she was feeling tired and sore and old. If Anne was glad to be released from her hiding place under the gunnysacks, and King almost delirious with his freedom again, she of all of them was the happiest the day's journey had been accomplished.

John's aunt and uncle made them welcome and as comfortable as they could. The farm was a poor place, not much better than a hovel, but there were fresh eggs from the flock that scratched around the yard, and a piece of country ham for tea. Anne insisted on helping to wash up, and she was soon chattering away with the elderly couple as if she had known them all her life. Miss Goodly, installed in state in the one comfortable chair, sipped her tea and rocked, watching her charge.

She could see that Anne was still upset, in spite of her gay airs, and she wondered what had happened in the earl's library the evening before. Anne had been strangely reticent

about it. Of course she was still distressed by her discovery
that Lord Bredon was not the knight in shining armor she had
thought him to be, Miss Goodly told herself. She sniffed. She
had never been an admirer of the male sex herself, and this
latest exhibition by one of its members came as no surprise to
her. Satan's Rake, indeed! The earl was just spoiled and
conceited; she had had his measure after only a day at Bredon.

But she wondered where this mad journey to escape him
would lead them all, and she was glad she had penned a few
lines to the Nettleses before she left, so they would not worry
about Anne. John Coombs had said he would post it for her.
She had told the vicar the whole story, promising to remain
with Anne and keep her safe. She had not expressed any of
her many doubts about their escape, nor how they were to
live until the earl lost his wager and it was safe to return
home to Tees. The Season was several months away, and
fifty pounds and the little she had in her reticule would not
last long, not with three women to feed and shelter, to say
nothing of a large dog and an elderly horse who appeared to
have lost everything but his appetite.

The Coombses waved good-bye to them shortly after dawn
the next morning. Settling down on several folded sacks on
the rough perch, Miss Goodly was glad the weather continued
fair. She had seen Mary Agnes giving the sky an intent
perusal as she backed the horse between the shafts and she
was glad the Yorkshire countrywoman was with them. Besides understanding horses, she had all kinds of practical
knowledge the other two knew nothing about, and they would
need her expertise. She hoped, however, that they would all
be able to abandon this particular disguise before much longer.
Playing a demented old crone might be amusing for a while,
but she longed for her own neat clothes and a proper bonnet
and gloves.

This morning Anne and King sat up in the back of the cart,
and the girl blew a kiss to the elderly couple as they pulled
away. She was prepared to dive under the sacks at the first
sign of life, but for an hour she was able to enjoy the crisp
November morning and the lonely countryside they were
passing through. She knew, from what Farmer Coombs had

told them, that it was a long two days' journey to the nearest large town, but unlike her companion, she was not distressed by their disguise. She seemed to feel a lot safer wearing an old gown and ragged shawl, her distinctive red-gold hair pushed up under an ancient mobcap. As she braced herself against the jolting of the cart, she patted King, but her eyes were far away. What was the earl doing now? she wondered. He was sure to be furious when he learned of her escape, and once again she prayed that the footmen, indeed everyone who had helped them, would escape his wrath. She did not like to think that by coming to her aid, others might bring punishment on themselves. Then she looked down at the old gown Rhea Carter had given her, and was glad she had been able to give her a better one in exchange. She hoped the earl would never see her in it, for then he would know her as their accomplice.

Anne sighed, exasperated with herself. No matter how hard she tried to think of other things, her mind seemed to return again and again to Lord Bredon.

Later that morning, she stretched out on the sacks and dozed, for she had not slept very well on the hard pallet that was all the Coombses had been able to provide. King was running alongside the cart now, the horse's slow pace making it easy for him to keep up, and she was alone except for the occasional remarks of her companions seated high in front of her. Half-asleep, she relived the earl's kiss.

It was as real as if he had released her only a moment before. She could still feel his lips on hers, eager and warm and consuming, and the way his hands had held her close. She felt her skin glowing and her lips tingling with the memory. A perverse part of her wished he would gallop up behind them right now, and after a number of scathing remarks, order them all back to Bredon.

But although she watched all day, half-expectant and half-fearful, Lord Bredon never appeared in their dusty wake.

Sometimes during the long afternoon, she pondered her decision to go to Cawfell first, the one place she had always promised herself to avoid. Perhaps it was because the earl had claimed to have purchased her from her uncle, and she wanted to find out if it were true. Or perhaps she wanted to find out where her father was. Maybe they do not even know, she thought in despair. Perhaps no one knew. She could remember very little about her mother now, although she thought long and hard. The only thing she could recall was how pretty she had been. Anne had often been left alone as a small child; sometimes her mother had not returned to their lodgings until dawn. I am probably a bastard, she told herself, determined to face the truth. But no matter who I am, I have to know the truth. Anything would be better than this limbo she found herself living in now, the little scullery-maid-turned-lady to win a wager made by drunken men one rainy night for their amusement.

Her lips tightened when she remembered that, and she felt no more remorse that she had run away from Bredon.

That night they camped in the open. Mary Agnes insisted on it, for she said the horse's slow pace left them much too close to Bredon still to seek shelter in an inn.

They found a deserted field bordered by a large wood, and Mary Agnes drove the cart into it until they were out of sight from the road.

Anne thought Miss Goodly would be horrified, but she entered into the adventure with a will, even insisting on gathering twigs for their small campfire.

Anne and the maid watered the horse at the small brook that ran through the field, and then hobbled him and turned him loose to seek what sparse graze he could find. While Anne tried to arrange the gunnysacks into a rough bed, Mary Agnes set about cooking sausage and slicing bread and cheese for their supper.

When the sun went down, it seemed very dark and lonesome and cold, and they were all glad King was with them for protection. That night they kept warm by huddling together in the cart bed under the blankets and tarpaulin Mary Agnes had insisted they carry, but the cold, frosty morning drove them back on the road shortly after dawn.

Mary Agnes wore a worried frown all day. She knew they must get Miss Goodly to shelter, and soon. Although she tried to hide it, and had won the maid's admiration for her courage, the effects of rough living were taking their toll.

Mary Agnes sought the less used roads, and as they plodded through small hamlets and past lonely farms, they were often jeered at and sometimes chased by dogs. King dispatched these barking mongrels in short order. Mary Agnes herself had discouraged a group of village louts who followed them calling out insults. If they had not understood her broad Yorkshire, they could not mistake the dangerous glare in her eyes.

That night they were lucky enough to find a deserted shed to sleep in, and the mounds of hay that Anne arranged seemed like a feather bed after the lumpy sacks. The maid wisely did not mention rats.

It was a long day later before they reached the outskirts of Market Deeping. They unloaded the cart, and then Mary Agnes left the other two and their belongings in a small copse while she went on ahead alone. She was sure it was safe now to sell the cart and the old horse, and she had convinced them that they should spend some of their money for a better rig, so they could travel in more comfort.

Miss Goodly was looking forward to a bath and a comfortable bed, and Anne herself was relieved. She had no desire to arrive at Cawfell dressed as if she were still the equal of her aunt and uncle. Somehow she knew she would need every advantage she could employ in her dealings with them.

While they waited for the maid's return, Miss Goodly sat patiently on a fallen log, a blanket as well as a shawl over her thin shoulders. She watched Anne pace about, knowing how hard it was for her to be cooped up in the cart all day with nothing to do.

At last Anne came over and sank down beside her companion. Her face was troubled, and there was a little frown between her brows. Wisely Miss Goodly did not inquire what the matter was, but sat and watched a squirrel as it scolded them for their intrusion from the safety of a high branch.

"Miss Goodly," Anne began after a moment, "may I ask a question?"

"Of course, my dear," the older lady replied. "Anything you wish."

There was a slight pause, and then Anne asked in a rush, "Is it true that English people . . . er, women . . . can be sold into slavery?"

Her companion tried to keep her expression neutral. Whatever question she had been expecting, it was not this. "Well, I am not sure, Anne," she said at last. "It is true there are indentured servants, but they are not slaves. In time they can work out the term of their indenture and gain their freedom again. Why do you ask?"

Anne did not look at her companion. She had picked up a fallen oak leaf and was turning it this way and that in her hands. "It was something the earl said to me. That last evening he told me I was his slave and had to do what he said because he had bought me from my aunt and uncle for a handful of guineas. And he said he had a paper to prove he owned me."

Miss Goodly tried to keep her horrified reaction to this news from showing on her face as Anne turned toward her and asked urgently, "Can that be possible in 1809?"

"I suppose so," Miss Goodly said slowly, and Anne looked even more distraught. "But the question is, were your relatives authorized to sell you? Unless they themselves had a paper from your parents, giving you up to them unconditionally, I do not think their signatures would stand up in a court of law."

Anne nodded eagerly. "I thought much the same myself. That is why I said we must go to Cawfell. There is no real chance my mother has returned to England, and I may never know who my father is, but at least I can find out if I really do belong to the earl . . . er, that way."

Suddenly she buried her face in her hands and sobbed. Dismayed, Miss Goodly put her arms around her. "Come, come, my dear! You must not lose your courage and composure at this jointure. You have always been so brave, so eager for life. And now, in spite of all your obstacles, you must continue to maintain your spirits. In doing so, you support

Mary Agnes and myself as well, for we depend on you, much the way you depend on King.''

Anne sat up and wiped her eyes, apologizing profusely for her lapse.

Miss Goodly patted her back. ''All women are subject to 'lapses,' as you call it. The successful ones refuse to give in to defeat and depression, and pick up the threads of their lives again. Life is hard, Anne, as you learned when still a very young child. It can also be unfair. Do not struggle against it, but let it take you where it will. In the end, I am sure all will be well with you.''

She sounded so calm and positive, Anne had to smile.

It seemed an age before Mary Agnes called to them, and they came back to the lane to see a pair of grays harnessed to an elderly landau. It was not a very impressive equipage, but Miss Goodly clapped her hands in delight, and Anne said they would be all the crack.

They changed their clothes in the copse then, and loaded the landau. Taking her seat, Miss Goodly, neat again in brown twill with her gray hair in a smooth chignon, looked much more her usual self. As she and Anne settled back, Mary Agnes climbed to the perch and took up the reins. The chaperon wished they might have hired a groom. Surely three women and a dog traveling alone must appear very strange. Then she smiled. After playing a senile old hag for three days, the role of eccentric gentlewoman would be a positive relief.

When they reached Market Deeping, they took a room in one of the smaller inns. No one questioned them, and they were all relieved that the earl's search did not appear to have extended to this place.

When Miss Goodly woke the next morning, it was to hear a cold, sleety rain striking the windowpanes with sharp, fretful taps. She snuggled down under the quilts next to Anne with a happy sigh. They had reached shelter just in time.

Many miles away, the Earl of Bredon was in a frustrated rage. He stood at his library window and stared out at the dismal November day, watching the sleet whiten the lawn before him and ruffle the calm of the lake.

Where is she? he asked himself yet again. Where has she gone? In his mind, he went over the few facts he knew.

He had discovered her absence the morning after his return to Bredon, when he sent a footman to find out why Miss Anne had not come down to breakfast.

Not a muscle had moved in the man's face when he reported that Miss Anne's room was empty. Not only was she not there, some of her clothes were missing as well, and the bed had not been slept in. A similar check of Miss Goodly's room and Mary Agnes' place in the attic told him Anne had not left by herself. Even the dog was missing. In fact, the only things that remained to show that any of them had ever been at Bredon were all of Anne's new clothes and a scathing letter to him from Miss Alicia Goodly.

His face had whitened as he read it, and a dangerous pulse beat in his forehead as he strode to the fireplace to fling it into the burning coals.

Careful questioning of the servants gained him nothing. They had answered him promptly, their faces honest and open as they denied knowing anything about it. The earl had been sure they were lying. Although he had longed to send each and every one of them packing, especially the entire corps of footmen who made up Anne's Army, he had realized he did not have a shred of evidence with which to do so. Midler, trying his best to be helpful, had been no more successful in his questioning, and when he took to slipping around trying to eavesdrop on the other servants, he had heard not a word. It was as if Miss Anne Ainsworth had never visited Bredon at all.

Will Ashton had arrived in the midst of the uproar. He heard the earl's thundering voice in the library and raised a surprised eyebrow at Midler, who had welcomed him at the door. Hawk very seldom had to raise his voice. The butler looked distraught as he shook his head.

"It's that Miss Anne, sir," he confided. "She's run off, and no one seems to know where. Her maid and chaperon are gone too." His gloomy expression brightened a little as he added, "The animal is also missing."

Will turned quickly and almost ran to the library. As he opened the door, he heard Hawk say in a savage voice, "Start the search at once, Simms! Someone must have seen them or helped them. They were here last night, they cannot have gone very far. Start with the stables and the village, and then conduct your inquiries in ever-widening circles. Three women, two of them ladies, that large dog, Anne's brilliant hair—they cannot have escaped without a trace."

After the earl's agent scurried away, Will was soon put in the picture. He learned that Sir Hartley's visit had precipitated the debacle, and he started up, clenching his fists. His hazel eyes glowed with a dangerous light.

"I'll kill him for this, Hawk!" he growled. "He is not fit to live!"

For a brief moment a ghost of a smile had crossed the earl's face. "I do wish you would learn to control yourself, Will. I thought you had outgrown your tendency to solve every problem by helping your fellows to extinction. No doubt Hartley was only trying to win the wager. When he saw Anne, he must have known immediately that he had lost. How could he think otherwise? There she was, so beautiful and perfect and ladylike. Naturally he did what he could to turn her against us and get her to disappear."

Will's furious look changed to one of speculation. Hawk had sounded almost gentle when he spoke of Anne. Was it possible that he had come to see how fine she was? That he was in love with her?

"But what are we to do?" he asked, hoping that the finer emotion that was love was beyond the earl's capabilities still.

"We will continue to search. But if she is not found today, the task will become more difficult. She might be anywhere." Lord Bredon's eyes were bleak, but then he added, his voice more cheerful, "I do not think she will make her escape so easily. She is hampered by her companions and that dog, and by a lack of funds as well."

"Surely she will go back to Tees, Hawk," Will pointed out.

''She would be remarkably foolish if she did so, for it is the first place anyone would think of looking for her. Anne is not foolish, far from it. No, she will not go back to Tees. But where will she go?'' he mused, rubbing his chin and then walking to the window as if he hoped to find the answer there.

The search had continued for two days, but there was no trace of Anne, not even the tiniest clue. The earl grew steadily more angry in his frustration, and his expression more forbidding as his eyes flashed an icy gray glare. Even Will Ashton stayed out of his way. His agents came and made their reports, and were sent out again. The earl himself spent hours studying maps and thinking, trying to discover the route the women might have taken. Not knowing their destination made this an exercise in futility.

Now he turned from the library window with a sigh. She was gone, but he promised himself he would find her, no matter how long it took. And when he did, Miss Ainsworth would discover how unwise it was to incur the Earl of Bredon's wrath.

A gust of wind blew the sleet against the window, and he found himself hoping that she was somewhere warm and safe. And then he scoffed at himself. Of course his concern was only for the wager, and because he had chosen her for his future mistress.

When Will entered the library, he found his friend brooding down into the fire, one booted foot on the fender. His eyes seemed calmer somehow, and he wore an air of quiet determination.

When asked what they were to do now, the earl did not reply for several moments. Then he straightened up and said, ''We continue the search and we wait. No matter how long it takes, we wait. It appears that we are about to be taught a lesson that I fear is long overdue. Satan's Rakes have never been known for their patience. Amusing, is it not, my dear Will?''

# 10

The Earl of Bredon was a member of the Quorn, one of the great hunts to be found in the Midlands. The counties of Leicestershire and Northamptonshire were the most highly enclosed sections of England, their many tight thorn hedges making the chase both challenging and dangerous. They were also blessed with low rolling hills and wide vistas, an ideal location for fox hunting.

Late one afternoon, a landau containing two ladies, and driven, somewhat surprisingly, by a sturdy countrywoman with a huge shepherd on the perch beside her, arrived at Cawfell. The hunting box looked deserted, and Anne could not restrain a shiver of disappointment as Mary Agnes halted the team before the shallow steps that led up to the front door.

Miss Goodly squeezed her hands and then pointed to where a thin plume of smoke could be seen coming from the kitchen chimney. Remembering all the hours she had spent in the adjacent scullery made Anne shiver again, this time with loathing. Then she put up her chin and set her lips in a composed line. She was back, back where she had vowed never to come again, but she would not be here for long.

The travelers had taken a room at the inn in the nearest village, and they had spent an hour washing and dressing in their best, all the while rehearsing once again the things they planned to say. Now Anne looked down at her smart blue traveling gown with its matching bonnet and hoped it would be enough to awe the Jenkinses into giving up the secret of her birth.

She helped Miss Goodly up the steps, and gave the knocker

a mighty crash. The two waited for several minutes, and Anne was about to knock again, when the door opened a few inches. Her uncle peered out at them.

Seeing two ladies, even unescorted as they were, he opened the door a little bit wider. "Yus?" he asked.

"Good afternoon, Uncle," Anne said, pushing the door wide. "Surely you do not plan to keep me standing here on the step this cold afternoon, nor my chaperon either. The earl would be most displeased if he knew!"

The butler's mouth dropped open, and he stepped back. The one candle he held did little to dispel the gloom of the hall as the ladies swept in. Miss Goodly looked around and sniffed her disapproval.

"Annie?" he croaked, his voice disbelieving.

Somehow his awed tones gave her courage, and she nodded even as she inspected him. The years had not been kind to Mr. Jenkins. He was almost completely bald now, except for a fringe of gray hair and a few greasy strands combed carefully over the dome of his head. His face was lined and sallow, and the dark eyes she remembered were set in even heavier pouches. She was surprised to see how thin and short he was. She remembered him as a much taller man, but of course, she reminded herself, to Little Annie Ainsworth, he must have seemed immense.

"Miss Ainsworth to you, my good man," Miss Goodly corrected him, her voice proud and icy. "How dank and unwelcoming this hall is, my dear Anne. We shall require some more candles."

Anne nodded and handed her uncle her pelisse and gloves before she helped her chaperon. "And a fire in the drawing room, Jenkins," she ordered. "I realize we were not expected, and I am sure you and my aunt will be relieved to hear that we do not stay, but perhaps a tea tray would not be beyond your capabilities. Such a raw day, is it not?"

Jenkins gulped and nodded. Her rich contralto, speaking as elegantly as ever the earl had, impressed him. He did not know why she was here, but it was obvious that the years she had spent since the last time he had seen her had turned her into what he would be quick to call a real swell.

"O' course, An . . . missus. Oi'll see to it instanter," he mumbled, backing away to light a branch of candles that rested on a side table.

Anne nodded and strolled about the hall, looking with a critical eye at the paintings of the hunt that adorned it. The butler hesitated for a moment, until she turned and raised one red-gold eyebrow at him, and the gesture reminded him of his master so vividly that he bowed and scurried away.

"Excellent, Anne!" Miss Goodly whispered when he was safely out of earshot. "Only continue that way, and we should have the information you need in very short order."

Secretly she prayed that that information would be good news. Their money was disappearing at a rate she could only deplore, and if they did not reach a place of safety soon, she would have to insist that Anne return to Tees and the vicar's protection, no matter how dangerous that might be.

Anne led her up the stairs to an empty bedchamber to freshen up, and when they came down again, it was to find the drawing-room candles lit, a fire started, and a bowing Jenkins ushering them to seats. He had removed a few of the holland covers from some of the furniture, but Miss Goodly ran a critical finger over a dusty table and sniffed again as she took her seat.

"Be so good as to ask my aunt to bring in the tea tray herself," Anne commanded as she took the seat opposite. "I wish to speak to you both."

Jenkins nodded and bowed again before he left the room.

It seemed an age to an impatient Anne before she heard him whispering in the hall, and then the door of the drawing room opened to admit her aunt, followed by her husband, who was carrying the tray.

Anne had to struggle to keep from trembling. She had almost jumped to her feet as Aunt Mabel lumbered in, for she could still remember her bellowed orders and the switch she used so frequently. Mrs. Jenkins was a tall, buxom woman with heavy arms and a truculent expression on her red face. Her curtsy to the ladies was shallow and insolent.

"Well, well," she said, folding her arms over her massive stomach. "And 'ere, so Jenkins tells me, is me niece. Quite the foine leddy, ain't you, Annie? But you're no more a leddy than I am! Ha," she snorted. "Less, mebbe. I got me marriage lines, I do, which is more than I've 'eard tell you 'ave! Oh no, you're still little Annie Ainsworth and my kin, for all the earl's dressed you up as foine as ninepence. And we all knows woi 'e did that, now don't we?" She laughed a sneering laugh as her eyes raked Annie's figure in its smart blue gown. Swept back almost seven years, Anne sat frozen, unable to speak.

"I doubt that you are any kin of Miss Ainsworth's anymore, Mrs. Jenkins," Miss Goodly said into the silence. The house-keeper turned to stare at her as she continued, "The earl has told me how you gave Anne up to him. In doing so you forfeited any rights to call yourself Anne's aunt. Now that I have seen you, I am sure Anne can only be grateful that such is the case. You must not look for any special consideration now that she is Lord Bredon's ward. From what she has told me, I would be very much surprised if she felt any charity toward you or your husband."

Mabel Jenkins' mouth fell open, but before she could speak, Anne handed her chaperon a cup of tea. "Sugar, Miss Goodly? Cream?" she asked, steady and assured once again. "I do apologize for these cakes. They look as if they had been baked some time ago. I wonder if m'lord knows how poorly Cawfell is run when he is not here?"

At her educated accents, her aunt frowned even more heavily and for the first time looked a little doubtful of her ground. Behind his wife's massive figure, Jenkins could be seen to cringe.

After passing the plate of dubious cakes, Anne took a sip of her tea, and then she said, "I have come here for one reason, and one reason only. But I assure you that if I do not get satisfactory answers to my questions, I shall be quick to report it to the earl."

Jenkins bobbed his head and hurried into speech. "Anything at all, Annie . . . er, missus. Wot can we do for you?"

Before Anne could begin, a respectful voice from behind him said, "I found a stableboy to watch the team, Miss

Anne. King is watching the stableboy. I thought perhaps you might need my assistance.''

The Jenkinses turned to see an unsmiling Mary Agnes putting her cloak down over a chair before she curtsied to their niece as if she were the queen. Her apron was dazzling white and heavy with starch, and the little cap she wore on her tightly coiled brown hair was trimmed with lace. It was obvious that she was a most superior lady's maid.

"Thank you, Mary Agnes," Anne said. "Sit down over there, if you please. We shall not be long."

With a glance around the room that told the Jenkinses the maid considered the location she found her mistress in most unsuitable, Mary Agnes retreated to a chair near the wall.

"Now, Mrs. Jenkins, I require an honest, straightforward answer," Anne commanded. Her aunt, looking at her beautiful haughty face, stiffened. It wasn't fair! Here was Lizzy's brat acting as if she were quality, and she knew she was no better than her mother had been. For a moment she felt a pang of regret and envy. She had been young like that once, young and comely and fresh. And now she was old and gin-sodden, married to a onetime convict and dependent on her niece's goodwill. She made herself nod, and kept her expression neutral.

"Yes, miss?" she asked. Jenkins breathed a sigh of relief, and the three visitors were able to relax. Their plan seemed to be working.

"I have come to discover if you have heard from my mother since I left Cawfell," Anne continued.

Now her aunt smiled, a sly smile that disclosed several gaps in her teeth. "Nah, that we ain't. Never a word from 'er since she left you 'ere," she told her niece as if she relished giving her the bad news. "Prob'ly dead, she is. Wouldn't surprise me none if she wuz."

"I see. I really did not expect you had. And so you will tell me instead where I might find my father."

"Your *father*?" Mrs. Jenkins asked, her voice insolent again. "Now, 'ow would I know 'oo 'e might be? Might be any number o' men," she continued, chatty now. "Lawd, yus. Lizzie was no better than wot she should be, woi—"

"Mind your tongue, my good woman, or it will go hard with you," Miss Goodly said, stiffening in her chair and pointing an accusing finger.

The massive, slovenly housekeeper seemed to wilt before the look in the indomitable little lady's eye.

"You will bring Miss Ainsworth any family papers that you have in your possession, and at once," Miss Goodly continued.

"Papers?" Mrs. Jenkins asked, her innocent voice sounding false even to her own ears. She was not surprised when her niece spoke up, her voice hard.

"Yes, *papers*. I know you cannot read them yourself, but I myself do not suffer that handicap. And if the papers are not immediately forthcoming, I shall have no recourse but to return to Bredon and lay this matter before the earl. I know he will be most displeased to hear I was not accorded every courtesy, and that my wishes, like his, were not instantly obeyed."

Jenkins seemed to see his master before him, that icy expression and hard jaw, and hear his soft, frightening words in his niece's ultimatum. He could also see himself and Mabel trudging down the drive of Cawfell, their possessions on their backs, and with no place to go.

"I'll get 'em for ya, missus," he volunteered eagerly.

His wife hissed in annoyance, as Anne nodded. "Do so quickly, if you please. I have no desire to remain here a moment longer than is absolutely necessary."

As her uncle scurried from the room, she turned and said, "Come and have a cup of tea, Mary Agnes. It is a cold day."

The maid curtsied again and accepted the cup she poured. As she retreated to her corner, she gave the housekeeper a look of disgust. Mrs. Jenkins was suddenly all too aware of her soiled apron and greasy dress.

She stood first on one foot and then the other, as the two ladies sipped their tea and discussed the dinner they had ordered at the inn where they were staying, and the plans they had for joining the earl in London in a week's time to do some shopping and attend the theater. It had all been carefully rehearsed, if Mrs. Jenkins could have known it.

The butler came back at last, clutching a worn cardboard box. Anne struggled to keep her expression cool as she took it from him and opened it. Inside there were very few papers. She looked each one over before she passed it to Miss Goodly. A leaden disappointment began to grow when she saw the papers were mostly canceled bills. She found the Jenkinses' marriage certificate, and read it aloud with no comment. Of her mother's, there was no trace. And then, almost at the bottom of the box, there was a fragment of a letter. It was written in an educated hand, and she looked up quickly to see her aunt leaning forward, her mouth open and her face avid as she stared at it. Had she saved this paper because it had belonged to her sister? Did she hope to use it someday, somehow?

It was not a very large fragment, and Anne could see there were only a few sentences written on it as she smoothed it out.

". . . will not be forced to support you anymore. You have shown me your true colors. As for the br . . ."

Here the paper was torn, and Anne swallowed her disappointment, before she continued to read, ". . . acknowledge her, even if we are marri . . ."

She could not make out the signature, and she passed the note to Miss Goodly, feeling a bitter frustration.

"Now, this is very encouraging, my dear Anne, very encouraging indeed," Miss Goodly was saying. Anne looked up to see her waving the paper in triumph. "It is proof positive that your mother was married." She turned to the Jenkinses. "You have been most uncooperative, but you will give us the name and direction of Anne's father at once."

" 'E wuz Archie Ainsworth," Jenkins volunteered eagerly. "Least that's wot Lizzie always called 'im."

"And where might this Archibald Ainsworth be found?" Miss Goodly inquired next. "Come now, speak up!"

Mrs. Jenkins looked mutinous, but she wilted before the stern eye of Miss Goodly. "I don't know, and that's the truth, ma'am," she declared.

"Really?" Miss Goodly asked, her voice frigid with disbelief.

Anne felt it was time she took a hand. "Come, my dear Miss Goodly," she said. "Of course they do not know, not now, for he would hardly remain in touch with such as they. But surely they know where he was from originally, and in which parish my mother married him."

She turned to her aunt, and that woman said, her voice grudging, " 'E was from St. Just. Lizzie used ta say that if 'e lived any closer to the end o' England, 'e'd be in the ocean. They got married in Plymouth, where ya ma and me grew up."

"Excellent!" Miss Goodly said, her manner applauding this hard-won information as if it had been freely given. She rose. "We will take this paper with us. Shall we be on our way, dear Anne? Oh, I almost forgot."

Turning to the butler again, for she wisely assessed him as the weak reed of the combination, she asked, "Where is the paper that Miss Anne's mother gave you, giving up her rights to her daughter when she went to America?"

"There wuzn't never no paper," the butler answered, seemingly confused. "She just left Annie on our 'ands one day and never come back."

Miss Goodly drew on her gloves and beckoned Mary Agnes to come forward to assist her mistress. "Indeed?" she asked. "That is very unfortunate, both for you and your wife."

She buttoned her cloak and picked up her reticule.

"Un . . . unfortunate, missus?" Jenkins croaked.

"Oh yes, I think so. You as much as sold Miss Ainsworth to the earl, and you put your mark on a paper saying you had done so," Miss Goodly announced. She shook her head as she took Anne's arm to lead her to the door. "I do not think the authorities would look at all kindly on such underhanded, cruel dealings, for it was not your right to give her away. You must hope that Miss Ainsworth never decides to prosecute, or you might very well find yourselves in jail."

At the door now, Anne turned back to stare into their stunned, frightened faces. For a moment she considered being as cruel to them as they had always been to her, but then she said, "I shall never do so, Miss Goodly. When Lord Bredon removed me from *their* tender care, it was the best day of my life!''

She swept from the room, her head held high, and Jenkins wrung his hands and moaned. It was obvious to him that Annie, for all her wealth and education, had not forgotten a single pinch or blow.

He did not even hear the front door close behind the visitors, or the strident exclamations of his wife, for he was remembering how many of those blows he' had administered himself, and he was afraid.

The carriage had turned out of Cawfell's gates before anyone said a word. Miss Goodly had tucked the precious paper in her reticule for safekeeping, and patted Anne's hand before she leaned back against the squabs to close her eyes in relief. But when the dour Mary Agnes flourished the whip over the grays' heads and cried, "Hurrah, we did it!" she opened them to smile.

"Indeed we did, Mary Agnes," she said, her voice rich with satisfaction.

Anne had to laugh at them. In the days they had been traveling together, she had come not only to depend on her companions, but to love them as well. The maid had been a tower of strength, driving the team and seeing to their welfare— everything from purchasing inexpensive meals they could eat on the road to finding suitable accommodations. And Miss Goodly, bless her, Anne thought, had never once let their spirits flag. By her cheerful conversation and indomitable presence she had held them all together, secure as she was in her belief that everything would end happily. Her calm good sense had been not only welcome but also necessary, for Anne, for all her love of adventure, was only seventeen, and Mary Agnes had a tendency to look on the dark side of life. Anne knew she could never have done it without these dear women to guide her and help her. Constantly together, they were easy in each other's company now. There was no mistress, no maid, no chaperon. There were only three very good friends.

"You were perfect, both of you," Anne complimented them now. "Miss Goodly, you cowed them completely, so superior and prim you appeared, dear ma'am, and as for that curtsy, Mary Agnes, I am sure Princess Caroline never had a better one!''

Mary Agnes laughed, and King barked a little, unwilling to be left out of the festivities.

''And now we know our destination,'' Miss Goodly went on, nodding in her satisfaction. ''We shall leave tomorrow for Plymouth and St. Just. Thank heaven we go to the south of England. It will be December in a few days, and I dreaded the possibility of a trip to Scotland during that frigid month.''

''Suppose . . . suppose we do not find my father there, Miss Goodly?'' Anne asked, frowning a little.

''We are sure to find some of his family, my dear, and so we will be able to discover where he is at present.''

''This St. Just, ma'am. How far is it?'' Mary Agnes asked over her shoulder.

''A very long way,'' Miss Goodly admitted, frowning in turn. ''We will have to be very careful with what funds remain to us, Mary Agnes.''

The maid nodded. She was already making plans for even more frugality than she had employed in the past, when Annie said, ''The earl will never think of looking for me there. That will be a relief.''

Miss Goodly thought she sounded a little pensive, and she looked at her sharply.

Under the brim of the smart blue bonnet, Anne's lovely profile was serene, and she told herself that she must have imagined the wistful note she thought she had detected in her words. Surely Anne, sensible, practical girl that she was, could not be falling in love with the wicked earl. No, that could not be. Handsome as he was, she knew him now for one of Satan's Rakes indeed.

The man they were both thinking about, one with revulsion and the other with regret, was seated in his library at Bredon. He was reading a reply he had had from the Vicar Nettles to his inquiry. It was short, almost terse, announcing that although he had learned that Anne had left Bredon, she was perfectly safe. He had no idea, however, where she might be found.

The earl folded the letter with a little smile. Unspoken, but implied, was the silent message that even if he did know, nothing, not even his instant dismissal, could drag the information from his lips.

The earl had not even bothered to order him to send him news of Anne's whereabouts, for he had known it would be useless. He and Will had discussed and abandoned the idea of a trip to Tees. They knew neither of them would have a pleasant reception, and not even the earl himself would be able to gain any new information. Instead, Lord Bredon wrote to his agent at the Grove, telling the man to keep a sharp ear out for news of Miss Ainsworth, news he was to relay to his master by express as soon as he had discovered it.

After several fruitless days of waiting, Will prepared to return to his own estate. He was doing no good at Bredon, and he did not want his sister to be alone when all the family descended on Ashton Abbey to celebrate Christmas.

"Where will you be, Hawk?" he asked that last morning as they stood at the top of the steps of Bredon, waiting for the footmen to finish loading the carriage.

The earl shrugged, his eyes staring at a far horizon only he seemed able to discern these days. "I have no idea. I may remain here, to keep in touch with the search, or I may travel to London to see Hartley and Reggie. Perhaps if I were to pretend that I knew where Anne was, I might find out something."

Will looked startled. "You don't think she has gone to them, surely, Hawk?" he asked, his voice incredulous. "Not Anne, and that . . . that devil!"

The earl's mouth tightened. "I do most sincerely hope not, Will. But we must remember she could not have had much money by her. I do not pay my vicars such a munificent sum that the Nettleses could have sent her to Bredon laden with gold guineas. And she has been gone so many days now. Desperation may drive her to them."

His gray eyes seemed to darken at the possibility, and then with a visible effort he shook off his abstraction. "If I do go to town, it will not be for long. You may always reach me here. Like the spider, I shall stay close to my web, spinning it in ever-widening circles and waiting patiently for the one prey I desire so much to stumble into the silken strands.''

He laughed at Will's sudden frown and startled exclamation, and clapped his shoulder in camaraderie. "That was an unfortunate simile, my friend. Do not regard it. You know me as a hawk; I think I would prefer to be compared to that bird, for it swoops down on its prey, rather than a fat patient spider using entrapment to gain its ends.''

He smiled and then said, "The carriage is ready, Will, so be off with you.''

The two friends shook hands, and Lord Bredon promised to send word as soon as he had any news.

But as the carriage bowled away, the easy smile he had worn left his face, and he said to himself softly, "But whether I am spider or hawk, Anne Ainsworth has no hope of escaping me.''

# 11

After Will Ashton left, Bredon seemed very cold and barren. There was no one to talk to, no one to share this difficult period of waiting for news that never seemed to come. Every day, the earl heard his agents' reports, either in person or by the post, and when they were invariably negative, he would order his stallion saddled and ride out as if the devil himself sat behind him on those powerful hindquarters.

And then, after three days of this unwelcome solitude, Lord Bredon decided to travel to London to see what news he could glean from the other two members of Satan's Rakes. He left early the next morning, telling his butler to expect his return within the fortnight.

Once again, his valet was treated to a silent trip, for the earl ignored him to stare out the carriage window with an unblinking gaze. Only the occasional clenching and unclenching of his hands told Barker of his stress.

They arrived at the earl's town house in the early-December dusk some three days later. Lord Bredon had pushed them all hard—coachman, grooms, and teams—by insisting on starting each day before sunrise and traveling well into the evening hours.

Now, after a bath and a tray of food brought to his rooms, he changed into evening dress. He had thought long and hard about the best way to approach his adversaries, and he had decided to begin with Lord Quarles. If he could find him early enough in the evening, he would still be coherent, and yet well-sprung enough to be careless of what he disclosed.

Accordingly, he made his way to two of Reggie's favorite haunts. When he did not find him there, he went to his rooms

133

on South Audley Street, where he was informed Lord Quarles was spending the evening with Sir Hartley Wilson.

The earl's gray eyes did not show any dismay at this unwelcome news as he thanked the servant and went away. It was well after ten now, and he told himself it made no difference whether Reggie was alone or not. By this hour he was invariably drunk.

On being admitted to Hartley's rooms, he discovered Reggie lolling in an armchair by the fire. Two empty wine bottles lay discarded at his feet, and he was clutching a third as he tried to pour another glass of burgundy. Of Sir Hartley there was no sign.

Lord Bredon's lip curled in disgust as he handed the butler his cloak, hat, and gloves. "Do let me assist you, Reggie," he said as he walked into the room. Noting the man's trembling hands, he added dryly, "I believe the object of drinking is to get the wine *in* you, not *on* you."

Lord Quarles looked up in amazement, his blue eyes vacant, and his mouth hanging open in astonishment. "Hawk! Tha' you, man?" he mumbled.

"As you see," Lord Bredon said, taking the bottle and pouring them both a glass. He leaned against the center table, casual and assured. "I trust I find you well, my friend?" he asked.

Lord Quarles gulped the burgundy, and a few drops ran down his chin. " 'M fine. Why'd you ask?"

Lord Bredon inspected him coldly. Reggie had put on another stone in weight, and his color was not good. The whites of his eyes were red-veined, and his fat lips almost purple. Hawk noticed he did not seem to be able to control the tremor of his hands.

"You do not look well," he said in reply. "Surely a repairing lease is in order before you drink yourself to death."

Lord Quarles pushed out his fat lower lip and glared. "Aye, 'member you said that to me once 'fore. But I' still here, Hawk!" He seemed to remember something then, for suddenly he guffawed and slapped his knee. 'An' I'll be here for t' Season, too! Must c'llect m' wager 'long with Hart . . . Hartley.''

Lord Bredon put his glass down on the table, his eyes growing colder. "Ah, yes, the wager. But where is Hartley this evening? Surely he is a poor host to leave you here drinking all alone."

Lord Quarles waved in the direction of another room. "He's in there. Brought a wench up, offered me first go." He brooded into his wine for a moment, and then he confided, "Couldn't do it. But no loss. Didn't like 'er. Skinny, yellow-haired jade."

He finished his wine and looked around. "Where'sa bottle?" he asked plaintively. Lord Bredon strolled back to pour him another glass, noting his stained linen and musty smell. The prostitute had been lucky, he thought in disgust as he retreated to a safe distance again.

Just then the door of the other room opened and Sir Hartley came in, tying the belt of his dressing gown. Behind him, Lord Bredon could hear a woman's muffled sobs.

Hartley's eyes were bright with satiation and opium, and they brightened further when he saw the tall, elegant figure of the earl.

"My dear boy, why did you not have yourself announced to me at at once!" he exclaimed. "It has been such an age since I have seen you."

Reggie's glass fell to the hearth and broke, and he began to snore, but neither of the other two men took their eyes from each other's faces.

The earl's expression was unreadable. "But you were busy, my dear Hartley. I did not care to interrupt your . . . your pleasure."

Sir Hartley waved a hand, and went to pour himself a glass of wine, stepping over Reggie's sprawled legs as if he were a piece of furniture to be avoided.

"Yes, it was rather pleasant. Not outstanding, mind you, but satisfying enough in its way." He smiled to himself, and then he added, "I would offer her to you, Hawk, but I fear she is in no—mm, shall we say condition?—to receive you, and won't be for some time."

The woman's sobs seemed to be growing in intensity, and

he called to his man, "Hanks! Remove the drab at once! Give
her the usual and take her down the back way."

Lord Bredon heard the butler's assent, and then Sir Hartley
shut the bedroom door.

"Do sit down, Hawk," he invited. "I cannot tell you how
delightful it is to have someone sober to talk to after all these
months. You must tell me everything you have been doing,
dear boy." He paused for a moment and then added softly,
"Oh yes, everything!"

"I should be glad to, and of course I am anxious to hear all
your news as well," Lord Bredon replied as he took the seat
across from his host. "But tell me first, is Reggie always like
this now?"

Sir Hartley did not turn to inspect their friend. "Not always.
You can generally get a halfway sensible word out of him if
you approach him before three in the afternoon. Of course, he
does not rise till two. It does limit the amount of conversation
that is possible."

Lord Bredon frowned. "Can no one stop him? He will be
dead if he continues to drink this way."

His host shrugged. "Who cares? Not I. But come, what
brings you to London, Hawk?"

"Some unfinished business. I do not make a long stay, for
I have found Bredon uncommonly amusing this autumn,"
Hawk said.

Sir Hartley's cat-green eyes glowed. "Now, that I did not
expect to hear you say. I was sure you would tell me you
found it devoid of much interest, being so . . . so empty."

"Empty?" the earl asked, holding Sir Hartley's gaze with
cold, steady gray eyes. "Whatever can you mean?"

He thought he detected a little unease in Hartley's long,
narrow face, and it gave him the confidence to continue, "I
am so sorry I missed you when you called. To think that I was
in London while you were at Bredon! Perhaps we even
passed each other on the road."

He sighed in regret, and then a little smile curved his lips.
"Of course, I probably would not have seen your carriage. I
was in such a hurry to return home to . . . Bredon."

He smiled into Hartley's eyes and sipped his wine, content

with his ploy, for the man was frowning openly now. Changing the subject, he said, "Will has asked me to relay his regards. He has gone to Ashton Abbey to play lord of the manor for the Christmas season. He has become so moral, you would not know him."

Sir Hartley bestirred himself from his reflections to ask a few questions about their absent friend, but it was clear his heart was not in them. The earl was amazed at the relief he felt. It was obvious that even if he had no idea where Anne Ainsworth was, neither did his opponent.

Having gained the information he sought, he rose a few moments later and begged to be excused, claiming a previous engagement.

Sir Hartley looked at the clock. It was past midnight, and he professed surprise. "At this hour, Hawk? What a shame that I was so . . . mm, enthusiastic this evening, for it can only be your need of a woman that could take you away from your friends."

The thought seemed to reassure him, for he added with a sneer, "But if you need to seek out a wench, then Bredon cannot have been anywhere near as . . . what did you call it?—amusing?—as you claimed."

Lord Bredon smiled. "I am not going to visit any of those houses that we both know so well. I find my recent memories, as well as my anticipation of future delights, more than adequate for my needs."

He bowed a little and strolled to the door. As he opened it to leave, he said, "We shall not meet again for some time. You see, as soon as my business is concluded, I am returning to the country."

"To Bredon?" Sir Hartley asked, leaning forward in his eagerness.

The earl pretended to think. "Did I say I was going to Bredon? I am sure I did not. No, lately Bredon has become much too notorious, especially now when I feel such a burning need for . . . mm, seclusion."

He waved his hand and left, closing the door softly behind him. Sir Hartley swore long and hard. So he had seduced her after all, and convinced her to continue to throw in her lot with him. Perhaps that redheaded servant slut who had taken his money had even laughed at him with Hawk.

Hartley rose to pace the room, his cat-green eyes almost closed in his anger. Well, we shall see, he told himself. The game's not done, not by a long shot. There were five long months to go before the Season began, and in that space of time he was sure to discover where Hawk had hidden the girl away. He could not be with her every moment, no matter how lovely and passionate she was. And when he left her, Sir Hartley would be there to take a hand in the business. His face grew contented as he contemplated what he would do to her so she would never be able to appear and win the bet. Why, this evening's little bit of fun would pale in comparison, he told himself in satisfaction.

He poured himself another glass of wine, and his eyes fell on his drunken, sleeping friend. Much help he is going to be, the drunken sot, he thought, kicking Reggie in the shin. Lord Quarles whimpered and moaned, but he did not wake.

Sir Hartley continued to stare at him, and then he rubbed his lean jaw. Reggie had done nothing to gain the wager, and it was not fair that he have any reward from it. And if he died, his thousand pounds would go to his partner. Sir Hartley sat down, deep in thought. There was every chance the man's excesses would carry him off next week . . . next month . . . maybe even tomorrow. But if they did not, and the time grew near . . . He smiled again, as he told himself he would be more than glad to assist in the matter. Having made this decision, he knew it was even more important than ever to find Annie Ainsworth. He nodded, his face determined, and then he raised his glass in a solitary toast.

"To my success, and to my coming wealth," he murmured, and then he laughed and swallowed his wine.

Lord Bredon went to bed with a lighter heart than he had had for some time. Anne had not gone to Sir Hartley for help, and no matter where she was, in whatever circumstances, she was safer than she ever would have been under his protection. As he waved his valet away, he was surprised to remember how this past evening he had felt such profound disgust at Hartley's sadistic habits, more even than the disgust he had for Lord Quarles, who was steadily drinking himself to death. And yet at one time, he reminded himself, he had found them amusing, sought out their company, and reveled in excesses of his own. He remembered Hartley's insinuation that he was going to a woman, and he was amazed when he realized how long he had been without one. Could it be that the wager was turning him celibate? And then he recalled his reaction to Anne's embrace, and he smiled as he adjusted his pillows. Somehow, every other woman seemed a mere shadow of her beauty, spirit, and vivacity, to the point that he wanted her above all others, and was content to wait until he could have her. *And to think I laughed at Will for falling under her spell,* he mocked himself as he drifted off to sleep.

Early the next day, Lord Bredon called on his man of business and at his bank. He ordered a new coat at Weston's, and purchased several dozen bottles of wine from his vintner, and he stopped at Brooks's and White's and at Tattersall's as well. He saw few of his acquaintance, for most people in society had gone to the country. Perhaps it was because London streets were so thin of company that he noticed that he was being followed. His eyes gleamed with amusement. Surely Hartley did not think him mad enough to install Anne in the house he maintained for his mistresses in town! Then he realized that he could further the myth that Anne's whereabouts were known to him.

Smiling a little to himself, he slowed his long strides to be sure the little man behind him would be able to keep up, and he paused for several moments on the doorstep of one of London's finest modiste's in Bond Street. When he emerged at last, he had several boxes in his possession which he gave to a boy to deliver at his house. He wondered if the shabbily dressed man who was tailing him would dare venture inside to find out what he had purchased, hoping he would. He also hoped that someday soon he would have the opportunity to see Anne wearing the filmy deep blue negligee or the transparent violet chemise.

He stopped once more at Rundell and Bridge, the jewelers. He could see his shadow peering into a corner of the window as he inspected several necklaces, holding them up to the light as if to admire them. Finally he purchased a delicate silver chain hung with a sapphire pendant. He had not intended to carry the game this far, but had found himself thinking how well she would look wearing it, the fine stone that would rest between her breasts, complimenting her dark blue eyes.

When he reached home, he went into his library to inspect the post. Only a few minutes later, his butler ran in in answer to his urgent call. He found m'lord smiling, his gray eyes ablaze with excitement in a way he could never recall seeing before. He waved the letter he was holding in one long white hand.

"Send Barker to me at once!" Lord Bredon commanded. "And order my fastest horse made ready." The butler was already hurrying to the door when the earl called after him, "Do not have the horse brought round. I'll go to the stables myself."

The butler looked surprised at this unusual procedure, but he had been in the earl's service for many years, so he had only nodded and went to do m'lord's bidding.

Behind him, Lord Bredon reread the letter he had received that had elated him so. One of his agents had discovered that Anne Ainsworth and her companions had been in Bath only a week ago. There could be no mistake, the agent wrote, for she had used her own name. They had stayed at a small poor inn, and the host remembered them well, not being accustomed to housing such a lady of quality, especially one so beautiful and with such unusual red-gold hair. He had even described her two companions and the dog.

Lord Bredon issued further orders to his servants, and wrote a letter of instruction to his agent at Bredon, telling him to recall the men who were searching and send them to Bath at once. Then, as he went upstairs to change to riding dress, he realized Anne must be feeling secure indeed, to take such a risk. Or was it that she did not think he would continue to look for her after so many days?

As he stamped into his riding boots while Barker packed a few necessities in his saddlebags, he smiled a little grimly. Miss Anne Ainsworth had a very great deal to learn about the

Earl of Bredon, beginning with how persistent he could be, and how he hated to have his will crossed. He was sure he would be instructing her in these things in a few days. And then, of course, after the wager was won, he would have a more pleasant task before him, showing her the ways of mutual enjoyment that lovemaking could bring. How he was looking forward to it!

He told his valet to bring the rest of his clothes, and his carriage, to York House in Bath. Barker was ordered to leave at dawn the following day. The valet had trouble keeping his expression neutral when he learned he was to slip out of the house the back way, telling none of the rest of the staff his destination. He was not even to give the coachman orders until the man was on the box and they were about to leave on the journey.

The earl himself used the back door a few minutes later, his saddlebags over his arm.

No one saw him ride away to the west road out of London, for the shabby little man who was hiding in the entry of a vacant house across St. James's Street was staring steadily at the earl's glossy black front door with its shining brass knocker.

By the time the Earl of Bredon was entering the outskirts of Bath, Anne and her companions were driving into Plymouth. It had grown warmer as they traveled into the south of England, which was a relief to Miss Goodly especially. Her older bones disliked the cold winter air.

Plymouth was a bustling port, and the fresh, tangy breeze that blew from the harbor and the channel beyond revived them all. Anne had never seen salt water, and her dark blue eyes showed her excitement. How beautiful it is, she thought, so wide and sparkling and full of motion, its dark waves adorned with necklaces of white lace. She realized suddenly that her mother must have watched it this way often. Perhaps she had even lived on this very same street. Maybe that was why she had gone to America, Anne mused. Why, she had spent all her girlhood watching the ships make ready, loading supplies and cargo and passengers. She must have seen so many of them raise anchor and slip away to the west, their sails filling and hulls heeling over as they began the long journey. No doubt her heart had followed a many and many of them until they were nothing but specks on the far horizon. It must have seemed like a wonderful adventure to her. Then she felt a pang. How could her mother have left her little girl to her aunt and uncle's care, even for such an exciting journey?

She was recalled to the present when Mary Agnes pulled the team to a halt before the municipal building. It was only two in the afternoon, and during their lunchtime picnic by the roadside a few miles from Plymouth, they had decided that while Mary Agnes found lodgings, Anne and Miss Goodly would begin the search for her father. Mary Agnes would return for them later. By this time, King was so used to them all, he did not complain when the maid held his ruff as his mistress climbed down from the landau and disappeared into the building with her chaperon.

The young clerk who hurried to help them was lost the moment Anne smiled at him. Although many people came to look for marriage licenses, these ladies were unusual. Not only did they not know the month the wedding had taken place, they had no idea whether it had occurred eighteen, nineteen, or even twenty years ago. The clerk began to drag out the dusty ledgers, hoping the search would take a very long time.

It was almost four o'clock before they discovered the entry they were looking for. In August, in the year 1791, a Miss Elizabeth Carson, spinster, of St. Stephen's Parish, Plymouth, had married Archibald Torrey Ainsworth, of Torrey Parish, St. Just.

Anne shook the clerk's hand in delight as Miss Goodly copied the information down, and then she thought to look for her own birth certificate. This one was much easier to find, for they knew the year and the month. Anne traced the black letters with a pink-tipped finger.

"Anne Rosemary Ainsworth, daughter of Mrs. Elizabeth Ainsworth," the entry read. She had been born on the eleventh day of March, and Anne was glad to know her birthday at last. And then she wondered why her father's name was not written down, for she could see that other entries had both parents named. The only other one on the page that did not was an illegitimate boy born to a spinster mother.

Miss Goodly had thanked the young clerk, and now she came and took Anne's arm. "Come along, my dear," she said. "Mary Agnes will be wondering what has become of us."

As they left the building, the chaperon added, "Time enough to begin looking for your father and his family tomorrow, Anne. I, for one, am weary and I could use a cup of tea."

She was to have this in short order, for Mary Agnes was indeed waiting for them, a welcoming King by her side. He jumped down from the perch of the landau, and even though he wagged his tail as Anne patted him, a gentleman who had been hurrying forward to assist Miss into her carriage drew back at the size of him and his big jaws.

The room Mary Agnes had found in one of the poorer inns was tiny, and the tea she had ordered was skimpy, even though she augmented it with two-day-old buns she had bought from a baker. Neither Anne nor Miss Goodly complained. They were used to poor meals and accommodations by this time. Anne told the maid of their success, while Miss Goodly sat back in her chair, her eyes half-closed. She and Mary Agnes knew to the ha'penny how much money remained to them. In a way, she wished she had not given in to Anne's pleading to stay in Bath for a day, so she might see the abbey and the famous Pump Room. She had agreed only because Mary Agnes had offered to try to find employment in Plymouth if their search did not prosper.

Under the chatter of her charge, Miss Goodly said yet another fervent prayer that they would find Anne's father in short order, and that he would be willing to provide for her. If they did not, there would be nothing for it but to travel back to Tees. From there, it would be only a short step before Anne was returned to Bredon and the earl's domination once again. Miss Goodly did not think the earl would invite her to stay as well this time.

There were many other travelers abroad that day. While Anne sipped her tea and chatted in the tiny room in Plymouth, the Earl of Bredon was ordering a three-course meal to be served in his private parlor at York House, Bath's finest hostelry. And unbeknownst to either of them, Sir Hartley Wilson, a grumbling Lord Quarles beside him, was tooling his phaeton along the road that led to Cawfell. He had learned from his spy of the earl's decampment, but by the time this was discovered, the earl and his carriage had long since disappeared. No one, not even his butler, had any idea where he had gone. Sir Hartley knew he would have been told otherwise, such an intimate of the earl's as he was.

Sir Hartley considered a quick trip to Bredon, but somehow he sensed that Hawk had been telling him the truth, and his quarry was no longer there. No, he would try Cawfell first.

As Reggie took yet another gulp from his flask, mumbling about "keepin' out the cold, y'know," he reminded himself that after all, Cawfell's housekeeper and butler were Annie Ainsworth's aunt and uncle. They just might have some information about the girl that would help him.

# 12

The three women and the big shepherd were on the road again the first thing the following morning. St. Just was a long two days' journey from Plymouth, and Miss Goodly had not thought it worth their while to remain in the busy port town on the off chance that someone might be able to give them further information about the Ainsworths.

Their way took them inland now through lush, gentle countryside, for the village they sought was on the west coast, facing the Atlantic. Mary Agnes insisted they camp out again that night. The weather was mild and there was no threat of rain, and she had kept the tarpaulin so they would not be troubled by the early-morning dew. When asked if she had any objection, Miss Goodly chuckled.

"I have become an old Gypsy woman this past month," she declared. "I shall have to learn how to make clothespins and tell fortunes." Her companions laughed at the picture she would make in such a role, and she smiled at them, tiny and prim and indomitable.

When they drove into St. Just at sunset the following evening, they attracted a lot of attention in the small fishing village. There was no inn where they might stay, but one of the women standing by the strand dickering for fresh fish was glad to offer them the spare room in her cottage for a few coins.

When asked, this Mrs. Blackwood admitted that she knew the Ainsworth family, but she was strangely reticent about them. Miss Goodly was tired, but she was sure she could discover more on the morrow.

By dint of careful, persistent questioning, they learned at

their meager breakfast that the Ainsworths lived a few miles inland on a sizable estate.

"Won't do you no good to go out there, though," their hostess muttered as she cleared the dishes.

"Why ever not?" Anne asked as she rose to help her.

The woman eyed her red-gold curls with some curiosity. "You be an Ainsworth, don't you, miss?" she asked.

Anne admitted that she was, but this time her winning smile did not gain an answering one.

"Thought so," Mrs. Blackwood said. "All the Ainsworths have that hair. Round here, they call it the mark o' the devil. But there's only two o' them about now. The others has all gone abroad or off to seek their fortunes. Peck o' trouble the Ainsworths 'ave 'ad over the years, for all their birth and money."

She shook her head at Anne's look of dismay. "Yes, there's just Mr. Archie left now, and 'is sister, and you've no chance of seeing 'im, no chance at all. 'E don't see nobody, and 'asn't these past ten years."

"How very peculiar," Miss Goodly said as she rose from the table. "Do you mean he is a recluse?"

"Don't know about that," Mrs. Blackwood said as she scoured the porridge pot. "Miss Rosemary, now, she comes into the village for supplies every so often, but no one's seen Mr. Archie for years. See, the story is 'e 'ad a big disappointment years ago, and it turned 'im sour on people."

She shrugged as Mary Agnes declared, "He'll see us! We've traveled a long way, and it's important."

After a brief conference, the three travelers decided to drive out to the Ainsworth home, in spite of their hostess's dire predictions. It was a cloudy morning that threatened rain, but being so close to journey's end, none of them wanted to delay. Telling Mrs. Blackwood they would return later, and dressed again in their best, they followed her directions and took the road that led out of the village, heading inland.

The way grew steadily more uncultivated as the few small farms and cottages they passed fell behind them. The land they drove through was wild and deserted, and in the gray, overcast morning, the mournful cries of the seagulls made it seem even more remote. With her countrywoman's eye, Mary Agnes noted the fields that had not been worked for years and now grew only weeds and nettles, the broken fences and rotting stiles, and she shook her head. The drive they sought was overgrown, and if King had not bounded up it as a rabbit ran across the opening, they would have missed it completely.

Anne jumped down to open a sagging gate. She had not said much since they left St. Just, and now Miss Goodly patted her hand after the landau drove through and she climbed to her seat again after closing the gate behind them.

"Courage, Anne," the older lady told her. "I admit this is not a very prepossessing place, but perhaps Mrs. Blackwood was wrong. In any case, we shall see. But you are not to be imagining all kinds of obstacles. Sufficient unto the day, my dear."

"We must hope there will be no evil indeed, ma'am," Anne said, trying to smile. She had called King into the landau with them, and the chaperon saw how her fingers were entwined in his fur for reassurance.

They made their way up the weed-choked drive, the unpruned branches on either side slapping against the landau. And then before them lay a large stone mansion. The Ainsworths were gentry, anyway, Miss Goodly thought in some relief. All the windows of the mansion were shuttered, as if no one had lived there for years, but then they smelled wood smoke and saw the thin trace coming from a back chimney.

Mary Agnes climbed down and went to the front door to pound on it several times. No one came.

At last she shrugged and returned to the carriage. "It's my belief this door isn't used at all, Miss Anne," she said. "Might be better if we drove around to the back."

Miss Goodly nodded, and the maid guided the team around the house. The kitchen yard showed more signs of life. There were a few hens scratching in the yard, and a small plot showed that someone had cultivated a vegetable garden there. Miss Goodly and Anne climbed down to join the maid at the back door.

For several minutes they took turns banging on it. Mary Agnes even tried to open it, but it was locked. Anne backed away to stare up at the second-story windows, and she saw a faded curtain twitch, as if someone was staring down at them. She could not help the shiver that ran up her spine, and then she pointed to the window, angry now at being spied on.

"I know someone is in there," she called. "Come down at once!"

Miss Goodly looked amazed, and Mary Agnes frowned at her words, but Anne remained where she was, her chin lifted in defiance.

"We are not going away until we speak to you," she called again.

The door opened just a crack then, and she marched back to the worn stone step. She could hear the chain by which the door was fastened to bar their entrance, chinking, and then a thin voice whispered, "Go away, you instrument of the devil, go away! We see no one!"

"Now, see here, my good woman," Miss Goodly declared, taking charge when Anne seemed struck speechless by this epithet, "this is Miss Anne Ainsworth. She has come a long way to meet her father, Archibald Ainsworth. You must—"

The disembodied voice interrupted, "My brother has no daughter. You lie!"

"Now, there you are wrong, Miss Ainsworth," Miss Goodly remarked, her voice calm and reasonable. She sounded as if she were sitting in the lady's parlor discussing the latest news of the royal family rather than locked out and forced to speak to a crack in the door. "We have a copy of his wedding certificate, and Anne's birth notice too. Her mother was Elizabeth Carson of Plymouth, and they were married there eighteen years ago. If you do not open this door and let us in to speak to you, I shall have to go to the authorities to gain admittance."

There was a long pause while whoever hid behind the door digested this threat. "Wait," the voice said at last, and the door was closed again.

Anne leaned against the side of the landau, disappointment on her face. "Do you . . . do you think they will let us in, Miss Goodly?" she whispered, almost as if she would rather not enter the house and have to meet such unwelcoming relations now.

"They had better," her chaperon remarked in a loud, carrying voice. "You are Anne Ainsworth, and their kin. We have proof of that."

It seemed a very long time before the door was inched open again. "My brother will not see you," the voice began, and then hurried on as Miss Goodly opened her mouth to protest. "But you may come into the kitchen and I will speak to you."

"Very well," the chaperon agreed, seemingly unmoved by this less-than-gracious welcome.

They all heard the chain as it was removed, and then the door opened almost grudgingly, to disclose a tall middle-aged woman. She was pale, as if she rarely spent much time outdoors, and her red-gold hair worn in braids twisted around her head was faded and streaked with gray. She wore an old-fashioned morning dress, and somewhat incongruously, a fine diamond necklace. As she stepped back to allow them to enter, her eyes never left Anne's face. She was not an attractive woman, for her face had fallen into petulant lines and her mouth had a distinct downward twist.

The kitchen they entered was low-ceilinged and dark. There was only a small fire, and one lit candle set on a big deal table. It cast long shadows on the smoke-stained walls. Anne took a deep breath to steady herself.

"Why ever don't you open the shutters?" Miss Goodly asked, peering around. "It's as dark as a cave in here."

"We . . . we never open them," the middle-aged lady replied, her voice husky, as if she seldom used it. Still, she did not take her eyes from Anne. "Now, what do you want?" she added.

"We want your brother to acknowledge his daughter," Miss Goodly announced, ignoring the woman's cry of denial. "We have proof that he is Anne's father, a fragment of a letter he wrote to her mother. Now Mrs. Ainsworth has gone to America, Anne is all alone in the world."

The other woman looked at them shrewdly, the older gentlewoman an obvious chaperon, the lady's maid, and the young girl dressed in fashionable clothes. "How came she to be so well dressed then, and acting the lady?" her newfound aunt demanded. "Her mother was nothing but a whore, from a family boasting no education or wealth." She sniffed her scorn, and Anne tried to keep from cringing.

"She has been raised by the Vicar of Tees and his wife in Yorkshire," Miss Goodly explained.

"But why?" Miss Ainsworth persisted. "Who paid for it?"

"The Earl of Bredon saw to her upbringing. Indeed, he is the reason we are here. We were staying at his estate in Leicestershire when Anne discovered that he had elevated her above a servant's status only to win a wager. The earl is not a good man. I feared for Anne, left in his hands, and so we came away."

"I never heard such a fairy tale," Miss Ainsworth grumbled.

"May we sit down, ma'am?" Miss Goodly asked. "I am not as young as I once was."

Their hostess indicated two benches on either side of the deal table. As Miss Goodly sank down gratefully, she asked, "But why won't her father see her? I should think he would want to make his daughter's acquaintance after all these years."

"He never sees anyone but me, and hasn't for years," Miss Ainsworth admitted in a hoarse whisper. Her eyes darted to a steep set of stairs set against the far wall, and Anne followed her gaze, lifting her head to peer into the shadows. Was her father there? Was he watching her? Listening?

"I should like to meet him, Aunt Ainsworth," she said, raising her voice a little. Her elegant accents proclaimed the lady.

Now her aunt looked at her even more intently, "You have his eyes," she admitted. "And then there is the hair. All the Ainsworths have that same reddish-blond hair. Can it be possible that the slut did not deceive him after all?"

She seemed to have forgotten the others, and Miss Goodly clasped her hands together on the table and said, "Come now, Miss Ainsworth. I think you had better tell us what happened so many years ago that made your brother leave his wife and child alone and helpless in the world.''

Her tone of voice pronounced her scorn for such behavior, but their hostess did not notice. She had settled down on one of the benches and seemed to be putting her thoughts in order.

''Archie met the woman in Plymouth when he was only eighteen. She was several years older, although he did not realize it then. She seduced him, and when she told him she was carrying his child, he married her. He was only a boy, an idealistic dreamer, full of chivalry. He did not know what he did.''

She stared at Anne again, her eyes full of dislike, and then she continued, ''He brought her here, and my father, Sir Reginald Ainsworth, took her measure at once, but it was too late. Of course Archie discovered in short order what kind of woman she was, as well. It was only a month later before he found her with one of the grooms. When he became distraught, she laughed at him and mocked him, telling him of all the men she had known, both before and after meeting him. My father overheard her and had a stroke. He died before morning. Archie loved his father; he never forgave her for that. And so he settled some money on her and had her driven to Plymouth. We were all sure the child could not be his, such a loose woman as Elizabeth Carson was.

''And then my brother began to feel that everyone was laughing at him behind his back for being taken in by a whore,'' she said, leaning forward to whisper, as if she did not want their unseen listener to hear her. ''He did not go to London or even to Plymouth anymore, and he dismissed all the servants. First the stableboys and tenant farmers, then the indoor servants.'' She sighed and looked down at her work-roughened hands. ''Soon there were only the two of us left. We had to close down most of the house, for I could not care for it alone.''

She looked at Anne again, her blue eyes cold. ''It was all your mother's fault, girl, that his life was ruined.''

''I am very sorry, ma'am,'' Anne said, trying to swallow the lump in her throat.

Her aunt gave a low, bitter travesty of a laugh. "Sorry, are you? Well, now you know why he will not see you, ever. You might as well get out. There is nothing here for the likes of you."

"But you are wrong, Miss Ainsworth," Miss Goodly interrupted. "Anne is her father's responsibility. You have admitted she is most certainly his daughter, and she is homeless and penniless. He must help her."

"Must?" Miss Ainsworth asked, her voice scornful. One hand came up to touch her diamond necklace, as if it gave her courage.

"Oh, yes, I believe so," Miss Goodly continued. "If he does not do it willingly, he must be brought to a sense of his obligations by the law. And for me to call in the authorities will have everyone talking about him, and you too, the very thing he dreads most of all."

The two women stared at each other, but it was Miss Ainsworth who looked away first. "She cannot stay here," she whined.

"She does not want to stay here, but she must have some haven, some place of shelter, and enough money to survive," the chaperon persisted.

"I don't know . . . You must leave! I must talk to my brother about this matter, but . . . go away now!" Miss Ainsworth cried, upset and petulant.

Miss Goodly rose and beckoned to Anne. "We shall return tomorrow. That should give you more than enough time to come to some arrangement for Anne's future. Good day."

Miss Ainsworth did not reply, for she sat frozen, staring openly at the stairwell now, but when the three travelers were in the yard once more, they heard the door slammed shut behind them. The chain was fastened in a hurry, as if the lady was afraid they would think better of leaving and try to force their way inside again.

Miss Goodly sighed as a subdued Anne helped her to her seat in the landau. "This is not quite the reception I would have wished for you, my dear, but you will see," she said, making her voice cheerful. "I am sure the Ainsworths, shunning notice and publicity as they do, will come to see they must provide for you.''

"Lord, yes," Mary Agnes said stoutly, clucking to the team. " 'Tis their duty, miss.''

Anne held King close to her, her eyes troubled. "But I cannot like it, Miss Goodly. They do not want to help me, or even see me. And if what they said about my mother is right, I cannot blame them.''

"Do me the favor of forgetting your mother, Anne. She has been gone for a very long time, and her behavior, no matter how unfortunate, has nothing to do with you,'' Miss Goodly said, her voice tart. "You, my dear, are a lady. You father is gentry, and so, therefore, are you.''

She continued to expound this theory and make plans for the future, but when they reached Mrs. Blackwood's cottage in St. Just again, Anne changed her clothes to take King for a walk along the shore. Mary Agnes did not want her to go out unattended, but Miss Goodly shook her head when she began to protest. She knew Anne had to be alone for a while, and there was little harm that could come to her in this tiny village, protected as she was by her dog.

Anne walked along the sands, but today she did not see the waves or the shore birds, or revel in the briny fresh air. King ranged up and down the beach, chasing a sandpiper here or barking at a gull there, but he always came back to her side to put his black muzzle in her hand as if to ask her what was wrong.

Anne patted him absently. The things she had heard about her mother had disturbed her very much. True, she had always known her mother was from the working class, and she had suspected she had not been any better than she should be, but to hear such hatred of her, such damning evidence of her lack of morality, was extremely depressing. I may be Anne Ainsworth and the granddaughter of a baronet, she told herself, but part of me is still Elizabeth Carson.

She bent to pick up a shell, turning it over in her hands without really seeing it. No, not even Elizabeth. *Lizzie*, who went with any man who had the price to pay for her favors. *Lizzie*, who pretended to be a good girl wronged to force my father to marry her. *Lizzie* who laughed and taunted him with all her lovers, and caused my grandfather's death. Lizzie Carson Ainsworth, who abandoned a ten-year-old child to run away to a new life in America.

How many of her traits have I inherited, she wondered, along with my father's hair and blue eyes? Maybe I am more like her than I know.

She paused then to stare out at the ocean, remembering the earl. She could still see him in her mind's eye as plainly as if he stood before her now. That silver-blond hair, the lean handsome planes of his face, the icy gray eyes, and the deep smooth voice that teased and seduced and wound around her senses like a golden net of silk. She could still feel the strength of his hands as he pulled her into his arms to kiss and caress her. She remembered the warmth of his breath, even how his cheek had felt against hers, rougher than her own with the tiny bristles of his beard making her skin tingle. And she remembered how a part of her had never wanted him to stop kissing her, to take away those demanding lips that moved and insisted until she was powerless to resist and opened her own lips to them. She remembered how her arms had gone up around his neck, so she might press even closer to him.

She put a fist to her mouth to keep from crying out, and closed her eyes as if that would blot out her memories. But that was even worse, for in the dark, her body remembered exactly how he had felt when she had been molded against his tall frame.

Admit it, Anne, she ordered herself bitterly. You have missed him every single day since you left him at Bredon. Missed him, and wanted to be back with him. You want him still, even knowing what kind of man he is, arrogant, selfish, evil. It cannot be that you love him, one of Satan's Rakes, so it must be just desire.

Her Aunt Ainsworth had called her mother a whore, and that was what Sir Hartley had called her, too. Was that what she was, in all truth? Perhaps even the Nettleses' love and care and goodness could not change that facet of her personality, for it was so deeply ingrained in her genes that she was powerless to act any differently.

Anne's soft lips tightened in despair. She felt like a freak, half-lady, half-ladybird. To pretend to the ranks of the gentry would be a sham, feeling as she did about the earl, yet she did not seem a servant anymore.

She called to King and turned back the way she had come, no wiser now that she had been when she left the cottage. Had anyone ever been so confused and bedeviled? she wondered. Who *was* the real Anne Ainsworth? And more important, what manner of girl was she?

# 13

When Anne and her companions arrived back at the Ainsworth mansion the next morning, it seemed as if nothing had changed from the previous day. The kitchen they were admitted to so grudgingly was as dark and cheerless as before, Rosemary Ainsworth glowered at her with the same hatred in her faded blue eyes, and there was not a sign of her father.

Miss Ainsworth inspected the birth certificate carefully, and the fragment of the letter they had found at Cawfell, and her face grew even bleaker.

"Very well, you are my niece," she said, touching her diamond necklace again in the nervous way she had. "But do not expect to be received by us with open arms. Far from it! You are still *her* daughter!"

She laughed in scorn then, and Anne tried not to show her despair.

Miss Goodly took a hand. "What you say is true, of course. We do not dispute the fact. However, I think you very wrong not to realize that Anne is nothing like her mother. She is a good girl, carefully reared to be honorable, kind, and decent. In short, she is a lady, and a lady in the finest sense of the word. If you knew her character and goodness, you would not treat her this way."

Anne felt tears coming to her eyes, and silently she begged her tiny champion to stop. Poor Miss Goodly had no idea what kind of girl she really was.

Her aunt sniffed. "So you say. My brother does not care to find out, however, and neither do I, for bad blood will always tell. But we agree she must have some means of support, left alone as she is in the world. To that end we offer her a stipend of two hundred pounds a year and the use of the dower house, which is located outside St. Just. It is furnished and should be ample for her needs.''

Mary Agnes stirred, for she had been busy since they left the day before, and she had learned from the villagers how wealthy the Ainsworths were. Two hundred pounds was nothing to them. Before she could protest the sum, Miss Ainsworth continued, "There are conditions, of course. She must never come here again, not even step onto the grounds, or the pension will cease. There is to be no communication with my brother and me, either spoken or written, after today."

She went to a shelf and took down a leather purse. "Here is next year's stipened. From now on, our solicitor in London will handle payment. I have written down his name and direction."

Miss Goodly looked at Anne. She had been expecting a more generous settlement, but the despairing, wounded look in Anne's eyes made her nod and take the purse and card. "Very well," she said. "Although it is hardly munificent, we accept."

"I must have my . . . my *niece's* word that she will abide by our conditions," Miss Ainsworth insisted, almost spitting the word.

"You have my promise," Anne whispered, and then she put up her chin and turned to face the dark stairway. "I am sorry my birth brought trouble for you, Father," she said, her voice louder now, and steady. "I would not do anything to disturb you further. Thank you for your assistance."

She turned back, and Mary Agnes could see her squaring her shoulders and she applauded the girl's courage. Miss Anne was growing up in a hurry, she thought as she gathered their things and moved to the door. It was too bad she had such miserable relations on both sides, but no one could help the kin they had been born to.

She climbed to the perch of the landau and Anne assisted Miss Goodly to her seat. Then she turned and removed her bonnet. The mild winter sunshine lit her red-gold curls until they seemed a fiery halo around her head as she stared up at the windows on the second floor. Her dark blue eyes searched intently, but the curtains did not move. At last she sighed and raised her hand in farewell.

Quickly Miss Goodly wiped away the tears she would rather Anne did not see.

As Mary Agnes clucked to the team, she shook her head and muttered, "They are fools not to see how Miss Anne could bring the sunshine back into their lives!"

Miss Goodly held Anne's hands tightly in hers. "Never mind, my dear," she said. "Remember it will all come right in the end."

"At least we have a place to live," the maid threw over her shoulder as the team trotted down the weedy drive. "Let's hope this dower house is not full of damp or leaks."

Thinking to cheer up her charge, Miss Goodly suggested they stop on the way back to St. Just to inspect it. As they drove in that direction, she began to make plans, and Anne threw off her sorrowful abstraction to join in the important discussion of hiring servants and purchasing supplies.

The dower house was not much bigger than a large cottage, but it was made of rosy brick and set in a garden surrounded by a low brick wall. The view of St. Just and the ocean in the distance was superb. Inside, the furnishings were old-fashioned but in good condition, and someone through the years had seen that the rooms were dusted and aired and that the windows were tight and the roof did not leak.

Over the ache in her heart, Anne found herself caught up in the others' enthusiasm.

"I'll be off to St. Ives for supplies this very afternoon, Miss Anne," Mary Agnes declared. "We can buy food here, but we need linens and blankets as well."

"And I shall ask Mrs. Blackwood to recommend a girl to help with the scrubbing. I think we should hire a cook, too," Miss Goodly said. "Mary Agnes has enough to do."

Anne shook her head. "Not maiding me, she won't. I doubt if any of the gentry hereabouts will take me to their hearts, and even if they did, it would not be wise to call attention to ourselves. No, it is just as well the cottage is somewhat isolated."

"We will need books, then, and some needlework," Miss Goodly agreed, adding to her growing list.

"First things first, ma'am," Mary Agnes told her, fastening her bonnet strings more securely. "I'll drive you back to the village now, and you can speak to Mrs. Blackwood while I'm gone."

"We shall pack our belongings as well, and have them brought here," Miss Goodly promised her. She went to the door with the maid then. Anne ran ahead to find King, and now as she watched her playing with him, Miss Goodly said softly, "Poor, poor child! I hope she will have peace here."

Mary Agnes looked at her shrewdly. "Don't know about that, ma'am. Miss Anne's not the type to want peace, if you ask me. More likely she'll be bored to tears after all the excitement we've had, and go out and find herself some more."

Miss Goodly twinkled up at the dour Yorkshirewoman. "Then we must keep her very, very busy," she decreed.

This turned out to be easier than anyone had imagined. After the first excitement of moving into the dower house and setting it in order, there were still walks and drives to take, and church to attend. Miss Goodly hired a large hearty woman to cook for them, and her young daughter to help with the scrubbing and the laundry. An old man who appeared one morning asking for a job was soon established in the stables and busy making plans to rejuvenate the gardens at the first sign of spring.

Anne tried not to think about spring, and the Season she had been raised as carefully as any hothouse flower to adorn. It was winter now, although the air so far south was mild and pleasant. Miss Goodly declared she had never been so comfortable and wondered she had stayed in Yorkshire so long.

Anne began to go out with King on long rambles such as she had taken with the vicar in Tees. The exercise helped her to sleep at night and quieted her dreams. Miss Goodly was content to remain by the fireside, and Mary Agnes was in her element supervising the other servants, but they did not worry about her. Everyone in St. Just knew Miss Anne now, and looked forward to her warm smile and kind words.

One of Anne's favorite walks was along the shore road away from the village. She liked the wind and the views of distant ships, and she would pause now and then to rest and stare out to sea.

One afternoon in January, three weeks after they moved into the dower house, she took the familiar path. King knew her habits, and when she settled down on a broad rock to watch the fishing boats pulling in their nets in the distance, he ran on ahead.

Lost in her memories of Bredon and the earl, Anne did not notice the phaeton coming toward her from the direction of St. Ives. Nor did she see it pull to a halt a little way behind her, the driver throwing the reins to his passenger before he climbed down and approached her.

She was recalled abruptly to her surroundings when a light tenor voice drawled, "Why, it is Annie Ainsworth herself! I knew I could not be mistaken."

Anne's hand went to her throat as she rose. The redheaded Sir Hartley Wilson smiled at her, his narrowed cat-green eyes cold and menacing. Anne looked around. Directly behind her was a steep, rocky embankment. King was just a speck far down the beach, and Sir Hartley was blocking any chance of escape to the road.

"I did tell you I would find you if you tried to trick me, did I not, Annie?" he asked, moving closer. His hand went to the pocket of his greatcoat, and he pulled out a pistol. Anne's eyes widened.

"You should not have done that, my girl. I do not like to think of how you and Hawk have been laughing at me. It makes me feel even more vindictive."

He was pointing the pistol at the ground, but Anne was not deceived. She could see the hatred and desire to do murder in his eyes, and she hurried into speech.

"You are wrong, sir!" she exclaimed. "I did not laugh at you with the earl! I left Bredon with my chaperon and maid, and have not seen him since that time."

Sir Hartley sneered. "So you say, but women will say anything to save themselves from pain. I know."

Anne shook her head, wondering if she dared to call her

dog. Then she realized the man would shoot her long before King could race to her aid, and she swallowed.

"If what you say is true, then why did Hawk come and make such a point of telling me how delightful a mistress you were, and how he had taken you away from Bredon to hide you from me?" Sir Hartley continued. "And why, my dear, *dear* Annie Ainsworth, did he slip away from London so surreptitiously? He is somewhere nearby, I am sure. Were you waiting for him to come to you even now?"

Anne shook her head again. "This is all a terrible misconception, Sir Hartley," she told him. "I swear I have not seen the earl since I left Bredon. I did what you told me to do. I went away to hide. He has no idea where I am."

"Then why didn't you write to me and tell me where you were, as I ordered, wench?" he demanded. "Why didn't you ask me to send you more money?"

"There was no need. I found my father here. He is the son of the late Sir Reginald Ainsworth. Under his . . . his protection, there was no need for yours," Anne said. She tried to keep her expression calm. She could see King running back to her now out of the corner of her eye. His powerful legs were covering the ground in great leaps, as if he were concerned by the man who stood so close to her.

Sir Hartley did not appear to be convinced by her words, and he shrugged, "Gentry, is he? It really does not matter. You are involved in a wager, and I have decided there is a much better way to make sure Hawk can never win it. Oh, yes, a much better way."

He smiled and reached out to pinch her cheek. "At least it will be better for me," he murmured. "And I see no reason why I shouldn't enjoy you too, as well as Hawk. Even if what you are telling me is the truth, it will only make it that much more exciting. Innocence is so hard to find these days."

Anne gasped in horror, and recoiled, and then King began to bark. He had reached the rocks below them, and he was climbing as fast as he could. Sir Hartley spun around at the sound, and his face paled. The big shepherd was snarling as he scrambled from rock to rock, drawing ever closer. With his fangs bared, he had never looked more vicious and dangerous. Sir Hartley raised his pistol.

"No, don't!" Anne cried, closing with him and trying to deflect his aim. He pushed her hard with his free hand, and losing her balance, she stumbled and fell. As the pistol was discharged, she hit her head on a rock, and mercifully knew no more.

When she regained consciousness, she found herself wedged into a phaeton between Sir Hartley and a fat, florid man. Her hands and feet were bound and covered by a light driving rug. There was no way she could move. Her head was throbbing in a way that made her feel sick to her stomach, and then in a rush, she remembered her dog.

"King!" she cried, hot tears rolling down her face. "You shot King!"

Sir Hartley chuckled. "Yes, I did. He left me no choice, for I could see he had every intention of tearing me to bits. Besides, Reggie is so fleshy, there was no room for him in the carriage. Oh, I do beg your pardon, Annie," he added sarcastically. "This is Lord Quarles, the one member of Satan's Rakes I do not believe you have met."

Anne turned her throbbing head carefully to stare at the dissolute face. She saw he was one of the men in her dream of Cawfell who had laughed at her. Now, his fat cheeks shaking with the speed of their passage, he reached into his pocket to get a flask and open it.

Wiping the lip on the soiled sleeve of his greatcoat, he offered it to her. "Care for a nip, m'dear?" he asked, his words slurred. "Nashty bump you have there."

Anne turned away in disgust. Lord Quarles was drunk, and he smelled, but she put him out of her mind. She felt as if her heart was broken. King was dead. Never again would he walk beside her or wag his tail and run to her when she called. Never again would he roll over on his back and squirm in delicious wriggles when she scratched his stomach, or put his big head in her lap as she sat dreaming before the fire. The tears she could not help ran unchecked down her cheeks, and a sob escaped her lips.

"Come, come, my dear. He was only a dog," Sir Hartley

said. Anne stiffened as he added, ''You will discover I am not a man who is at all moved by tears.''

To keep from thinking about King, Anne began to wonder where Sir Hartley was taking her, and how soon it would be before she was missed at the dower house. And then she realized in despair that it would not matter. Miss Goodly and Mary Agnes would have no way of knowing where she had gone, or with whom. And even if they did, how could they help her, two women alone? No, she must see to her freedom herself.

''Where are you taking me?'' she asked in as even a voice as she could manage.

''To a house I own west of London,'' Sir Hartley told her. His green eyes raked her face for a moment before he added, '' 'Tis nothing like Bredon, to be sure, but it serves the purpose.''

''How . . . how far away is it?'' Anne asked next, trying to make plans.

''Several days. But you must curb your impatience, my dear wench. I plan to travel with all speed. We shall stop only when it is absolutely necessary.''

He glanced at her again, and then he smiled, that smile that never reached his eyes. ''You are thinking you will be able to escape me somewhere along the road, are you not? Do not build up any such hopes, Annie. I intend to drug you at the first opportunity. Then Reggie and I will claim we are taking you to a doctor, for you are very ill. No one will think a thing of it, and you will be in no condition to run, or even speak.''

He laughed then, contented with his plan, and Anne felt a murderous rage. Beside her, Lord Quarles pulled on his flask and ignored them.

They stopped at last at a run-down hedge tavern some miles from Truro. Dusk had fallen, and as soon as Lord Quarles climbed down and staggered forward to hold the horses' heads, Sir Hartley dropped the reins and turned toward her. Without a word, he struck a sharp blow on the side of her jaw, and she crumbled.

She regained consciousness to feel someone holding a cup to her lips. ''Drink this, Anne. It will make you feel better,'' a soft voice whispered, and she obeyed. She was thirsty and she swallowed eagerly. Too late she remembered Sir Hartley's threat to drug her, just as darkness overcame her again.

The days that followed would forever remain a blur in her mind. They seemed to be made up of endless hours in the phaeton, what seemed like a few minutes in uncomfortable beds, and always the laudanum-laced drinks that she was given. When she tried to protest, Sir Hartley forced the liquid down her throat. She was never left alone unless she was unconscious. Sir Hartley even remained in the room when she had to retire behind a screen to see to her needs. She felt dirty, for she had no change of clothes, and dizzy and despairing and completely helpless.

In her few lucid moments she found herself praying that this nightmare of a journey would be over soon, no matter what came to her at the end of it.

The weather grew progressively colder as they traveled to the north and west. Sir Hartley was forced to give her his own greatcoat when he saw she could not control her shivers.

"Can't have you dying on me, Annie," he remarked as he buttoned the coat.

Anne stared at him through drugged eyes, her face vacant even when his hand closed over her breast.

"I can wait," he told her. "When I take you, I want you to know it, slut. Besides," he added as he picked up the reins, "you are dirty."

"When we goin' get to Greenwood?" Lord Quarles asked, his voice querulous. "Been travelin' f'rever."

"Has your flask run dry, old friend?" Hartley asked. When Lord Quarles began to protest, he laughed. He had been in a high good humor ever since he had found Anne. "Never fear," he added now. "We should arrive this afternoon, and then you may have all the bottles you like."

Lord Quarles brightened. "Hafta keep out the cold, y'know," he confided. "Never seen such weather. Brr."

Sir Hartley spared a glance at the sullen gray clouds that raced overhead. "If I don't miss my guess, we'll have snow before morning. But we won't care, will we, Reggie? We'll be snug at Greenwood, you with your bottles to keep you company, and I . . . I with Annie Ainsworth.''

Fortunately, Anne had dozed off again, and she did not hear his remark, nor the exultant laugh he gave.

# 14

Two days after Anne disappeared without a trace, a distraught Miss Goodly and a frowning Mary Agnes sat in the parlor of the dower house, discussing the incident once again. The groom had found King's body and buried him in the garden, but Anne had not been seen since.

Miss Goodly sighed and wiped her eyes. "It had to be the Earl of Bredon who took her away, Mary Agnes," she said. The maid did not disagree as Miss Goodly continued, "But how could even he be so cruel and wicked as to shoot her dog, the one thing she loved above all else in the world?"

From the doorway a deep smooth voice remarked, "Unfair, ma'am. The only animals I have ever shot in cold blood were those who had to be put out of their misery."

Miss Goodly gave a little shriek, and the maid spun around to glare at where the Earl of Bredon stood lounging against the doorjamb. He was so tall, he made the parlor seem very small and low-ceilinged.

"Where is she?" Miss Goodly demanded. "Where have you taken her, you devil?"

The earl looked astonished to hear this form of address from the prim chaperon. "You are speaking of Anne, ma'am? I have not taken her anywhere. I have only just arrived with the purpose of doing so."

He straightened up then, and moved into the room, tossing his gloves and hat on the table. His handsome face was stern now as he said, "Do you mean to tell me she is not here? I'll have a straight answer, Miss Goodly, and at once."

Miss Goodly sniffed. "You know she is not here. You took her away two days ago."

The earl stared at the indignant chaperon and glowering maid. The worry and concern on their faces told him what had happened. He swore silently. Sir Hartley had found her first after all.

When the earl had reached Bath, he had been sure he would find Anne in a matter of days. His agents had begun to search the neighborhood, and had been quick to discover that Anne Ainsworth had gone to Plymouth. There the trail ended. Will Ashton, summoned to the port by Lord Bredon, had been perplexed.

"But what is she doing here, Hawk?" he had asked. "Why would she travel such a distance, and where is she now?"

The earl had not even attempted to reassure him. "If I knew that, Will, she would be with us this moment. Once again, we must wait for news."

But this Will Ashton had been unable to do. He had set out himself, ranging up and down the countryside around Plymouth, searching for her.

The earl had forced himself to remain where he could be sure to hear whatever news was brought at once. He could see the ships in the busy harbor from the window of his room, and he was afraid. Afraid that somehow Anne had managed to leave England. The sense of loss he had felt as he had faced this possibility amazed him.

But fortune had finally smiled on him. One of his men, traveling from Bredon to join him, had stopped to spend the night at Cawfell. There, being entertained by the Jenkinses, he had learned of their visitors. Mrs. Jenkins, still bitter at a fate that had decreed she must spend a life of drudgery while her worthless niece paraded as a lady, had been only too anxious to tell him all the details.

"Yus," she had said with a toss of her head, "marched in 'ere, proud as a peacock, she did, demanding this and that. And tellin' us wot the earl would do to us if we didn't 'elp 'er."

"What help did she want?" the agent had asked, hiding his elation.

"Wanted to find out 'oo 'er pa wuz, she did," Jenkins had

chimed in. "And when she found out 'e wuz from St. Just, she and them others wuz off like a shot."

The agent rose, anxious to be on his way to the earl with this good news. As Jenkins walked with him to the door, the butler said, "You'll tell milord 'ow we 'elped 'er, right? An' not only Annie. There wuz that Sir Hartley and Lord Quarles 'ere as well."

The agent, who knew all of Satan's Rakes, had paused in the act of mounting his horse. "Sir Hartley Wilson?" he had asked. "Tell me what happened. Quick, man! The earl will want to know everything!"

In a servile voice, Jenkins revealed that he had told the two rakes where Annie had been going. The agent had cut short his whining that he had given the earl's friends every assistance, by mounting and galloping away.

When Lord Bredon heard the news of Anne's trip to Cawfell, he had smiled at last, but the intelligence that Sir Hartley was already on her trail had him frowning again. He had ordered his horse saddled, and set out at once for St. Just. Once there, it had been a simple matter of a question or two, to discover where the girl he had sought for such a long time had taken refuge.

Now he folded his arms across his chest and said, "I assure you I had no hand in Anne's disappearance; Miss Goodly, nor did I shoot her dog." His mouth was set in a hard line, and his gray eyes were like chips of ice as he added slowly, "But I think I know who did take her away, and where."

Mary Agnes could control herself no longer. "Who, sir? Where is she?" she cried.

"We must go to her at once," Miss Goodly said, and even in his anger, Lord Bredon had to hide a smile at the sight of her. There she stood, not quite five feet tall, middle-aged and gray, with her eyes flashing behind her spectacles, and her little hands clenched in purposeful fists.

"You must leave this to me. Speed is important, and I can move faster alone," the earl said as he picked up his hat and gloves. "You return to Bredon and await Anne there."

"Go to Bredon? Never!" Miss Goodly exclaimed. Her tone implied she would rather go directly to hell.

The earl raised his brows. "Yes, to Bredon, Miss Goodly. I shall be taking Anne there when I find her, and besides your consequence, she might need a woman's assistance." He paused and frowned, and then he added, "St. Just is no longer safe. Bredon is."

He walked to the door, moving quickly, and then he turned and bowed. "In this instance, dear ma'am, you must agree that even *I* am a safer companion than Sir Hartley Wilson."

Remembering the things Anne had told her about the other rake made Miss Goodly gasp and quickly agree to his plan.

Anne woke up in a dark room. She was lying fully clothed on a big bed, and for a moment, in her drugged state, she panicked. Then all the memories of the past few days came flooding back. She raised her head cautiously and peered into the blackness. Outside of a small, dying fire on the hearth, there was no light. Suddenly she heard voices, and her eyes searched the darkness for some clue to their whereabouts. It took only a moment for her to spot the little strip of light coming under a door. She rose slowly, testing her muscles and reflexes, before she went as quickly as she could to put her ear against the wood.

"More burgundy, Reggie?" she heard Sir Hartley ask.

There was silence for a moment, and then the teary, tremulous voice of Lord Quarles saying, "You're m'best friend, Hartley, know that? Good fellow you are. 'preciate it. Man's friends 'portant, right?"

Anne heard a chair being scraped back, and in a moment the sound of logs being thrown on the fire.

"Indeed they are, Reggie," that hateful light tenor agreed. After a moment he added, "What a bitter night! I'm glad we reached Greenwood when we did. My man tells me it's colder than he can ever remember."

"Tha' so?" Reggie asked. And then he exclaimed, "Whoops! Spilled m'wine."

Anne heard him begin to cry, mourning his clumsiness, and it was several minutes before conversation was resumed.

"Wha' you goin' do with the gel, Hartley?" Lord Quarles asked next.

His host laughed. "What do you think I'm going to do with her, Reggie?"

"Er . . . tonight?" the other asked.

Anne found herself inhaling sharply as she waited for the answer. "No, not tonight. She's still feeling the drug and I'm tired. Besides, she needs a bath. But I have been most remiss! We must have some of my special brandy, to celebrate, my friend."

"Cel . . . brate?" Lord Quarles asked, perplexed.

"But of course," came that soft purr. Anne had to press her ear against the wood to hear. "We have won the wager, my boy. A thousand pounds apiece if Hawk couldn't turn a servant wench into a lady. You remember the terms."

"But she *ish* a lady," Reggie argued.

"She gives the appearance of one, that is true. But in a few days, surely no more than a week, the only thing that will be left of her will be a whimpering, pleading servant slut. You'll see."

Anne shivered. Sir Hartley had sounded so triumphant, so sure of his power to break her, but it was not that that made her recoil in horror. It was the pleasure and anticipation in his voice as he looked forward to whatever he had planned to do to her.

She was backing away from the door when she heard him say in a persuasive voice, "Care to join me, Reggie? I cannot drink anymore until I go outside."

"Thass good idea," Lord Quarles agreed, scraping back his chair.

Anne heard them move unevenly to the door, Lord Quarles giggling at his inability to walk a straight line. In a moment they were gone. Anne wondered if she had any chance of escape now, but her head was still spinning, and she did not seem to be able to think coherently. And when she tried the door, she discovered it was locked. She put her hands to her head and moaned, slumping against it in despair.

She heard a door close in the other room, and then, very clearly, one set of footsteps. As the decanter clinked against a glass, she heard Sir Hartley say, "And now I shall drink the toast I have been saving for such a very long time. To Lord Quarles, the drunken sot! You'll freeze out there in no time, even with all the liquor in you, and then I'll win your share of the wager as well as my own."

There was silence for a moment, and then he added as if continuing an earlier conversation, "I quite agree with you, Reggie, for you turned out to be my best friend, too. I drink to that friendship—and to the wealth it will bring!"

His laugh and the enormity of what she had just heard sent Anne creeping silently across the room to climb into bed again. She pulled the covers up over her dirty gown and hid her face in the pillow. By leaving his friend outside to freeze, Sir Hartley became a murderer.

And then she remembered she was alone with him now, and it was a long time before she slept, in spite of all the laudanum he had given her.

She woke with a start to find him tying her to the bedposts. There was a pale gray light in the room now, and she could see his face clearly. She began to struggle, but he slapped her so hard that she made herself lie still.

"That's better, wench," he said easily. As he put a gag over her mouth, he saw the terror in her eyes, and he laughed. "Not yet, Annie, not yet! I am expecting visitors, and it is most important that they do not learn you are here."

He tested the bonds and gag again, and then he went to the door. Anne could hear him locking it behind him.

She lay there unable to move for what seemed a very long time. The sky lightened slowly, and as it did so, she remembered everything she had heard last evening. And then she heard voices coming into the next room, and she strained to listen.

"Some coffee, Justice Gibson? Doctor?" Sir Hartley asked.

Strange voices agreed, and for a moment there was only the clinking of china.

"Sad business, this," one stranger remarked. "On any other night he might have regained consciousness and been able to save himself, but the frost last night was so deep, he did not have a chance."

"I shall always regret that I did not insist he stop drinking before he broached the fourth bottle," Sir Hartley mourned. The regret in his voice was so genuine, Anne did not see how anyone could doubt his words. "As I told you, I was tired from our journey and went to bed. Reggie assured me he would be along shortly. If only I had made him come up . . ."

"Now, sir, you must not blame yourself," the other, gruff voice said. "You could not know he would go outside, drunk as he was, and fall and hit his head. Besides, from his appearance, he might have died at any time. I have seen cases like his before. It is obvious he was drinking himself into an early grave. The freezing conditions last night only speeded up the process."

"Yes, I suppose so," Sir Hartley said, and then he sighed and added in a choked voice, "But he was my dear friend!"

Anne shivered at his wickedness.

"Your sentiments do you credit, sir, but his untimely demise cannot be laid at your door. I shall sign the certificate 'death by misadventure.' Is that agreeable, Gibson?"

"Certainly. It can't be anything else in a case like this," the justice agreed. "Now, don't you concern yourself, sir. The body will be removed this morning and sent to his home for burial, as you directed. I will handle all the details."

After a few more minutes' conversation, the officials left. Anne had strained against her bonds, but Sir Hartley had tied them too securely, and there was no way she could remove the gag and scream for help unless her hands were free. She felt a wave of despair. Sir Hartley was a murderer, but he was going to go free. And if she revealed what she had overheard last night, he would kill her too.

She was left alone for a long time, a time she spent in deep thought. She was thankful that at least her head was clearer this morning, although after considering several plans, she still had no idea how she could possibly escape this evil man. She could not help but wish that Lord Bredon would suddenly appear, like a prince in a fairy tale, to whisk her away after he ran Sir Hartley through with his rapier. She began to cry then, for fairy tales had nothing to do with real life. Then she realized that crying would make it hard for her to breathe with the gag in her mouth, and she made herself stop.

Sir Hartley came back at last. He removed her bonds and the gag, chatting easily all the while.

"I have ordered you a bath, Annie, and a tray of breakfast as well. You cannot escape this room, and it will do no good to scream. My man and his wife are used to screams. I chose them for their ability to ignore 'em."

He chuckled, and Anne drew away from him to sit up, holding her head. In a moment, he brought her a glass of water. She looked at it with suspicion, and he laughed out loud. "There is no laudanum in it, Annie. It will not suit my purpose to have you drugged now."

The door opened, and a man dragged in a copper bath. He was followed by a slatternly-looking woman carrying brass cans of water. Both of them gave her no more than a cursory glance. Anne eyed the steaming cans with longing. It seemed to take forever before the rest of the water was brought in and the servants bowed and left.

Sir Hartley eyed her soiled gown with distaste, and then he went and opened a wardrobe. "After your bath, you will find clean clothes in here," he said, and then, instead of leaving, he paused to consider her, tapping the key to the room against one palm. "I wonder if I would find it amusing to watch?" he mused, as if she weren't even there.

Anne was aghast, and she stood up, clutching the bedpost for support. When she saw him coming toward her, she had to stifle a gasp of horror.

"How calm you are, Annie," he marveled. "You won't be so for long."

His hands reached out to undo the buttons of her gown, and she tried to twist away from him. At once he grasped the material at the neck of her gown and slapped her hard with the other hand. His half-closed green eyes glittered with anticipation. Anne began to fight him as hard as she could, sobbing as she did so. When he slapped her again, she screamed.

And then she heard hurried footsteps and men's voices, the manservant and also the deep wonderful tones she remembered so well. Her heart leapt and she cried out, "Lord Bredon! In here!"

The door was flung open, and through her tears she saw the tall figure of the earl. Still held tight in Sir Hartley's grasp, she watched him stroll in and place his hat and gloves on the table. He looked about with contempt, and then he said, his deep voice sinister, "But I find I must object, my dear Hartley, to your treatment of Miss Ainsworth. You should have remembered that the lady is . . . er, mine."

Anne heard her captor draw a startled breath as the earl withdrew a pistol from his greatcoat pocket. Suddenly she found herself pushed away, and she fell sprawling on the bed.

As if in some horrible dream, she watched Sir Hartley reach into his own pocket, and she cried out, "Be careful! He has a gun!"

And then a loud retort echoed through the room and she closed her eyes in fear that she might have to see the earl lying dead at her feet.

"What a shame you moved when I fired, Hartley," she heard him say, and she sobbed in her relief. "I was, of course, aiming for your heart," the earl continued, and she opened her eyes to see him standing there, a smoking pistol in his hand.

Wondering, she turned to see Sir Hartley drop his pistol, his other hand coming up to clutch his wounded arm. His eyes were full of pain and hate. Fascinated, Anne watched his shirt sleeve turning red, and then she saw the blood that dripped from his cuff to stain the floor.

Taking a deep breath, she slid off the bed on the other side and ran into the earl's arms, weeping as if she never meant to stop. Lord Bredon held her close, his free hand caressing her tangled red-gold curls.

"Oh, m'lord, he . . . he killed Lord Quarles, and he shot King! And he was going to . . . to . . ."

"Forget what he was going to do," the earl said, his voice unsteady. And then he put her away from him a little so he could look at her.

He saw her dirty face, and the ugly bruises on her jaw, as

well as the dazed look of someone who has been drugged, and his mouth tightened.

"How badly have I wounded him?" he asked the servant over her head as he drew her close to cuddle her again when he felt her trembling.

"The bullet's deep, sir, but not fatal," the man answered in a frightened voice.

"Fetch some bandages," Lord Bredon said easily. "I suppose we cannot let him bleed to death, even if he does deserve it."

The servant bowed and left the room. The earl saw that Sir Hartley had fainted, and he took advantage of this respite to bend his head and ask, "You are all right, Anne?"

She raised swimming dark blue eyes to his. "Yes, m'lord. Now."

His glowering look vanished, and he led her to a chair. "Sit here, my dear. I have some unfinished business, but as soon as it is completed, we will be on our way."

By the time the servant returned to bandage his master's arm, Sir Hartley had regained consciousness. His narrowed cat-colored eyes glared at Anne and his former friend, but he did not say a word.

At last the servant gathered up the stained cloths and the basin of water he had brought, and Lord Bredon said, "Leave us! There is no need to fetch a doctor, and I am sure Sir Hartley would not care to have the authorities summoned to what was, after all, a private matter."

The man nodded and left the room. Lord Bredon strolled up to the bed where Sir Hartley was lying now and said, "Miss Ainsworth and I will be on our way. May I suggest you leave the country as soon as you can? I am afraid that the climate here is going to be as injurious to your health as it was to poor Reggie's."

His soft, smooth words made Anne shiver. Sir Hartley paled.

"Oh, by the way," the relentless voice continued, "the wager is forfeit, sir. Miss Ainsworth is a lady, not only by her upbringing, but by her birth. There is no question that she will be accepted by the *ton*. Besides, now that Reggie has died—mm, in such an *unusual* way, too—and you are going abroad for your health, there is no one to settle it. Will and I don't care to continue the farce.''

Sir Hartley glared up at him, but when he saw the searing look in Hawk's eyes, he closed his own.

Lord Bredon came back to draw Anne to her feet. ''You have a cloak, ma'am?'' he asked, his voice mild again. When she shook her head, he went to the wardrobe and found a heavy cape to wrap around her.

Anne tried not to look to where Sir Hartley was propped up on his good arm watching them.

''Hawk!'' he called suddenly. ''Wait! I can explain, and . . .''

The earl spun around quickly, his arm flung full length as he pointed at the man on the bed. ''Not a word, sir, if you value your life,'' he said, his harsh voice totally unlike his usual smooth, drawling tones.

And then Anne found herself being taken from the room, held tight in his strong arm. He did not speak, nor did she, until he had helped her to her seat in his racing curricle, and wrapped a heavy rug around her knees.

The morning was overcast, and so cold she could see his breath. She stared down at him through a misty haze of tears, and she tried to smile. At that, he pressed her hand.

''Easy, Anne,'' he said. ''Time enough to tell me all about it when you are safe at Bredon.''

As he came around to take his seat and nod to Sir Hartley's groom to let 'em go, Anne murmured to herself, ''It seems I was wrong. Fairy tales can come true after all.''

# 15

To Anne's surprise, the earl took her first to London. It was less than a day's journey from Sir Hartley's house near Wallingford, and he could see Anne was in no condition to travel the long miles to Leicestershire. Especially not in freezing weather in an open racing curricle that had not been built with comfort in mind.

They arrived at his house in St. James's Street late that afternoon. Anne had slept most of the way, her head resting on Lord Bredon's shoulder. Every so often he would turn and look down at her, and once he halted the team so he could tuck the hood of her cloak more securely around her red-gold curls. Anne slept on, unaware.

She woke as they approached the streets and squares of Mayfair. In spite of the number of houses that were closed, she appeared stunned by the size and richness of these mansions, the amount of traffic in the streets, and the noise and clatter and smells that were London.

The earl helped her down from the perch, and then as she stumbled a little, he picked her up in his arms to carry her up the steps. Anne gasped and clutched one of his lapels.

The butler, who she could see was a very superior person indeed, showed no surprise at the earl's burden, and he only nodded at the orders he was given.

As he carried her on up the stairs, Lord Bredon said, "A bath and some supper are what you need, Anne, and then I want you to go to bed. I will send a maid to attend you. Do not feel pressured about leaving for Bredon tomorrow. If you do not feel able for the journey, it will be an easy matter to delay it."

As he carried her into a large bedroom on the front of the house, he added, "Miss Goodly and your maid are on their way to Bredon now. It will take them some time, so any postponement of ours does not matter."

"Miss Goodly is coming back to Bredon?" Anne asked, her eyes wide.

The earl did not smile at her as he set her on her feet. "But of course. You must have a chaperon, Miss Ainsworth."

She thought he sounded sarcastic, and she lowered her eyes.

"No more conversation now," he said. "Your immediate concern is a bath, I am sure. At least it should be."

Anne looked down at herself and made a face, and he smiled a little then.

"Good night, Miss Ainsworth," he said.

He turned to leave her, and she reached out and grasped his sleeve. "M'lord," she said.

When he stopped and looked at her, she smiled a little shyly. "Thank you . . . for everything," she whispered.

They stood staring at each other for a long moment, and then a maid came in with a pile of towels and the earl nodded. "Sleep well," he murmured before he went away.

The bath was glorious, and so was the luxury of being clean again from the top of her curls down to her toes. Anne ate everything on the tray that was brought to her, wearing one of the housekeeper's voluminous nightgowns, and then she was helped into the huge bed with its soft sheets that smelled faintly of lavender, its large downy pillows, and its satin coverlets. She was sure she would not be able to drop off after dozing all day, but the instant her eyes closed, she was in a deep, dreamless sleep.

She woke early the next morning. For a moment, she wondered where she was, but then the sound of carriages rumbling by outside, and a dairyman calling "Milk O! Milk below!" made her remember. She snuggled down in the sheets and said her morning prayer, adding a special thanksgiving for her deliverance.

The maid who came in to make up the fire and bring her

breakfast told her the earl was having some clothes sent, and suggested she remain in bed until they arrived.

Anne agreed, and after the tray was removed, she settled back on her pillows to wait. She found herself thinking as well, now she was alone. She realized that yesterday she had been so exhausted mentally and physically, and so relieved, she had not thought beyond her rescue. Now she must consider what lay ahead. True, the earl had saved her, and he had said the wager was forfeit, but had he also abandoned his plans for her future? It was entirely possible that he had not. Perhaps he had only been angry with Sir Hartley for touching what he had decided was to be his. Anne remembered her father. Would it make any difference that she was the granddaughter of a baronet? She did not think the Earl of Bredon would allow that to deter him. He was so autocratic and demanding, so used to getting his own way. Surely the daughter of a whore who had abandoned her, and an eccentric recluse who had not even bothered to speak to her would not be much of a threat to him. Besides, in bringing her to his house to spend the night, he had as much as proclaimed her status. No young lady of quality would ever be treated this way.

But why, then, had he invited Miss Goodly and Mary Agnes back to Bredon? That was a puzzler. A chaperon would be the last person he would want in attendance. Or was that perhaps just a ploy? Bredon was very large, and Miss Goodly could not be with her every moment. And she had to remember that the earl, even though he had rescued her, was still one of Satan's Rakes.

Her blue eyes were troubled as she thought these things, and absently she pleated the bedsheet. As her fingers touched the monogram, she looked down. The large raised satin letters of the earl's crest were soft to the touch, and she smoothed out the bed linen to study them.

And if the earl asked you to be his mistress, Anne, she whispered to herself, what would be your reply? Do you really want to leave him and all this to go back to St. Just and two hundred pounds a year? Do you really want to live only with Miss Goodly and Mary Agnes for company in a quiet fishing village?

She looked around the luxurious room, the wide, comfortable bed, and the chaise heaped with delicate pillows and a soft cashmere throw; the elegant dressing table and gilded mirror, and the silver candlesticks and porcelain bibelots that adorned every surface. Admit it, she told herself fiercely. You love it here, just as you loved it at Bredon. You want to be wealthy and pampered; you always have.

Besides, if the earl came through that door right now, you know what you would like to do—hold out your arms to him and beg him never to leave you. You are a shameless girl, no better than your mother. It was very hard to admit these things, even to herself. She did not know what she was to do, or how she was to act when she saw him, now that she understood her true nature.

Fortunately, the maid came back then in company with two others, burdened with all manner of large white boxes filled with new clothes.

The earl had gone out very early to do his shopping, taking Anne's soiled gown and a sandal for a pattern. He had not been able to resist the blue morning gown that was the color of her eyes, nor the fur-lined cloak of gray velvet, as well as a number of other outfits he could not wait to see her wear.

He had shopped for many women through the years, for he had always deplored his mistresses' taste. They had loved flashy finery and loud colors, and since he would not permit them to appear that way while they were under his protection, the only answer was to choose their clothes himself.

When he left the modiste's at last, he was frowning, although he did not realize it.

Anne joined him in the library just before luncheon. She came in somewhat shyly, wearing a traveling gown of deep scarlet wool. The earl inspected her keenly. He had wondered if the color would clash with her hair, but it was as stunning as he had hoped.

As she curtsied, she said, "I must thank you again, m'lord. The clothes are beautiful. But surely there was no need to buy so many."

Lord Bredon waved his hand. "I am glad everything seems to fit. And now, won't you be seated and allow me to pour you a glass of wine? We have plans to make."

Anne could see that speaking of her new clothes seemed to disturb him, and she nodded and went to sit by the fire.

As she took the wine from his hand, she tried not to touch his fingers, and she hoped he would think that it was the heat from the fire that made her face so rosy. But Lord Bredon had noticed, and for a brief moment his lips twisted in a grimace.

"Are you feeling better, Anne?" he asked, his face and voice expressionless now as he took the seat opposite her.

When she assured him she was quite recovered, he asked, "When do you think you will be able to travel? I am anxious to return to Bredon."

"As soon as you like, m'lord," she replied, looking up into his gray eyes. What she saw there made her lower her own in haste to stare into her glass.

"Then we will leave right after luncheon. We can put several miles between us and London by nightfall," he told her. "I have ordered my coach made ready so you may make the journey in comfort. One of the maids will be with you, to assist you."

"Will you also ride in the coach, m'lord?" Anne asked.

Lord Bredon thought she sounded distressed at the possibility that she might be cooped up with him for several days, and he frowned. In actuality, she was regretting the maid's presence if he was going to be beside her.

"I shall travel by horseback," he told her, his deep voice cold as the butler came to announce luncheon.

The coach left London at two. Anne rode in solitary state, a maid beside her. The servant thought her very quiet, for she spent most of the time staring out the window. She did not know that Anne was watching the earl whenever he rode alongside, admiring his straight, broad back and shoulders, his long legs in their polished boots, even the tilt of his hat that showed her a glimpse of his silver-blond hair.

In the days that followed, the only time that Anne saw

Lord Bredon alone was at dinner in the inns where they stopped each evening. And even there, they had no opportunity to talk, for the inn servants came in and out bearing trays and firewood and fresh candles. She was surprised that Lord Bredon left her right after dinner every night as well, and never asked her any of the details of her life since she had run away from Bredon, or what had happened to her with Sir Hartley and Lord Quarles.

He is probably still angry with me for running away in the first place, she told herself. I have put him to a great deal of expense and bother, to say nothing of the way I defied him. He has probably decided to send me back to Tees as soon as Miss Goodly reaches Bredon, not wanting to be bothered with such a willful chit.

This thought depressed her so that she became even quieter and more morose. The earl, who watched her as carefully as she watched him, was sure she was reliving her experiences at Sir Hartley's hands, and many times he cursed the man as he rode beside the carriage and saw her set little profile framed in the glass.

They arrived at Bredon six days later. The earl had set an easy pace, with plenty of stops for rest and refreshment. As he helped Anne up the steps, between the footmen who stood at rigid attention, to where Midler waited to greet his master at the door, Anne was so bemused she did not even smile at her old friends. John Coombs clenched his hands in their white gloves. Miss Anne was different. She looked as beautiful as ever, but some of the light had gone out of her face, and he mourned the loss.

Back at Bredon again, but for how long? Anne wondered as the earl took her fur-lined cloak and handed it to the butler.

"We will have tea served in the library, Midler," he said, breaking into her thoughts. "Has Mr. Ashton arrived? Miss Goodly and the maid?"

On being told that nothing had been heard from any of them, Lord Bredon nodded. He felt as if a burden had been lifted from his shoulders. Let me have some little time with her alone, he begged fate as they walked to the room where he had seen her first, the day she came to Bredon, and then he wondered why that was so important to him.

They chatted of the journey, and speculated about Will's and Miss Goodly's present locations, and then Anne excused herself.

The earl rose as she curtsied, and then he came and took her chin in one hand. As he caressed her jaw with his thumb, he said, "I am glad to see the bruise has faded, Anne."

He could feel her trembling as he stared down into that beautiful face, those luminous dark blue eyes. When he saw the trouble in them, he added, "I am afraid it will take a much longer time for the bruises I cannot see to fade, if they ever do. I beg your pardon."

Anne did not understand his soft, regretful words, and she lowered her eyes. "If I may be excused, m'lord?" she whispered. She was sure he must be able to tell how she was aching to be in his arms. Why, it was all she could do not to put her own arms around his neck and draw that handsome head down to hers until his lips were possessing hers again. She was ashamed of herself and her wantonness.

The earl stifled a sigh and let her go. "Yes, go and rest. We will talk this evening," he said.

He watched her move away from him down the long room, and it was only when she shut the door softly behind her that he recalled himself and went to glance at the post that awaited his inspection on the desk.

That evening he was before her in the drawing room. She did not come down until the last bell, and as she joined him near the fireplace, he studied her. She was wearing one of the gowns he had bought for her, a slip of misty yellow silk, but he did not admire the way it clung to her breasts and supple waist and displayed her soft shoulders and rounded arms. Instead, he searched her quiet face. It showed no emotion at all, and even when she smiled briefly in greeting, she seemed to be only a pale copy of the vivacious girl he had known before. And I have been the cause of this, he told himself as he took her in to dinner.

During the meal, he managed to keep the conversation

light and general. Anne replied when he asked her a question, but she had little to contribute, and tonight no one could look askance at the amount of food she ate. She toyed with her fish and took only a bite of the breast of pheasant, and when dessert was served, she waved it away.

Lord Bredon could stand it no more. "Bring me the port, Midler, and then leave us," he ordered, and there was something in his voice that made Anne dart a glance at him, her heart beating faster.

Pouring a glass of wine, the earl waited until the butler had seen his minions from the room and closed the doors behind him, and then he said, "And now I think we must finish this affair, Anne. I have waited, in hopes you would recover from your experience with Sir Hartley, but it appears it is still affecting you. I am sorry for it, but I can wait no longer."

He looked up to see her watching him intently, her face composed.

There was a little silence, and then he said, "Tell me now everything that happened to you. Begin with the night you left Bredon, and leave nothing out."

He saw her hesitation, and he added, "I think you owe me that much."

Anne nodded, and began her story. She did not implicate the footmen, or tell of Rhea Carter's and the other villagers' role in her escape, and she was glad the earl did not question her about it. When she reached her arrival at Cawfell, he stirred in his seat at the head of the table.

"Why was it so important for you to find your father, Anne?" he asked.

They were the first words he had spoken since she began her story, and his even, quiet tones reassured her a little. At least he does not sound angry with me, she thought.

"I had to go somewhere, and the money Sir Hartley had given me was running out," she told him. Then she stared at him as she added, "Besides, I wanted to find out who I really was. I had been a scullery maid, a beloved foster daughter, a lady, your ward, even a pawn in a wager—and now it appeared I was about to become your mistress if I could not escape you. I . . . I was confused. Who was Anne Ainsworth, truly?"

She lowered her eyes to the tightly clasped hands in her lap, and so she did not see the light that flashed for a moment in his eyes.

"When I reached St. Just, my father would not even see me. He agreed, through my aunt, to give me money to live on, but he hated my mother so for the way she had deceived him, that he would not speak to me. I never even saw him."

At the sad note of regret in her voice, the earl interrupted. "Parents are not always loving and kind, Anne," he said. "My own mother left me to her servants' care. I heard her telling one of her friends once that my father's death was a happy release for her. Now she did not have to ruin her figure producing any more brats for him. I was only a nuisance to her, someone who intruded on her life of pleasure."

He stopped as if he wished he had not told her that, and then he said, "Go on. How did Hartley manage to spirit you away from Miss Goodly and that fierce maid of yours?"

Anne told him about her walk, and for the first time, how King had been shot. Her voice quivered a little, and he wished he might take her hands in his for comfort, but she held them in her lap, sitting straight and proud as if she scorned his sympathy.

She told him what she could remember of the mad dash to Sir Hartley's home, the blows and drugs, the cold and humiliation. And then she told him what his friend had planned for her, and how he had taken Lord Quarles outside, and struck him and left him to freeze to death.

Will is right, the earl thought as he listened to the horrors coming from her lips. We are none of us worth a ha'penny. We are more than dissolute and debauched. We are evil. But I have always known that, so why do I regret it now? Is it because I am hearing innocence describe it? Innocence that I have caused to be corrupted? He shook himself, knowing it was far too late for regret.

He sipped his port to give himself time to recover. The story he had just been told had affected him deeply, and he was amazed at how fervently he wished there was some way he could make it up to her, some way he could bring back the laughing, unsophisticated girl she had been. But unlike the last time, he could not charm her with his smiles and teasing now. Anne Ainsworth deserved better than that; there was nothing a man like him could do to help her.

"May I ask you a question, m'lord?" Anne asked, interrupting his sad musing.

He looked up from his contemplation of the ruby liquid left in his glass, and nodded, his throat still too tight for speech.

"I heard you tell Sir Hartley the wager is forfeit. You do not need me to win it for you anymore, so why have you brought me back to Bredon?" she asked, her head held high. "What happens to me now?"

The earl made himself look into her eyes. "I brought you back because I felt I owed you that much. I am not sure even now that Hartley will not try to murder you, just for revenge. Until he has left the country, you are not safe."

The words sounded lame even to his own ears, and he was not surprised when she persisted, "But after that, what happens? I am not your ward, and without the wager, there is nothing between us."

Her blue eyes continued to hold his gray ones. How handsome he is, she thought, despair in her heart. Those lean, aristocratic features, that blond hair turned to silver in the candlelight. She looked down to where his hands rested on the table, and she remembered how they had felt caressing her, and she had to swallow.

"There you are wrong, my dear," he said softly. "There is still something between us. Something that has yet to be resolved."

He got up then, pushing back his chair abruptly to come to her side. After a little hesitation, she took the hand he held out to her, and rose to stand before him.

For a moment he stared at her, and then he took her face in his hands as he had done that afternoon in the library. They were firm and warm as they lifted it to his, so he could search deep into her eyes. Anne had the strange feeling he was trying to tell her something, something he could not put into words, and she wondered at it. And then, after what seemed an age, he bent his head and kissed her.

It was not the kind of kiss she associated with the Earl of Bredon. Rather, it was only a soft, reassuring touch on her lips, the kind of kiss someone might give a child.

He drew back a few inches, still holding her face as he whispered, "And how are we to resolve it, I wonder?"

Anne ached to move forward until her body was touching his. She wanted him to put his arms around her and pull her closer still. She wanted the kiss he had given her before, demanding, passionate, relentless in its intensity. That kiss, and then a hundred more.

"If you are asking me to be your mistress, m'lord, I will," she found herself whispering back, helpless with her desire for him.

He dropped his hands, and she heard his sharp intake of breath as he stepped away from her. Anne had to grasp the back of her chair to keep herself from falling as she waited for his reply.

And then she saw him shake his head. "No, Anne, you will not," he said, and the words burned into her, all the more cruel for the golden, smooth tones they were spoken in. "I do not want you that way anymore," he continued.

She turned away so he would not see the hurt in her eyes. "Then how are we to resolve this problem, m'lord?" she asked, her lips stiff.

The earl sighed. "For you and one of Satan's Rakes, there is no way," he said. "I see that quite clearly now. I shall take you back to Tees, of course. I should never have brought you away from there in the first place. But by returning you to those who love you, I shall be doing what I can to make reparation."

Anne almost cried out that she didn't want to go back to Tees, she only wanted him, in any way she could have him. But then she remembered that he had rejected her when she offered herself to him. Her shoulders slumped. He did not love her, and worse, he did not even want her.

She made herself straighten then, although it took every ounce of courage she possessed. "I see," she said, and then she looked to where he was standing so quietly a few feet away and asked, "When should I be ready to leave?"

The earl watched her. He saw the tears she was hiding, and how frozen and white her face was. She looked like a marble statue, with only the flaming color of her hair to remind him she was a living, breathing woman. His hands curled into fists and he made himself say, "You will thank me someday, Anne, no matter how you feel now." And then he seemed to recall her question, and he added, "We leave tomorrow at dawn. We will not wait for Miss Goodly and your maid to arrive as I had planned, for I am sure Bredon has become too painful for you to wish to remain."

Anne nodded. "If you will excuse me then, m'lord," she said with a curtsy.

As she walked to the door, her head held high, he cried, "Anne!"

She stopped at once, and turned back to him, her heart in her eyes. He stifled whatever he had been going to say in his moment of weakness to think she was leaving him. "You will take all the clothes I bought for you. Do you understand?" he said instead.

She bowed her head in acquiescence and left him. Lord Bredon stood alone in his massive dining salon, and then he strode back to the table and the decanter. As he poured himself another glass of wine, he cursed softly and at length.

The decision he had just made was the only way he knew to rectify the harm he had brought to her, and perhaps the finest thing he had ever done in his life. But it had been by far the hardest, especially after she had confessed her love by offering to be his mistress. She would never know how that artless confession had stabbed his soul.

He did not know if what he felt for her in return was love, that elusive emotion he had always sneered at before this, but he did know how much he had come to care for her. Perhaps it was love; he did not know. He only realized that with Anne there was none of the mistrust and scorn he had always felt for other women, that her well-being mattered to him so much that he was letting her go. She was young. There would be someone else for her someday, someone finer and cleaner than he, someone who was not debauched and evil and unworthy of her.

He wondered if the bleak pain he felt now would ever lessen, or if he would have to bear it until death released him. A fitting punishment for one of Satan's own, he thought, and the bitter groan that escaped his lips was full of his agony and regret.

# 16

The earl's mud-spattered traveling coach came into the village of Tees four days later. The journey had been difficult, for Lord Bredon insisted on haste. Anne was so emotionally exhausted and drained, she did not even notice the wicked pace he set. Once again the earl had ridden beside the coach and left her to the company of a maid, and not once during those days had he spoken a word to her that the entire world could not have heard. He was the polite gentleman, serving only as her courier, and so remote she felt the journey was only a necessary chore he had to perform.

He helped her down from the carriage himself at the manse, and then he stood back as she ran into the vicar's arms. It was only when she turned aside to kiss Mrs. Nettles, the tears running down her face, that he stepped forward.

"I am Bredon. If I might have a few minutes of your time, sir?" he asked the vicar. Reverend Nettles' face grew cold and grim, but he nodded and led his unwelcome visitor to his study.

When Lord Bredon came out half an hour later, his face was expressionless, although a small muscle moved for a moment beside his mouth as he took his hat and greatcoat from the hands of the awed little maid. There was no sign of Anne, but he had not expected to see her again. As he left the manse, he told himself it was just as well. Any formal leave-taking would be too painful for her to bear, after what she had offered him at Bredon—and he had refused.

He had spoken candidly to the vicar, for he had wanted to prepare him for the change in Anne Ainsworth, and he had not spared himself in the telling. He had kept his voice and his expression emotionless as he told him everything that had happened to her. Not even the vicar's look of disgust for his raking, and dislike for what he had done to this beloved girl, had stayed his tongue. If I were a Catholic, he told himself, that would have been a confession.

But there had been no absolution to be had from Davis Nettles, nor had he expected any. The man abhorred him, as well he should. But it had been important that he understand. Otherwise, he might press her unwisely before she was ready, and the earl had been afraid of the despair he had seen so clearly in her eyes.

She will forget me soon, he told himself as he mounted his horse and prepared to leave Tees for the Grove, where he would sleep only for one night.

From her window, Anne watched him ride away, followed by the lumbering coach. She could hear Aunt Ellen clattering down the stairs in response to her husband's call, and she was glad she had left. It had been hard to answer all her breathless questions, hard not to break down completely and wail. And that she knew she could not do.

She was glad when Aunt Ellen did not return or even send the maid to help her unpack, for she felt if she could not be alone, she would collapse, all her good resolutions gone.

In the study, the vicar was telling his wife the story he had heard, and patting her hands as he did so. This good woman looked horrified, and she agreed with her husband that they must not question Anne too closely.

"She will come to us when she is able to speak of it, my dear," he told his wife. "Until then, we must pretend that nothing has happened, nothing at all."

He paused for a moment, and then he added, "I cannot believe that what that evil man told me is true. How could Anne love such a man as he? He must be mistaken. Perhaps he intrigued her and she was drawn to him, for he's a handsome devil, but love him she could not. As for his supposed love for her, it is no such thing. He feels only lust; he does not know the meaning of the word 'love.' "

"But why did he bring her back then, Davis?" Mrs. Nettles asked, her little eyes round with wonder.

"I can only think a good angel took a hand for the first time in his life. Or perhaps it was the remorse he felt in effectively destroying such a good girl." He shook his head. "I doubt she will ever recover from this, Ellen, and for that reason I cannot find it in my heart to forgive him."

Miss Goodly and Mary Agnes arrived a week later. The weather had moderated a little, although it was still only January, and Miss Goodly knew there were several more weeks of winter to endure. For a moment, as she stepped down from the earl's coach drawn up before her cottage, she felt a pang of regret for the dower house above St. Just she had left behind.

By the time she arrived, Anne had herself well in hand. She was not cheerful, nor did she hum or sing as she went about her familiar duties, but she smiled and chatted when addressed. Only the sadness on her face when she thought she was unobserved told the inhabitants of the vicarage that she had not recovered from whatever was bedeviling her.

Surprisingly, it was Granny Nettles who broke through the shield of ice she hid behind. The old lady was almost blind now, and bedridden, and Anne spent a lot of time sitting with her and reading all her favorite verses from the Bible to her. Most of the time, Granny recited them with her from memory. But one snowy afternoon she put her wrinkled old hand over Anne's and said, "You are so sad, my child. I cannot bear to see you this way."

Anne looked at her sharply. The clouded eyes could not possibly see her face clearly. It was one of the reasons she sought the old lady's company so often. With her, she did not have to school her expression as well as her words and tone of voice.

"Oh, yes, I can see, but with the heart now, Anne," the old lady crooned. "It is too bad, too bad. He was an evil man, and I am sorry that you love him, but I know women cannot direct where their love shall be given."

Anne stared at her, feeling helpless. She had not told Granny of her love for the earl. Did she have second sight?

"I cannot see into the future, my dear," the old lady

continued. "I wish I could. It may be that you will never see him again. That is what Davis and Ellen wish, but I do not know if it is best for you. Perhaps you will. Perhaps it will all come right for you after all. I shall pray for you, and pray God will give you what you truly want, if He, in His loving kindness, deems it right."

Hand in hand, the two sat quietly for a long time without speaking, and then Granny Nettles said, "I think I will sleep a little now, Anne. I love you, and you are a good girl. Remember it always, for no one but yourself can take that away from you."

Granny Nettles died in her sleep that night, quietly and peacefully. And all the tears, all the sorrow Anne had felt since leaving Bredon, she was able to release at last.

A few days later, she seemed more her old self again, although the vicar noticed she did not refer to the earl, or to the time she had been away from them, even now. Those weeks might never have happened at all.

In late February, Will Ashton came to Bredon. He heard from Hawk how he had found Anne at Sir Hartley's estate, and it was a good thing that that man had taken the earl's advice and left the country forever, for Will was hot for revenge.

"If he ever comes back, no matter how many years from now, I shall most certainly kill him, Hawk!" he declared, his open, handsome face contorted with rage.

The two friends were sitting in the library at Bredon. Will had arrived for a visit only that morning. He had had a letter from the earl right after Anne went back to Tees, asking him to contain his impatience and delay his visit. He had wondered at it, at the time. What was the business the earl claimed, that could possibly take so much of his time?

Now, as he studied his friend's face, he did not think he looked at all well. He was thinner, more finely drawn somehow, and his carefully controlled expression never altered. And although his deep, charming voice was the same, it seemed somehow colder and more leaden. Hawk had never been mercurial, but Will had never seen him so devoid of animation.

When he asked about Anne, he learned only that she had returned to Tees. Somehow, the brevity of that answer did not please him.

Stealing a glance at his friend's profile where he sat gazing into the fire, Will said, "I am glad you let her go, Hawk, but somehow I am surprised."

The earl did not turn. "I know. So out of character for one of Satan's Rakes, was it not? I should have seduced her instead. I meant to, you know."

His words were careless, and in his anger, Will did not hear the pain there. "Do not speak of her that way, Hawk! Anne is too fine, too good."

Lord Bredon hid a yawn. "So you keep telling me, Will. You must learn to control your enthusiasms, lest you begin to bore me. You know I cannot stand to be bored."

Then he stood up and stretched. "I think I have rusticated at Bredon too long. Perhaps a trip to London is in order. I find I am in dire need of some diversion. Oh, no, no," he said, raising a hand at Will's indignant look. "I do not mean you are not a diversion for me, my old friend. I was speaking of a softer, more yielding kind than you can provide."

Will frowned a little, and then he said diffidently, "I had it in mind to make a journey north, Hawk, after I left you."

One mobile blond eyebrow rose as the earl eyed him intently. A tinge of red colored Will's cheekbones.

He waited for the sarcastic remark he was sure was coming, but Hawk only said slowly, "Ah, I remember how you said if you could win Anne, you would ask for nothing more." He paused, and then added, his voice even quieter, "I must wish you good fortune, Will, although, like you, I think Anne deserves someone better than one of Satan's Rakes."

"But I am not like that anymore, Hawk!" Will protested. "And with Reggie dead and Hartley gone abroad, I think we should discard that silly sobriquet once and for all. I do not think your heart is in the game anymore either."

"How shrewd of you, Will. You continue to astound me," the earl said in rejoinder. "And of course it is true you have not killed your man for many months."

"Months?" Will asked. "The last duel I had was five

years ago, as you well know. And even then I did not shoot to kill.''

The earl smiled, albeit weakly. His ploy had worked, he thought, as Will kept insisting that his wish to dispose of his fellows was a thing of the past.

And now Will Ashton stood in the vicarage hall and waited to see if Reverend Nettles would receive him. He twisted his hat brim impatiently in suddenly nervous hands. Suppose he sent him away? Suppose he would not even allow him to speak to Anne?

As the door of the study opened and the little maid beckoned him in, he made a firm resolve to be as persuasive as he could. He loved Anne Ainsworth. He would not give up the chance to marry her, and have her with him always, no matter how he had to abase himself.

He was received with more kindness than he had expected. The vicar had never thought Mr. Ashton anywhere near the villain of the piece the Earl of Bredon was, and now, although his manner was stiffly formal, he motioned his visitor to a seat, and heard him out.

When Will finished, his voice was hoarse. He had spoken for a long time, first confessing his part in the debacle, and not making any excuses for his wrongdoing. Reverend Nettles admired him for his honesty. A lesser man would have put all the blame on the absent earl.

And then Will told him of his love for Anne Ainsworth. "You know of it yourself, sir," he said. "Even before we left Tees, I implied it. But she was so young, and it was so soon, I did not dare to speak of it openly. I have not changed in my feelings since then. Although I was not able to protect her as I should while she was at Bredon and afterward, there is nothing I desire more in the world than to be able to protect her now, as my beloved wife.''

The vicar looked into the good-looking, open face before him and saw the truth of what he said in his hazel eyes, and he nodded.

"Very well, Mr. Ashton," he said slowly, as he rose from his chair. "Stay here, and I will ask Anne if she will see you.''

He went away, and Will spent the intervening time pacing the worn Turkey carpet and murmuring fervent prayers. It seemed a very long time indeed before Anne slipped into the room alone. Will was stunned. She was so different it was as if a paler twin of the girl he loved was standing before him, holding out her hand and trying to smile.

"Anne, have you been ill?" he asked as he took her hand and pressed it.

She shook her head, and then she indicated a seat. "I think it is this depressing winter weather, Mr. Ashton," she said as she took a seat herself.

Will could see from her tightened lips that she did not care to speak of the reason for her altered appearance, and he made himself sit down and say more calmly, "Yes, it has been a hard one. But I must tell you first, Anne, how I regret I did not see you before you came home. I wanted to apologize, to tell you how very sorry I was that I ever let myself be drawn into that stupid wager in the first place. And to beg you to forgive me for what happened."

She held up her hand and turned a little away from him, and his voice died away. "Please, Will," she said, her own voice breaking a little. "I cannot speak of that time, not even to you. I do forgive you, and I beg you to forget it. It is over now, and whatever happened to me is over too."

He saw the sad twist of her mouth, and wished there was some way he could make her happy again. And then he recalled his errand, and he got up and went to kneel at her feet, capturing both her hands in his own warm ones. She turned back to look at him, and he was startled at the terrified look in her eyes. Horrified, he hurried into speech.

"Yes, it is over, thank God. And now I can come to you, knowing that you realize the kind of man I was, and hoping you will believe me when I tell you that man is no more. No, instead, here is only simple Will Ashton, offering you his hand and his heart."

She tried to pull her hands away, and he tightened his grip. "No, Anne, hear me out! I love you. I have loved you since that first afternoon we met here on the hillside above the manse. You were so young then, so very young—I could not tell you, for I did not want to frighten you. Besides, I knew what Hawk had planned for you, and until I could convince him to give up the scheme, I did not have the right.''

"You did not manage to do that, did you?" she asked, her voice bitter.

He shook his head. "No, I did not. I have always followed Hawk in everything in the past, but even though I tried and tried, I could not get him to discard the plan. Finally he told me he was considering it, and a little reassured, I left you at Bredon. I thought, you see, that when he grew to know you better, he would come to understand why the whole idea of the wager was an obscenity.''

He pressed her hands as he smiled at her. "But you have not answered me, Anne. I know you do not love me, not yet, but won't you give me some hope that you might learn to do so in time? I will wait for you forever.''

Anne looked down into his fervent, pleading eyes. She knew Will Ashton was a good man, and part of her wished she might give him the answer he wanted so badly to hear. But she knew that was impossible. The earl's handsome face came to her mind, and the look in her eyes showed she was far away.

A little pressure from his hands recalled her to the present. "I can't, Will," she said sadly. "I am sorry, but I can't promise you that, ever.''

He searched her face, looking for some clue, some hope, but there was nothing to read there but sadness and regret.

He dropped her hands then, and got to his feet. "So this is to be my punishment," he said slowly. "Ever since I was a child, I have always heard that we must pay for our sins someday. And now I see that it is true. Reggie is dead, and Hartley fled abroad," he continued as if he were alone. "I wonder what punishment awaits Hawk?''

"How . . . how is the earl?" Anne asked, her voice wooden. "I trust you left him well?''

Will turned back to her, to see her head lowered and her hands clasped tightly in her lap, and with a blinding clarity he knew he had discovered the truth.

"You love him, don't you, Anne?" he asked hoarsely.

Anne wished she might deny it when she heard the pain in his voice, but she could not. "Yes, I do," she admitted.

Will's shoulders slumped in defeat. "I see," he said in a voice from which all emotion had been carefully removed. "Then there is no hope for me indeed."

Anne rose and went to take his arm. "And none for me either, Will," she said. "The earl knows of my love, for I told him of it, and yet he sent me away."

The two stood close together for a moment, united in their sorrow, and then she said, "I must leave you now. Forgive me, I did not mean to hurt you."

Will nodded, unable to speak, and she went away. He remained standing there in the middle of the room until the vicar came back. That wise man could see his suit had not prospered, and he was sorry.

Without speaking, he poured his guest a glass of wine and led him to a chair. "She would not have you, my boy?" he asked after Will had taken a sip.

"No, she will never have me," Will told him. "She loves Hawk—Anthony Hawkins, the Earl of Bredon, I mean."

The vicar leaned forward, frowning. "Are you sure?" he asked as if he could not believe his ears.

Will nodded. "She told me so. She also told me Hawk knows of her love, and yet he still sent her away. I do not understand that part of it at all. It is so unlike him, for I know he wanted to make her his mistress in the beginning, and . . ."

Suddenly recalled to the company he was in, he stopped speaking, alarmed at what he had revealed, and by the vicar's frowning face.

"And I didn't believe him," Reverend Nettles murmured. Then he looked at his guest and said, "Tell me more about the earl, if you please, Mr. Ashton. I begin to think I have been mistaken in his character."

Will began to describe Anthony Hawkins, and in doing so, he made the vicar feel much better. The picture he painted of the man showed a good friend, loyal and honorable in spite of his raking.

When Will took his leave a little while later, Reverend

Nettles sat on in his study, his hands clasped to his chin and his blue eyes serious behind his spectacles. He thought for a very long time before he asked his wife to join him so he might seek her advice.

# 17

As soon as William Ashton left Bredon, the earl made arrangements to go to town. He was disgusted with himself. Here he had been all this time, wallowing in self-pity and regret that he had let Anne go, like some weak, spineless simpleton. He had indulged himself for too long. It was time he took up his life again and forgot her.

As he posted up to town, he realized that that was probably an impossible feat, but he meant to try. For once he had done the noble thing, the one thing that could save her from him, and he must have no second thoughts of its wisdom. After all, her present predicament, and all the horrors that she had endured in the past weeks, could be laid at his door. It was his fault, and his alone. Reggie had been not so much evil as weak, but knowing Sir Hartley as he had, he should have guessed the man would try something foul. And Will had warned him, and begged him to let Anne go, and he had refused simply because he wanted her, as he had wanted so many others. And what Hawk wants, Hawk gets, isn't that right? he snarled at himself. He was selfish, conceited, and evil. Named Satan's Rake when he had barely reached manhood, Satan's Rake he would remain, now and always.

His servants were not spared his bad temper, and if Midler was delighted to shut the door of Bredon behind his master, his London butler steeled himself for the unpleasantness he was sure would come.

In a few days, the earl slipped back into the life he had always led. He went to his clubs and gambled hard, as if he did not care how much money he lost. But perversely, he won. The cards and the dice fell to his hands, and his friends

began to remark on his luck. He also drank heavily, sometimes not falling into bed until dawn, for then he knew he
would be able to sleep. And he looked around at all the pretty
demimondaines and opera dancers with a connoisseur's eye,
and coolly chose his partner.

The young lady had brilliant red hair. Indeed, it was for
that reason alone he chose her, for she had little wit, and
outside of the time spent in her scented bed, nothing in
common with him at all. But he had laughed until he had to
hold his sides, the first time he discovered that she dyed her
hair that flamboyant color.

And then he discovered that unless he had been drinking,
she could give him no pleasure. Many nights, unsatisfied, he
would leave her abruptly, to dress and walk the London
streets. His new mistress, installed in the little house he kept
for that purpose, shrugged her round shoulders. She had
heard the earl was a virile man with insatiable appetites, but it
appeared the gossip was wrong. But what did she care? He
was less bother to her this way, and as long as she was fed
and housed, and clothed, she was content.

Of course, she wished he would not insist on dressing her
in such die-away colors, she thought as she eyed her ecru
muslin gown that had only one small knot of ribbons at the
bosom for decoration, but that was a small matter. The earl
was handsome and well-built, and if he was not precisely
kind or overly generous with gifts of jewels and carriages,
neither was he cruel to her. She had had worse protectors.

She set about trying to please him in all the ways she
knew, but sometimes, not even her most inventive seductions
were enough.

Lord Bredon did not see Will Ashton, or hear from him,
and he was a little surprised. He could not help wondering
often how his suit had prospered in Tees, and finally he wrote
him a letter at Ashton Abbey to inquire. It was some weeks
before he had a reply, but in the meantime, something happened that drove Will right out of his mind.

He was riding in Hyde Park with two acquaintances one
afternoon in late March, when he saw Anne Ainsworth again.
His horse tried to rear at the sudden pressure of the bit as the

earl pulled at the reins hard. It could not be! Anne! Why was she here? he wondered as he brought his nervous mount under control.

She was seated in an open landau traveling on the carriageway, with an older lady seated beside her. Across from them, Miss Goodly sat, facing back. Anne was talking with great animation, and she looked just as she had when he first met her, gay and alive and beautiful. The older ladies laughed at something she said, but Lord Bredon had eyes only for Anne as he kept pace with their carriage from his own position on Rotten Row. He saw Anne was wearing one of the gowns he had bought for her, the blue afternoon gown with the dashing bonnet of feathers that swept up on one side to show off her red-gold curls. She had put her hair up, he noted, and she looked stunning.

One of the men he was with noticed the direction of his stare, and he whistled. "Now, who is that goddess?" he wondered aloud. The other man turned to inspect the vision in the landau as well.

"I have no idea," Andrew Barret admitted. "She's with the Duchess of Lyme, however. Could she be a relative come up for the Season?"

"The duchess's children are all married, so it must be a cousin or a niece," the other man remarked. "But who cares who she is? I must meet her!"

"Hawk saw her first, Percy," Andrew Barret reminded him. "And I do have to say that if Hawk sets about attaching her, you don't stand a chance."

The other man sighed. He was only of medium height and build, with ordinary features. Then he brightened. "But Hawk don't care for debutantes, Drew! Not his style at all. He's too much the rake for any of their sweet innocence, isn't that so, old boy?"

Percy Garth was startled for a moment at the cold gray glare in the earl's eyes, but it was gone so quickly he was sure he must have been mistaken.

"As you say, Percy. Debutantes are not for the likes of me," the earl agreed, his deep voice easy.

"Can't think why you'd want 'em to be, Hawk, not with

all those lovely ladies you have had under your protection. Silly things, debs,'' Percy continued as the landau rounded a curve and disappeared from sight. ''Nothing but love-love-love on their minds for years, but after they take that walk down the aisle, all white satin and lace, they revert to their true natures in a twinkling. Icicles, every one of 'em! My cousin told me so.''

Andrew Barret laughed at him, but the earl did not hear their banter, for his mind was working furiously. Anne was here in London, and he had to find out why. Was she staying with the duchess? And how had they come to meet?

He excused himself rather abruptly as soon as the trio reached the Stanhope Gate, and trotted back to St. James's Street, still lost in thought.

After he had given his horse to a groom, he entered the house and went immediately to the library. As he had known, the tray that held invitations was piled high. He rarely looked at them, for he had found the dances and tea parties and routs boring in the past. But still, his name was always included on the guest list by every society hostess. Anthony Hawkins, Earl of Bredon, might be a handsome rake, but he was from an old family with an excellent title, and he was wealthy beyond belief. For those attributes, there were many mamas of eligible daughters who would not hesitate to overlook a murder or two in his past.

He studied the cards. There was a dance to be given tonight by Lady Warren, and a ball in two days' time by Mrs. Rogers. Mrs. Rogers had two daughters in their twenties still at home, but he could see she had not given up hope. She would be delighted to welcome him, as would Lady Warren, who seemed to have a never-ending supply of wispy nieces from the country to present.

And perhaps Anne will be there as well, he thought. He might even see her tonight, and be able to talk to her again.

And then he dropped the cards back on the tray and went to stare out into the street. He knew he should not go. He had made his farewells when he took her back to Tees. It would only be painful for both of them if he renewed their acquaintance.

He smiled a little then, for he knew there was no power on earth that could stop him from missing the opportunity to be close to her again.

He arrived at Lady Warren's long after she had abandoned the receiving line, and for a moment he stood in the drawing-room door and surveyed the crowd. Several people noticed him, for his height and startling blond hair drew many eyes, as did his lean, broad-shouldered figure. He was dressed entirely in black, with only the white of his linen to relieve it. In the folds of his cravat, a black onyx stickpin, surrounded by diamonds as icy as his eyes, blinked, and he wore a matching ring on his right hand.

Across the room, half-hidden from his sight, the Duchess of Lyme drew in a delighted breath. "He is here, Anne," she murmured to the girl seated beside her, and she patted her hand when Anne paled a little. "I told you that seeing you in the park would fetch 'im, now didn't I?" she asked, her voice triumphant.

Glorianna Fanshawe, the Duchess of Lyme, was a tall, slim woman in her fifties. She had been delighted to receive her cousin's letter, for she had been feeling low this winter. Having married off her youngest daughter in the fall, she was missing the thrill of the chase. Besides, the duchess was an incurable romantic. And of all the letters she had had from the Reverend Davis Nettles in the past, none had ever been as exciting as this one. Why, it was better than any romance she had ever read. And since the girl was so beautiful and accomplished, she would be delighted to assist her win her handsome rake. My only problem, she thought with a chuckle after inspecting Anne on her arrival in town, will be to discourage other suitors. Perhaps I should keep a sturdy sailor or two handy to repel all boarders. Even now, she could see Percy Garth heading in their direction, and she gave him her most forbidding frown. Mr. Garth might have been intimidated if he had seen it, but he had eyes only for the vision at her side.

He was kissing Miss Ainsworth's hand and wishing she were not quite so tall, when a deep, smooth voice spoke up behind him. "Miss Ainsworth. What a surprise to see you in town."

Percy rose from his bow to see delicate color coming and going in the lady's cheeks, and he uttered a silent curse. Damn Hawk, he thought, that's torn it!

He was forced to relinquish Miss Ainsworth's hand when Her Grace ordered him to fetch her a glass of negus, and as he moved away, he heard the girl say, "Now, how can that be, m'lord, when you know I was always meant to come for this particular Season?"

Anne wondered if she had gone too far when she saw his eyes flashing, but then she put up her chin and smiled at him. She knew now he loved her, for he had told the vicar so, and she was not going to walk away and accept this exile he had imposed on them both without a fight.

"Might I beg a dance, Miss Ainsworth?" Lord Bredon asked next.

Anne consulted her card. "I should be pleased, and I see the next waltz is free."

For a moment they stood there staring at each other, and the duchess became a little alarmed. She hoped no one was watching them too closely, for it must be obvious to anyone with even less than perfect eyesight that there was something between these two. The air between them almost crackled with emotion.

"It would be kind of you to greet me too, Hawk," she scolded, hurrying into speech before heaven-knows-what happened. The earl looked as if he would like nothing better than to sweep Anne into his arms for a passionate kiss right this minute, and Anne looked as if, should he not do so soon, she would be glad to initiate it herself.

"Your Grace," he said, turning aside to bow and raise her hand to his lips. Anne's attention was claimed by another eager beau, come to sign her dance card.

"Behave yourself, Hawk," the duchess murmured.

"Oh, surely not, ma'am," came the cool rejoinder. "When have I ever behaved myself? And how disappointing if I should begin. Whatever would people find to talk about then?"

"Have a care then, rake, if not for yourself, for Anne," the duchess continued. "She is a good girl and I will not have her hurt."

The earl took the seat beside her and looked at Anne as she stood chatting with her admirer. She was lovely tonight in a simple gown of pale blue, and he admired the expanse of smooth white skin the low cut of the dress displayed.

"Where did you meet her, ma'am?" he asked. "And are you aware of our . . . mm, former acquaintance?"

"I have heard all about it from your vicar at Tees. Davis Nettles is my cousin," the duchess told him. "He asked me to sponsor Anne this Season, and I was delighted to do so." She chuckled, and then she added, "I do not think I will have her on my hands for long."

She thought the earl looked a little bleak then, but his voice was calm as he said, "She is very lovely, I agree, and sure to be wed shortly."

Before they could continue, Percy Garth was back with the duchess's negus, and then the orchestra began to play. The earl rose and excused himself. Bowing before Anne, he led her away from a pair of disappointed gentlemen. He could feel her trembling as he took her in his arms and hoped she did not notice the slight quiver of the hand at her waist. He stared down into that lovely face, now so close to him, as if he never wanted to look away. His gray eyes caressed her mouth and that full lower lip, her patrician nose and soft, smooth cheeks. Her dark blue eyes with their thick lashes returned his gaze steadily.

"I did not expect to see you here tonight, m'lord," Anne remarked. Her voice was light and easy, and the earl would never know the effort it took to make it so. She had seen him in the park that afternoon, and although she had wanted to beckon him to her side at once, she had been restrained by both the duchess and Miss Goodly. Indeed, she had had to endure an hour's lecture on how she was to behave tonight from both of them as they sat over the teacups in the drawing room later.

"I am generally invited to most of society's events," Lord Bredon answered.

Anne nodded. "I am sure you are, but I did not mean that. I cannot imagine, you see, that this is the type of party you generally frequent. Can it be that you have reformed, sir? Seen the error of your ways?"

The earl heard the teasing note in her demure voice, and his hand tightened on her waist.

"Why did you come to town, Anne?" he asked abruptly.

"Why, to see you, m'lord," came her prompt reply.

He inhaled sharply, and then over the fierce exultation in his heart he said, "Perhaps that was unwise, ma'am. You of all the world know best the kind of man I am. I have not 'reformed.' I have no intention of doing so."

Miss Ainsworth appeared to be considering his words. "Doesn't it grow tedious after a while?" she asked, as if she were genuinely puzzled.

"Tedious?" he asked, not understanding.

"Being a rake, I mean," she explained. "Always having to think up new excesses, new adventures, new sins to keep everyone gossiping about you? And how many mornings can you enjoy waking up with a thick head, surrounded by a harem of beauties?"

The earl's eyes flashed an icy warning. "I have never slept with a harem, ma'am," he said through gritted teeth, sounding like a man hard pressed.

"Ah, well, then I see that reform is out of the question, at least until you do so," she said seriously. "One would not like to think you had missed anything."

"Anne, if you do not behave yourself, I am going to . . . to,—"he began, but she interrupted him, laughing up into his stern face.

"Oh, do so at once, I beg you! Then you will be able to relax, for this evening at least, for you will have called everyone's attention to your role as premier rake of the realm."

He turned rapidly, and he noticed she did not falter, but followed his steps perfectly. "I do not intend to take this . . . this baiting for much longer, Anne," he warned her.

"The dance will be over soon," she soothed him. It was so wonderful to be in his arms again, to be close to him, that she could not help the happiness inside her that bubbled over and made her tease him. And then she recalled something, and she smiled at him and asked, "No doubt you are planning to silence me as effectively as the last time? I can hardly wait."

"The last time?" he asked, his brows coming together.

"Why, yes, at Bredon. Don't you remember? You told me to be quiet, and when I would not obey you, you kissed me."

Suddenly the earl stopped dancing. All around them, couples continued to move to the three-quarter beat of the music, but he put his hands on her shoulders and stared down into her eyes as if they were alone. Those gray eyes were not icy now.

"Shall I kiss you, Anne?" he asked softly, one brow quirked. "Shall I?"

Anne became aware of the growing whispers around them, and the stares of the other dancers. And then someone tittered, and she blushed.

"Not here!" she whispered fiercely, trying to take his hand again.

The earl put back his head and laughed, and then he swept her into the dance again. "That will teach you to play with me, baggage," he murmured in her ear.

"You called me that once before, too," Anne said, a little more at ease now that they were indistinguishable from the others on the floor.

The music stopped, and she stepped back to curtsy. As she rose to take his arm, she murmured, "And where you are concerned, my dear rake, you are completely correct. I admit I am a baggage."

Lord Bredon stood still, and Anne looked up at him, her eyes full of love and laughter. "I shall do myself the honor of calling on you tomorrow morning, ma'am," he said. His deep, smooth voice seemed constricted somehow, and she smiled.

"I shall look forward to it," she said. "There is something between us that has not been resolved to this day, m'lord. Perhaps we can resolve it then?"

His face seemed to grow immobile, and the hooded lids came down to hide his eyes. "On the contrary, Miss Ainsworth, any . . . er, problem between us was resolved at Tees some weeks ago.''

"Now, there we are not in agreement, but we shall see, shall we not?" she asked, and then Mr. Garth was beside them and there was no opportunity for further speech. The earl could only be glad.

He left the dance a few minutes later, but that night the candles burned in his library almost until dawn.

By contrast, Anne fell asleep as soon as she closed her eyes, a little smile playing over her lips. When she woke, Lord Bredon came into her mind at once, and she lay in bed savoring her happiness. In a few hours I will see him again, she told herself. And then I am sure I can convince him that we belong together, and I do not want any other man, no matter how good he is. I only want my dear rake.

She remembered when the vicar had asked to see her alone in his study shortly after Will Asthon's call, she had been a little disturbed by the request. She hoped he would not question her too closely about her reasons for refusing Mr. Ashton's hand. To her surprise, he barely mentioned the visitor at all.

Instead, he asked her if what he had been told about her love for Lord Bredon was the truth. All the color drained from her face as he spoke, and he took her hand in his. "Listen to me, Anne," he said. "I did not realize you loved him, but if you do, I must tell you something I have kept from you."

"I do love him, Da," she whispered. "I cannot help it."

The vicar patted her hand. "Then I must confess. When the earl brought you back, and after he had put the whole tale before me, he told me that you loved him, but I did not believe it. Nor did I believe that he meant it when he said he loved you too. How could I believe anything from such a man as he? Why—"

"He said he loved me?" Anne interrupted, and the vicar almost groaned aloud at the glowing light of hope that came into her eyes.

"He did indeed. It was for that reason that he brought you back here. He said you would forget him in time and that you should not marry a man like him, that you deserved someone younger and finer and cleaner. I agreed with him.''

''No, no!'' Anne cried, jumping to her feet. ''I don't want any other man. Oh, how could he be so blind, so noble? Didn't he realize what it would do to me, to be sent back here, rejected? Didn't he know I would never forget him because I would always love him?''

Suddenly she ran around the desk and took the vicar's hands in hers. ''Are you sure, really sure, he said he loved me, Da?'' she asked eagerly.

Reverend Nettles nodded, and she whirled around, her skirts spinning. He watched her through misty eyes. Anne was her old self again, gay and confident, and ready to grab hold of life and savor every bit of it. If only he had known of her love, he would have told her what the earl had said at once. He might still wish a better man for her, but if the Earl of Bredon was what she needed to make her happy and content, he would not stand in her way.

The Nettleses and Anne sat in the parlor for a long time that evening, making plans. Anne had been amazed when he mentioned his cousin the Duchess of Lyme. She had not known that Da had such exalted relations. She asked a few questions and learned that he was the younger son of a marquess. He had left his position in society gladly, to pursue his true vocation, serving the Lord. Davis Nettles was a happy man. He had a wife he loved, he told her, his flock to minister to, his books and music and painting. And he had had Anne these past seven years to add to his joy. Anne had smiled up at him from her old position on the footstool at his feet.

The next morning, the vicar sent a letter to Her Grace, and Anne put on her cloak and bonnet and hurried to Miss Goodly's cottage to tell her the news and beg her to come to London with her when the invitation arrived.

She knew from what the vicar had told her that the duchess never left town unless she was forced to it. She considered the country boring, and had been heard to say that the duke's mansion in Kent was a pile of stone that reminded her forcibly of Newgate Prison on a gloomy day. Hearing some of these stories had made Anne sure she would get along famously with such an outspoken lady, and so she had. They were now fast friends, for she had been in town for two weeks before she saw Lord Bredon in the park.

Now Anne lay in the duchess's best guest chamber in her house in Park Lane, planning what she would wear for their meeting. Certainly her prettiest gown, and certainly one of those he had chosen for her. Beyond that, she would have to wait and see, she thought, wishing Mary Agnes would hurry with her breakfast. She was starving!

# 18

It was after eleven o'clock that morning when the duchess's butler knocked on the drawing-room door. Anne jumped to her feet. At last! she exulted as she smoothed her gown. She had been waiting there since nine, and she had long since given up dreaming of what she would say, or how he would reply, and how soon it would be before she was in his arms again. Now she was only impatient for it to begin, and thinking of how she would punish him for making her wait so long.

But there was no tall, handsome Earl of Bredon entering the room behind the butler. He was alone, and he bore a letter on his silver salver which he presented to her with a bow. Anne took it in nerveless fingers, the smile of delighted welcome she had worn gone from her lips.

She turned it over and over as if she had never seen such a thing before, and the butler asked, "Will there be anything further, Miss Anne?"

Anne did not take her eyes from the red wax that sealed the letter and was marked with the earl's crest. "No, thank you, that will be all," she murmured.

She did not hear him leave the room or close the door as she continued to stare at the heavy folded paper in her hand. And then she took a deep breath and broke the seal.

It was not a very long letter, but it was very thorough. He told her he had had second thoughts about the wisdom of any further private meetings between them. He begged her to remember their previous meeting, when he had said everything he had to say on the subject of any liaison between them. He wrote that his mind was made up and that he had no intention of changing it. He admitted he had been attracted to her beauty, and said he apologized if she had misinterpreted any of his actions. He reminded her that he was a rake, and as such he insisted he had no inclination toward marriage. He told her she was very young, too young to interest him, and he assured her that in time she would forget him and her girlish infatuation for him. And he remained her humble servant, Anthony Hawkins, Earl of Bredon.

The drawing-room door burst open then, and the duchess ran in, followed closely by Miss Goodly. They saw Anne standing with her back to them, her shoulders shaking, and Miss Goodly demanded, "What has that horrid man been writing to you, Anne?"

The duchess cried, "Oh, do not weep, Anne! He is not worth it, none of them are! You must not be so distraught, my dear!"

Anne turned, and both older ladies were stopped in their tracks at the sight of her laughing face. "I am not in the least distraught, dear ma'am. I am in whoops. I have never read such . . . such *fustian* in all my life! Here, see for yourselves."

She thrust the crumpled letter into their hands and began to pace the drawing room while they read it.

"Men!" Miss Goodly exclaimed when she reached the end.

"They are all of them impossible," the duchess agreed.

"And Lord Bredon is the worst!" Anne said. "Oh, I will make him pay for this, just see if I don't. 'Girlish infatuation' . . . 'no inclination for marriage' . . . merely 'attracted to my beauty'—and implying I was so young I bored him. Bah! He cannot really believe I will accept this dissembling, this pack of lies, meekly!"

The duchess came and led her to a sofa. "Of course he does," she said cheerfully. "You *are* very young, you know, Anne, and so you have yet to learn how dense men can be. Having written his dismissal, Lord Bredon is in a fair way of believing it himself by now."

"I would never have thought he would be so noble," Miss Goodly marveled, reading the letter again.

The duchess laughed. "Oh, there is nothing so noble and

so tediously moral as a reformed rake. And that reminds me.'' She paused and turned to Anne, her face serious now. ''Are you quite, quite sure, Anne?'' she asked.

At the girl's look of incomprehension, she explained, ''I mean, are you sure you love him enough? He will lead you a miserable life, you know. He will watch you like the hawk he is named for, suspect every man who ever so much as smiles at you of being your lover, and hedge you about with every kind of restriction he can think of. No doubt you will be buttoned to the chin in Quaker-gray gowns two sizes too big for you. Why, I am willing to wager he will all but imprison you at Bredon, and I would not be surprised if he had a moat and drawbridge built! You see, knowing firsthand all the darker sides of men's nature, he will never be easy. He *knows* what men are thinking and what they want. I do not think I could bear it myself, so you must be very sure you can stand his future jealousy and constant attendance.''

Anne's eyes were dancing. ''It sounds heavenly,'' she sighed. ''Although I do hope I can talk him out of the moat.''

''I am afraid she is a lost cause, your grace,'' Miss Goodly said tartly, and the duchess laughed.

''Now, then, what are we to do to bring this tiresome man to heel?'' she wondered. ''Perhaps I should write and ask him to call on me . . .''

''That might do it,'' Miss Goodly agreed. ''Or perhaps when he continues to see Anne this Season, so sought after and admired, he will be so jealous he will change his mind.''

Anne rose from the sofa. ''But it will be far, far too late by then. I am sure he is arranging to leave London right this minute.''

The duchess looked up, her eyes shrewd, as Anne continued, ''Oh, yes. He will make a bolt for Bredon or Cawfell, or even for the Americas for all I know. He will not stay here where he can see me and be tempted. And for that reason, there is only one thing that can be done to stop him.''

The two ladies waited, and then she nodded and announced in a militant voice, ''I must go to him at once.''

''*Anne*!'' Miss Goodly breathed, much shocked. ''That would not be seemly—''

The duchess interrupted her by placing her hand over Miss Goodly's and pressing it slightly.

"I think you are right, Anne," she said. "Surely the conventions must be disregarded in an urgent case like this. And since I have every confidence that Anne will be able to convince him of her love, and get him to admit his, and in a very short time too, Alicia, there can be no impropriety in an engaged couple meeting alone. Run along, my dear. We will not expect you until much, *much* later."

Her young guest laughed and ran to the door.

"Take Mary Agnes with you!" Miss Goodly called after her, still not convinced that this was the correct way to approach the reluctant earl.

Anne nodded and blew them a kiss, and then she was gone.

When informed of her destination, Mary Agnes looked even more dour than usual, but Anne was having none of it. Arranging her bonnet on shining red-gold curls, she said, "Come along at once, Mary Agnes, and none of your lectures, or I shall leave you here and go by myself!"

The maid opened her mouth to protest, and then, seeing the look of resolution in Miss Anne's eyes that told her she would do just that, she meekly removed her apron and cap and picked up her shawl.

The duchess's carriage took them to St. James's Street and was dismissed, and Anne climbed the steps the earl had carried her up in his arms before. Her mouth was curved in a reminiscent smile as the butler opened the door to her knock.

"Good afternoon, Beavers," she said, stepping past him into the hall. "I trust I find you well? Be so good as to inform the earl that I have come to see him."

She was removing her gloves as she spoke, but she stopped for a moment when the astonished butler said, "But the earl is not here, Miss Anne!"

"No?" she asked. "When do you expect him, then?"

Beavers was all but wringing his hands. "As to that, I could not say, miss. He went out early this morning, and he has not been seen since. I . . . I have no idea."

Anne thought for a moment, and then she nodded and

handed her gloves and stole to her maid. "I will wait for him in the library, then. Mary Agnes, remain here."

The butler was forced to hurry ahead of her to open the door of the library as she went in that direction. Behind them, Mary Agnes settled down in one of the straight chairs that lined the hall, resigned to whatever mischief Miss Anne was up to now, and to however long a wait she would be forced to endure.

The earl had finished his letter to Anne at dawn, after wasting a great many sheets of paper. Alone, late at night, he had come again to see that it was his responsibility, and his alone, to make sure this dearest girl would not be burdened by such as he. No matter how he would regret it all his life, he must see to it that she was spared any future with Satan's Rake.

He had gone up to bed feeling saddened and frustrated, and not in the least noble. But he was awake early, for his dreams had been troubled and his sleep restless. He wondered, as Barker shaved him, if he would ever be able to forget her face, her laugh, her eyes, that glorious hair and the feel of her crushed in his arms, and he suspected he would not.

He had worn a grim frown as he left the house for an early canter in the park. And then, still restless, he went to Gentleman Jackson's for a sparring lesson. After only a few blows, the pugilist shook his head and dismissed him.

"You come back when your mind is clearer, m'lord," he told him kindly. "Shockingly abroad you are today."

From there Lord Bredon went to White's, and then, when that club seemed to be filled with nothing but bores and idiots, to Brooks's. Finally, at three, he returned to St. James's Street.

The first person he saw as he handed his hat to his butler was Anne's maid. Mary Agnes scowled at him from where she sat against the wall, and he returned a ferocious frown.

"Where is she?" he growled, and his butler was quick to tell him that Miss was waiting in the library, and had been for some time. He assured his master he had given her every assistance, and served her a luncheon as well.

Lord Bredon did not hear him, for he was striding to the

library doors. In a moment he slammed them shut behind him. Mary Agnes sat up straighter, her eyes avoiding any contact with the butler's.

The earl stood just inside the doors, his gray eyes cold under glowering brows.

Before he could speak, Anne rose from the leather wing chair where she had been curled up reading. She wore another gown of his choosing, a deep violet muslin with a simple white lace collar. It made her look very innocent, and his frown deepened.

"There you are at last, m'lord," she said, coming toward him with a smile. "Wherever have you been for such a long time? I am quite, quite angry with you."

"Nowhere near as angry as I am with you, Anne," he said, his deep voice abrupt.

She looked up into his face, noting the icy gray eyes and the rigid set of his taut mouth. "I can see you are, but surely you must have known I would not accept that ridiculous letter you sent to me, and meekly retreat to wring my hands. What a great deal you have to learn about me, dear sir, if so you thought."

"I certainly did expect you to accept it," he answered quickly. "What I did not expect was for you to come here, here to a known rake's house, in such a brazen manner. Are you determined to ruin your reputation?"

Anne appeared to consider this seriously. "How could I? You ruined it long ago."

He started, and she continued, "I fail to see why a visit with my maid beside me is at all brazen. Especially when you consider I have spent the night here, unchaperoned, too, with not even Mary Agnes to lend me consequence. How can a morning call—oh, I do beg your pardon!—a morning *and* afternoon call compare?"

The earl started to speak, and then thought better of it.

"Just so," Anne told him sweetly. "I could really insist you marry me, couldn't I, for you have compromised me quite thoroughly and completely, long before this."

Lord Bredon moved away from her then, and went to pour them both a glass of sherry. Anne watched him, a little puzzled. He seemed more relaxed suddenly, and easier, as if he had decided what he was going to do. As he handed her her glass, he said, his voice amused now, "Somehow I find it difficult to remember that you are only just turned eighteen."

He sounded as if he were laughing at her, and Anne was quick to say, "So do I, for I have felt a hundred these past weeks."

The earl lounged against the heavy table that held the London journals. He sipped his sherry, and then he said, "Do you really want a husband this badly, Miss Ainsworth, that you feel you must use entrapment?" His voice mocked her, but Anne was not fooled.

"I can assure you there is no need for it," he went on. "Oh, no, none at all. I could tell last evening that you may have your pick of the *ton,* for you are about to become a blazing success, the Incomparable of 1810. You do not need to . . . mm, pursue such a poor thing as I am, quite so fervently."

He smiled a little, as if to take the sting from his words, and Anne said, "Oh, none of your conventional gentlemen would do for me, m'lord. I have some very serious faults. I have had, as you know, a very unusual upbringing, and my background is suspect. Then too, I am impulsive and I have a shocking temper. I also find I love luxury and wealth, and being pampered by armies of servants. And I have discovered I am not at all reserved and shy and . . . shall we say 'ladylike'? I am sure I would scandalize most gentlemen with my ardor. No, no, they would not do for me at all. I would frighten them, and they would bore me."

There was a little silence, and then Lord Bredon said, "I believe I told you I have no inclination for matrimony? Since we are making confessions here, I will tell you that I really do not like women."

Anne's eyes never left his. "Then you are a fine actor, sir," she complimented him.

"I have always disliked them, starting with my negligent, unloving mother," he went on, as if she had not spoken. "I loathed my prim, cold, quick-to-punish nanny, and I can assure you that my governess could have given lessons to

Attila the Hun. No, at a very early age I was determined to avoid any permanent relationship with your sex. My intent was only strengthened when I grew older and discovered, in a most painful way, how devious and shallow and untrustworthy all women are. I am not capable of loving anyone. I use women, Miss Ainsworth, as I thought to use you at one time, and when I am tired of them, I discard them.'' He paused, and then he said slowly, "I tire very quickly and I am easily bored. You should be thankful I discarded you before I enjoyed you. I am not always so forbearing.''

He stared at her, his face cold and set, and for a moment Anne felt a little doubt.

"I am being very honest with you, my dear," he continued. "I still feel guilty about what happened to you at my hands, you see. But now you must realize that there can be nothing further between us.''

Anne took a deep breath. "Thank you for your candor, sir. And now I must be candid too. There is no need for you to feel guilty about what happened to me while I was under your protection. Have you ever considered, m'lord, what my life would have been like if you had not intervened all those years ago at Cawfell?''

She saw an arrested expression in his eyes, and, emboldened, she continued, "Try to think of how I would have grown up, left in my aunt and uncle's hands. It would have made no difference at all that my grandfather was of the nobility, for I would never have known it. I would have remained uneducated, hungry and work-worn, and beaten. Perhaps I might even have become the whore my mother was to escape it. Oh, no, you have nothing to reproach yourself for, for you saved me from that, and I can feel only gratitude.''

She sipped her wine, and then she put the glass down on the table and came toward him. "As for your hatred for women, m'lord, you know you do not hate me. You admitted to my dear vicar that you loved me.''

"I was mistaken. I do not know the meaning of the word," he said quietly. When she shook her head, he added, "And even if what I feel for you now is love, perhaps in time I will tire of you, too.''

He wished she would not look at him so intently. He felt as if she were looking into his soul, and he did not want her to see what was written there.

"Perhaps you will," she agreed. "But I think I will take that chance."

And then she put her hands on his arms and gripped them hard. "Enough, my dear! You may comfort yourself that you tried everything you knew how, to discourage me, and none of it has served. You see, what I feel for you is no infatuation, no silly girlish crush that I will outgrow. I love you. When you left me in Tees, I almost died with wanting you back. If Will had not told the vicar that I would not marry him because of my love for you, I would never have learned you felt the same way. Da did not tell me that, you see. Like you, he thought that I would forget you. I will never forget you, and I don't want the good young man that you and Da think I should have. I want you. And if I cannot have you, I want no one."

As she spoke, his arms had come up, almost reluctantly, to circle her waist, his hands firm on her back. Now she leaned against them. "Whoever would have dreamed it would take so much effort to win a kiss from one of Satan's Rakes?" she teased.

His hands caressed her back. "You may have all the kisses you like, and you know it, but I must be sure—"

"Oh, Anthony!" she cried. "You are such a fool!"

And then she reached up and drew his head down to hers and she kissed him. He hesitated for only a moment as those soft lips opened under his, and then he caught her to him with a savage need. Anne said a little prayer of thanksgiving, but then she forgot everything but the earl and how it felt to be held so close to him again, his mouth warm and hungry and insistent on hers. They had reached safe harbor at last.

When he raised his head finally, her shining eyes were wet, and there was an answering moisture in his own.

"Are you sure, my dearest Anne?" he asked, his voice pleading. "This is your last chance to escape, for if you agree to marry me, I will never let you go."

Anne shivered as the deep, loving tones of his voice wrapped around her and caressed her, and then she nodded and put her cheek against his.

"I am very sure, my love," she whispered in his ear. His hands came up to cup her face as if it were the most precious thing in the world to him, and she smiled.

"Besides, you made a promise to me once that you have yet to keep, m'lord," she told him. "Know that I hold you to it."

"What promise?" he asked absently as he loosened the pins that held her red-gold hair. He buried his hands in the richness that tumbled to her shoulders, his eyes absorbed.

"How quickly men forget," she mourned, her voice a little breathless. "And to think I have been waiting all this time for you to teach me my sums."

He smiled then, his gray eyes warm with his love, and he drew away to bow to her. "I should be delighted to instruct you in that ecstatic state of affairs in which one and one make one," he said. And then, with one blond eyebrow quirked, he added softly, "I can hardly wait to begin."

"Nor can I," she told him, and then, laughing, she went back into his eager arms.

*About the Author*

Although Barbara Hazard is a New England Yankee by birth, upbringing, and education, she is of English descent on both sides of her family and has many relatives in that country. The Regency period has always been a favorite, and when she began to write seven years ago, she gravitated to it naturally, feeling perfectly at home there. Barbara Hazard now lives in New York. She has been a musician and an artist, and although writing is her first love, she also enjoys classical music, reading, quilting, cross-country skiing, and paddle tennis.

# ROMANTIC ENCOUNTERS

# SIGNET REGENCY ROMANCE
## COMING IN JULY 1990

---

### *Mary Jo Putney*
The Rogue and the Runaway

### *Roberta Eckert*
Lady Angel

### *Carol Proctor*
The Drawing Master's Dilemma

---